MATA HARI OF THE HEADLINES

Carla MacMurphy knew what she wanted. She wanted
to be the best foreign correspondent in postwar Europe
so that she could show her socially prominent mother
that she was just as good as she was. And she wanted
to prove to the men correspondents that she was better
than they were.

Intensely ambitious, unscrupulous and amoral, Carla
was utterly indifferent to the misery in vanquished Germany. For her, the only thing that mattered was to beat
the other reporters at their own game—and any method,
fair or foul, would serve her purpose. Perfectly willing
to use her beauty to crack the impossible story or score
the important scoop, she offered her charms freely to
any man who would feed her drive for success.

More than a picture of a power-ridden woman, Carla's
story is a frightening report on life behind the headlines
in devastated and demoralized Germany. Although it is
fiction, its characters and events could be real.

We, who seven years ago
Talked of honour and of truth
Shriek with pleasure if we show
The weasel's twist, the weasel's tooth.

William Butler Yeats, 1919

Shriek
with
Pleasure

by
TONI HOWARD

WILDSIDE PRESS

CHAPTER ONE

THE GIRL pulled the jeep off the road onto a grassy bank and stopped under a white-stockinged appletree. She climbed out, unleashed the dog from the front seat, and walked a little way into the meadow.

My God, she was tired! Her head throbbed hot and feverish, and her back ached from seven hours' steady driving. She stretched her arms wide over her head and immediately a dizziness came over her so that she sat down abruptly in the grass. Always a hangover, whenever she had anything important or difficult to do, like driving a jeep from Paris to Frankfurt-am-Main. No one else on earth would stay out dancing and drinking till dawn and then try to make a trip like that on a nervous system like curdled milk. She rolled over in the grass and groaned.

The dog, a young Irish setter, came up and she rubbed the back of his head. "But we generally squeeze through, don't we, Timmy?"

Far off to the left the fields of the Moselle Valley rose and dipped, swayed backward and rolled in again. So neatly the squares were pieced together, light green, dark green, fields of bright yellow linseed, whipped all around with a blanket-stitch of low green hedge. A strong wind blew across the grain under the warmth of the late afternoon sun, and on a distant hill a plow moved methodically back and forth. La douce France! What a beautiful country it was, beautiful and quiet and fertile, only stirring faintly as a woman asleep. From here there was no sign that a war had just passed this way, no sign that the land remembered anything but sun and rain and the slow pricking of a plow, the surface quilting of man's cultivation.

And the day! The day was like a state of grace.

She lit a cigarette, and for the first time today it tasted good. She began to feel a little better. She didn't mind going to Germany at all, it was probably a much better assignment than France, more front-page stories, more by-lines, and undoubtedly a lot more exciting. Besides, she was sick of Paris.

She hadn't done too well in Paris either, she had to admit. But that hadn't been her fault but the fault of circumstance. Of circumstance and of the machinations of people who were jealous of her, who hated her for being successful at what she had set out to do. All newspapermen were the same—a bunch of long-nosed pundits who worked off their own disillusion by denouncing every woman journalist as a fake and a poseur. Well, to hell with them. She could beat them all at their own game. And she would.

She looked out over the fields. Seven-thirty, and already the beginnings of an evening wind were ruffling up the grasses; long brown shadows buttressed the hedges. "Come on, Timmy, time to shove on," she called, and the dog bounded obediently into the jeep.

All that distinguished the border between France and Germany was a cluster of shacks like outhouses and a big red-and-white peppermint pole lowered across the road. Within three minutes a natty little French lieutenant examined her papers, lifted the pole, saluted and waved her on. Shoving down on the gas pedal, she picked up speed. "We'll make it by ten o'clock," she told herself. "That's better time than Patton."

Once across the border the land changed, became more urban. Every fifth or sixth house along the road showed bomb damage; many of them were pock-marked by machine-gun fire. The highway here was dotted with holes, and only infrequently was there a sign to indicate the route.

As she came down into the Saar Basin the sun was setting fiery and magnificent behind blackened slagheaps, the ruins of abandoned mines, derricks and collieries standing lifeless as stage props along the rim of the valley. The streets of Saarbrücken were dark and deserted, with only one or two German civilians walking slowly among the piles of debris and fragments of houses that lined the road. Stores and shops were boarded up; the houses showed no lights. In the deepening dusk the city seemed an eerie graveyard, the gray skeletons of buildings staring down at her with sightless eyes, the jeep a noisy, coughing, human thing rattling and banging over the roads, shrieking insult to the unquiet dead.

Unconsciously, she began to drive faster.

Why weren't there more signs? It seemed hours since she'd seen a Highway Number 10 marker. A truck passed her going the other way, its open top filled with German PW's who called out unintelligible words to her as they passed. It was the first vehicle she had seen since she entered the valley.

6

Hunched over the wheel, she peered ahead for signs, driving as fast as she could over the washboard roads.

The road had been getting worse and worse, until now it was only a narrow alleyway through steep walls of piled-up rubble. It was dark now, the wind was getting colder; must hurry.

A fork ahead, picked up by the headlights. But as she came upon it she realized that she had lost the main route. No signs at all. She braked to a stop, started to turn around.

The motor stalled, letting in such a deathly silence that she instinctively glanced around in apprehension. She was surrounded by a pack of ragged children who had appeared out of the ruins like little gnomes and were standing in a circle around the jeep staring wordlessly at her, their pale faces singularly visible in the half-light, intent and without expression.

One of them, a skinny, dark-haired boy taller than the rest, pointed to the right-hand road and said loudly: "Ist nicht gut." As if set in motion by his boldness they all began to clamor: "Ist nicht gut!" "Gesperrt!" "Nicht gut!" pointing to both roads. Then: "Modom, modom, zu essen!" "Zu essen!" pointing to their mouths. "Bitte, bitte, zu essen!" They clung to the side of the jeep, some of them began crawling up onto the back. "Zu essen!" Timmy started to bark.

In desperation, the girl looked around to the back seat. Somewhere she had some chocolate, she could buy them off with that. She found the musette bag and started to open it. Immediately, dozens of pairs of dirty hands were snatching at her arm, at the bag, an hysterical mob scrambling all over each other screaming and clawing. Their faces close to hers were anguished and tense, mouths open like young rats, their voices shrill as they howled, scratched and fought for the last bits of food. The bag was emptied, chocolate, sandwiches, everything, gone, but they screamed and fought on. "Zu essen!" "Modom, modom!" In a frantic tug of war for the musette bag a small boy fell; the rest scrambled right over him. "Zu essen!"

In the background, near the shadowed doorway of an almost demolished house, several adults stood watching the scene, coolly curious but making no move to stop it.

"Allez-vous-en!" she shouted. "Geht weg! Out of the way!" She started the motor, threw the jeep into reverse and backed fast, with her left arm pushing off a boy who still clung to the side. He fell back crying, and in the dark she couldn't see if he was hurt or not. She shoved the gear into first and turned, and as the headlights swung past the huddle of men and

7

women in the doorway she could see in the full glare the dull unwavering hostility of their faces. The jeep plunged forward and she was off, roaring back in the direction she had come.

Like a bad dream. Like Gulliver in an Army jeep and the Lilliputians wild with hunger. Her hands were gripping the wheel as if to squeeze it dry, the cold wind was whipping her hair across her face, somehow in that fracas she had lost her cap; probably one of those little bastards had stolen it. Bouncing and clattering, the jeep banged on, twisting and turning through deep canyons of blasted brick and timber, over labyrinthian roads that sagged and dropped a foot at a jolt.

Now she was completely lost. No street lights, no road signs, no evidence anywhere of human life, except once in awhile a faint gleam of light from the boarded-up window of a battered house. Doggedly, she kept going.

In the telescopic corridor of light that was the road, everything the headlights hit was magnified, distorted, thrown up out of the blackness as a malevolent leering thing threatening the existence of this tiny hurtling jeep and its panicky girl driver. The shadow of a twisted rusting street-lamp was a coiled snake; a hollow building was a lurching, toppling cadaver; a creaking makeshift bridge might be a trap to the unholy dark on either side. Like Gulliver still, but now a frightened miniature Gulliver on a wild careening ride through a Brobdingnagian forest of supernatural cement and steel monsters.

Frightened of a bunch of ruins? Nonsense. Frightened of what, then? Of being alive and personal in a dead and desolate land, the war so recently over and so much hatred still at large, a dark impersonal sea of human hatred washing quietly around the crumpled pillars and caved-in roofs of a destroyed nation, gently nudging up the bloated grey flotsam of hostile tense faces, those men and women watching from the doorway, the wide screaming mouths of filthy, hunger-crazed ragamuffins. Of being an American alone in Germany, the solitary and defenseless conqueror tossed by accident to an avenging mob of the conquered.

Somehow there was guilt mixed in with it too, as if she personally had bombed these cities, reduced them to paleolithic boneyards of dust and rubble, and now had to face the dazed, uncivilized cavemen who crawled out of their holes to stare at her. And stare at her not as an innocent individual American named Carla MacMurphy but as a responsible cell in the military brain that had directed and achieved this destruction.

8

She tried to relax, to reassure herself that there was nothing to be afraid of as long as she kept going. Sooner or later she would come out on a highway. All roads led somewhere, didn't they? Yes, and some led to dead ends.

As she rounded a sharp turn, she caught sight of a woman, a light dress visible coming up toward the road from some alleyway. She made a quick decision to take a chance and ask the way. She stopped the jeep.

"Bitte."

The woman approached the jeep squinting in the brilliance of the headlights. She was young, with neat dark hair drawn tightly down from her face, and with her was a one-legged man on crutches. "Bitte," she replied.

The girl leaned out. "Bitte, wo liegt die Strasse nach Frankfurt?"

"Nach Frankfurt?" The woman hesitated, spoke inaudibly to her companion, who pushed himself forward into the circle of light and said in English: "You want to find the highway toward Frankfurt, yes?"

"Yes, please."

Inexpertly, as if unaccustomed to his crutches, he turned and gestured down the road. "Take the second turn to the left, it is a very small street but you can find it if you watch for a street that goes down. This little street two hundred meters and you will come upon the highway to Homburg. Then turn left. In Homburg you will find the highway." He finished and stepped back out of the light.

"Danke," said the girl.

"Bitte schön," said the man pleasantly.

Speaking softly to each other, they moved on down the unlighted street.

The girl shifted into first and started up again, looking carefully for the little street that went down and repeating to herself: two hundred meters, that's about two hundred twenty yards, then turn left, Homburg. She found the street, a cleared cobblestone alley that dipped steeply down around a mountainous pile of used brick, then just as steeply climbed up again onto, O miracle! a highway, a two-lane macadam road. She turned left.

She was moving fast, her hair was blowing in her face, she could picture one of those little savages strutting around in front of the others in her khaki cap, chocolate smeared all over his ugly Nazi face. She wished she had it back. My God, how could that dog sleep through everything? That couple she had talked to didn't seem so resentful, wonder how they liked being occupied by the French. He was obviously a returned PW, probably captured by the British, spoke pretty good English with a British accent, one leg gone and not very handy on crutches yet. The woman seemed polite, even anxious to help. But you couldn't trust them. Maybe it was just a trick and they had deliberately misdirected her into some other godforsaken hole and were now laughing quietly together over their cleverness in fouling up an American, like the French used to do when the Germans were there.

Nonsense, the road was lousy but it was a road and in all probability it went to Homburg. Was Homburg on the way to Frankfurt? She couldn't remember. Wonder where that couple was going, which of those uninhabitable wrecks of houses they lived in, bet they're happy, Lili and Hans reunited after his brave years at the front shooting down Allied soldiers.

Must be almost ten o'clock by now. The sky was murky, a watery moon slipping surreptitiously in and out of low dirty-looking clouds. She reached in the compartment, got out a bottle and took a stiff slug of Scotch. She was hungry, she could use a little "zu essen" herself, wish those brats had left her the cap and one sandwich.

A sign loomed up, big black-and-yellow letters: HOMBURG. With a feeling close to elation she skimmed through the town, a dark cavern of blasted tenements and demolished factories, and was out on the highway heading toward Frankfurt. Another enormous sign: FRANKFURT 158 km. She figured it quickly. About 100 miles, two hours should do it, she might get into the press camp before the bar closed.

The highway was good, the jeep running smoothly, and once in awhile a car passed her, making her feel less insecure. A railroad track ran alongside the road on the left, its switch towers and stations half-demolished; long lines of rusting passenger coaches littered the sidings. Gondolas and freight cars lay smashed and prostrate across the tracks, exactly as they had been after the Allied bombings a year and a half ago. She wondered how the French ever shipped the coal they claimed they were now producing in the Saar.

By now it was bitter cold, the wind like an icy wet towel on her face. Her trenchcoat seemed as light as a silk shirt and not much warmer.

Near Kaiserslautern she stopped to refill the tank with gasoline from one of the jerrycans, and while she was prying the can open two Dutchman in UNRRA uniforms driving an American Army sedan stopped to help her. One, named Willem, was young and good-looking. He loaned her his enor-

10

mous long khaki overcoat to keep her warm and his black beret to hold her hair down in the wind, and she combed her red-gold hair and put the beret on, and knew from the feel of it that it looked wonderful on her, very dashing. Then they opened some sandwiches they had and she got out the Scotch and the three of them stood companionably by the side of the road eating sandwiches and drinking Scotch, passing the bottle from hand to hand. Willem gave her his UNRRA address in Cologne, so she could send the overcoat and beret back after she got to Frankfurt, and she was sure he squeezed her knee when he tucked her into the jeep and wrapped his coat around her slim and lovely legs. In the light of the dashboard she could see he was very handsome, and when they waved her off he shouted "Wiedersehen!" Well, maybe she would see him again. You never could tell in this country.

From here on to Mainz, they had told her, the road was good and so well marked that she couldn't possibly lose her way. So she picked up speed, some of the old confidence came back. Cuddled down in Willem's big coat, warmed inside by the Scotch and digestively occupied by the sandwiches, she held the jeep at a steady sixty miles an hour. The moon had risen high, still ducking low black clouds but giving a clearer light. The towns she went through were small, unlighted, a square stocky church with a perfume-bottle spire silhouetted against the pale grey sky, white picket fences whizzing past in the wide darkness.

Langmeil, Kirchheimbolanden, Alzey, the towns went by quickly. The road was good, the signs clear and frequent. At Mainz, about 20 miles ahead, she would cross the Rhine into the American Zone. She leaned over and tucked Timmy securely into his Army blanket. "Almost there," she told the dog. "I told you we'd make it."

In clear moonlight she crossed the Rhine, its dark hills low and distant under the moon. At the other end of the bridge— "General Patch Bridge," the sign announced—was a white shanty and a white-helmeted American MP. His face was brown and leathery under the helmet-liner. "Where you heading?" he asked.

"Frankfurt. What's the best route?"

"Straight ahead, Route 40."

"Thanks, fellow," she called, pulling away.

She was off the bridge, still following N 40 but now in the American Zone, which, though just as dark and just as devastated, seemed somehow safer and better guarded. The road ran off the main street and through a narrow black alley

11

marked Frankfurter Strasse, and as the jeep bumped through its headlights surprised a party of colored soldiers and German girls gathered around three or four Army trucks. Several of the girls were entirely naked and shrank back into a doorway against the light; two or three couples were lying in the street.

"Hey!" shouted one of the soldiers, waving a bottle. His shadow on the building in back of him was a grotesque of drunkenness.

Without answering she clattered on through, and after a few minutes' driving was back on the highway.

In a cloverleaf turn the jeep climbed onto the autobahn, a four-lane speedway leading directly into Frankfurt. Taut as a string, her weariness pulling her ahead, she whipped into the city without incident, through a suburban area thick with trees, along two heavily bombed streets, past the Hauptbahnhof, an enormous hemispherical web of twisted steel, and pulled to a triumphant stop in front of the Park Hotel. "U.S. Army Press Center," the marquee read.

Under the light of the canopy, she looked at her watch: 11:45.

At the desk a sleepy grey-haired German clerk took her name and assigned her a room. He was effusively polite, explaining that, although they had received her reservation a week earlier, they unfortunately had no rooms with bath available. He seemed secretly delighted with his sad news, shrugging his shoulders in smiling melancholy, repeating over and over with exaggerated deference that he personally had done everything he could but the Army officer in charge had given him his orders, what could he do but obey? The only room with bath in the house was 205, a suite reserved for colonels, he would love to give her suite 205 but unfortunately—and he spread his hands in eloquent disavowal of the U.S. Army, which showed so little understanding of Miss MacMurphy's right to the finest room in the hotel and prevented him, an honest and resourceful German, from running things on a fairer, more civilized basis.

Fatigue, nervousness and the Scotch she had drunk on the trip combined to make her angry and indignant.

"I don't care what the Army's rules are, I'm taking suite 205 and I want my bags sent up immediately."

"But, Miss MacMurphy——" With lugubrious enjoyment he ran through his explanation again. Here was a complication, Americans quarreling with Americans, and an efficient, knowing German who could so easily rectify everything had not been given enough authority to help her. It was an injustice typical of postwar Germany, where the intelligent, such as she and he, must band together against the stupidity of the occupier.

Furious, she lashed out at him again. "Do as I tell you, send my luggage immediately to 205 or I'll talk to the Captain about your impertinence."

The deference became docility. "Yes, Miss MacMurphy, right away."

She was turning from the desk in self-justified anger when a tall slender young man in a correspondent's uniform burst out of the bar and across the lobby yelling "Carla!"

"Bill Somers!" Her voice dropped an octave in tone.

He held her by the shoulders, leaned over and kissed her warmly.

"God, I'm glad to see you. The PRO told me you'd be in tonight, but I was afraid it would take you two days to make it from Paris." He was looking at her closely. "What in hell have you got on?"

She laughed, looking down at herself. Willem's UNRRA overcoat hung on her shoulders like a blanket, so long it touched the floor at her heels. She had rolled back the sleeves in a thick bunch but still they completely covered her hands. "Oh," she said lightly, "hadn't you heard? I'm working for UNRRA now. But I think the job is a little too big for me."

"You look like a kid all dressed up in daddy's old uniform. Let's take the damned thing off and get a drink before the bar closes."

He took the coat, hung it up on a rack and waited while she went to the ladies' room to make up her face. When she came back to the lobby he was authoritatively instructing the German porters on the disposition of her luggage, care of the dog, and the parking of her jeep in a guarded parking lot.

She watched him with affection. He hadn't changed a bit in the eight or nine months since she had last seen him: the same deeply circled brilliant dark eyes, the same lanky, lean build, the same dynamic forcefulness. He was a damned good wire-service man; he could help her a lot with her first stories out of Germany. Maybe a little cynical, you had to be to stay in this profession, but generous as a fool if you worked him the right way. She remembered the night she'd first met him; it was at the press camp in Brussels during the war. She had had a terrible headache and hadn't felt like getting dressed, so she had walked across the hall and knocked on his door and asked him if he'd mind filing a story for her on his way down to dinner, and then, if it wasn't too much trouble, would he bring

13

some aspirin for her when he came back. When he came back with the aspirin she was sitting up in bed and he had sat down just to talk a little. And then—of course. Funny thing was, she hadn't found out his name until the next morning. Somehow it seemed a little too casual to ask a man's name just as he's climbing out of your bed. "Oh, by the way, what did you say your name was?" She'd solved it next morning by going over the list of war correspondents and finding which one had the room opposite hers.

He came toward her, smiling, and put his arm around her waist as they walked toward the bar. "How was the trip? Any trouble?"

"Oh no, nothing to speak of. I could use a drink, though."

"That you shall have, sogleich."

She recognized a lot of people in the bar: Polly Wilson, that simpering old bitch, and her husband Mike; two photographers whose names she had forgotten; a PRO major who used to be with the Ninth Air Force; the dumb dame who slept with Art Massey of the *Chronicle;* several reporters who called to her as she came in.

She and Bill found a table. He ordered Scotch.

"Don't let's stay too long in here, though," he said. "It's been a hell of a long time since we've been alone together."

She looked directly into his eyes. "It's been an awfully long time." Then softly: "I've missed you terribly, Bill."

He took an enormous gulp of Scotch. "Carla," he said fervently. "You're wonderful."

CHAPTER TWO

SOMERS was at the typewriter, at a table near the window of room 205. Every once in awhile he would stop to paw over some of the papers spread out in disorder on the top of the table, then after a minute or two the peck-pecking of the typewriter would start up again.

"What did you say their coal production was now?" he called.

"What?" It was Carla's voice from the bathroom.

"Coal production in the Saar. What is it now?"

"It's on that sheet of statistics. About 50 percent of prewar, I think."

He repeated his search of the papers. "Oh, I've got it. Yeah, 52 percent."

Carla was taking a bath. From the half-closed bathroom door came the sound of water running furiously into the tub, the slamming of a cabinet door, a thin babyish voice singing snatches of "Lili Marlene" in American-accented German. In a big armchair in the corner the Irish setter lay curled in sleep.

The tap-tap of the typewriter commenced again.

There was a knock at the door and a waiter in a much-laundered yellowish-white jacket came in carrying a bowl of ice and two glasses. "Auf 'en Tisch," said Somers, scarcely looking up from his page. He handed the waiter two cigarettes as a tip and went on with his typing.

"Hey!" he called above the roar of the bathwater. "Hurry up. I've got a drink waiting for you."

"Wunderbar." The sound of the bathwater stopped. "How are you getting along?"

"Fine. Almost finished."

The typewriter commenced again its deliberate staccato, chugged along steadily for several minutes. "I love the French," said Somers. "They're such realists. They fought this war against the Germans, they fought the last two against the Germans, obviously Germans are always going to be Germans, so why bother with these tricky unsubstantial distinctions between Germans and Nazis? Solution: put them all to work helping France get back some of the things she lost in the war, including French prestige. Especially including prestige."

Triumphantly he pulled the last page out of the machine. "Done! And if I do say so myself, a damned good story."

There was no answer.

He looked out of the window to his right. The other side of the street was a long desolate row of ruins. Only one building in the entire block had been left standing and that one was sliced off at the corner from roof to ground like a many-layered cake with one enormous bite taken out. In the rubble-heaps that spilled over the sidewalk, rusting steel girders stuck up like giant toothpicks. The ground floor must once have been a restaurant. He wondered if the proprietor had been a Nazi or just an ordinary little businessman like the businessmen back home.

He got up and poured himself a drink. "How'd you make out your first day in Frankfurt?"

"Just as you'd expect. Nine full hours tramping around from one office to another and all I got out of it was an incomplete set of identification papers. Our great peacetime

15

army! It's got everything so beautifully organized that you can't get anything done anymore."

He laughed. "Young lady, this is Headquarters European Theater. If a thing isn't impossible here, it isn't impossible anywhere." He was collecting the pages of what he had just written. "Did you get to see our four-star boy wonder?"

"General Blakely? I want you to know I was granted ten long minutes with His Elongated Highness, solely on the strength of having covered some of his more brilliant near-victories in the Mediterranean." She was evidently in a conversational mood, lying relaxed and still in the tub. "While the interview was going on, there was a German sculptor in the room making a bust of the great liberator, and throughout the entire time the General mugged and gestured with one eye on me and the other on the sculptor. Or shall we say one eye on public opinion and the other on posterity."

He clipped the pages together and put the story down on the table. "What did he talk about?"

"Blakely? Oh, mostly about food. Food is now, he says, a 'political factor.' "

"It sure is. Only I wonder who told him. What else did he say?"

"Nothing much. Everything is going along wonderfully with the occupation, progress crawling forward all over the place. American military government is a paragon of wisdom and efficiency, through whose peerless example the Germans have all become confirmed free-enterprising democrats. All we have to do now is teach German kids to play baseball and drink cokes, and we've got it made."

She was out of the tub now, he could hear the water noisily sucking out, her padded footsteps on the bathroom floor. He poured out another Scotch and tossed it down.

"Hurry up, honey, the drinks are getting cold."

"I'm hurrying." Her voice was sweet and unhurried. "What time is it?"

"What difference does it make? About eleven."

"You're through with the Saar story?"

"All through. Just waiting for you to get out of that bathroom and have a drink with me."

She came out in a white housecoat tied smugly at the waist. Her hair was piled on the top of her head, and she looked very young and pink and glowing. "Voilà!" she said, walking straight toward him.

"Jesus, you're beautiful, Carla."

"Am I?" looking up at him and smiling.

He tried to put his arms around her to kiss her, but she pushed him gently away. "I thought I was offered a drink," she said poutingly.

"You were. How do you want it?"

"Neat."

He poured her a stiff one, about a third of a glass. She picked it up and drank it thirstily, with evident enjoyment. "Still a competent little drinker, I see," he said, and reached over and took the glass from her hand and put it on the table.

This time he took her in his arms and kissed her, a long determined kiss.

At first, she pulled away from him a little, then her mouth began to tremble under his kiss. He tightened his arms around her and pressed himself hard against her, against the excruciating softness of her body. When he reached down to untie the housecoat, she made no move to stop him.

"Carla," he said against her mouth. "Carla. Now."

Slowly she extricated herself from his arms and walked over and turned out the lights. When she came back, the housecoat was wide open, floating behind her like a train. In the dim light of the room, he thought she had the most beautiful figure he had ever seen, slender and delicately formed but with wide full breasts. Without a word she came back into his arms, holding her face up like a child to be kissed.

"Do you know," he said later, lying on his back and staring up at the ceiling, "that you're absolutely terrific in bed?"

Carla made a little soft sound of dissent. "It's the bed," she said amiably. "It's a good bed." She reached for the sheet and pulled it up over them. "Could I have a cigarette?"

He lit two and handed her one in the darkness. He put the ashtray on his chest and then directed her hand to it. "There. Try not to miss it."

She laughed softly. "With that matting, you'd never know it if I did. Until maybe tomorrow, when smoke would come pouring out of your shirt-front."

He lay quiet for a long moment. "Carla," he said. "You know I'm very much in love with you, don't you?"

"I hoped you were, but I didn't know." In the darkness her voice had an appealing little-girl sincerity. "I thought if you were you'd tell me. And then I'd be very glad, because I've wanted so much for you to be in love with me."

"You have? Why?"

"Because——" The answer was hesitant but direct. "Because I've always been crazy about you, Bill. Ever since that night in the press camp in Brussels."

He reached out to put his arm around her.

"Bill," she said slowly. "What do you think of the food situation here? All this talk of Germans starving."

He raised himself on his elbow. "Gee, that's funny," he said. "You know, for a minute there I thought you were asking me about the food situation."

She giggled. "I was."

"'Food?"

"Food." Still laughing, she tugged at his arm. Then, more seriously: "Aw, please, Bill, please just tell me what you think of it. Two hundred words. Short sentences. It won't take more than a minute."

"Okay, okay. Well," he said, withdrawing his arm, "there's no doubt that as a nation Germany is goddamned hungry. Particularly the people in the big cities who haven't any way to scrounge around for anything extra. Up in the Ruhr, for example, where even the legal ration—which they seldom get— isn't much above the level of Buchenwald."

"Then why don't we send more food over from the States?"

"We're going to. You watch. Within a couple of months all America is going to go sentimental on the poor starving German."

"But what else can we do?"

"Nothing. It's too bad we have to go maudlin about it, and cite all the wrong reasons for doing the right thing. But the fact is we've *got* to send food over here, and keep sending it, and keep sending enough of it. Not out of mawkish pity or professional sentimentalism, but out of intelligent self-interest.

"How do you mean?"

"I mean you can't teach people anything when their stomachs are howling for food. Neither can you get any work out of them. I belong to the hard peace school. I think we ought to give these people a good stinging lesson in how to behave like human beings. But even I admit that starvation isn't going to do it. Starvation never taught anybody anything, except the value of bread. Wait till you've wandered around this godforsaken country awhile, you'll see that they'd slit each other's bellies for a premasticated potato. How are you going to teach a people human rights and constitutional government when all they're thinking about is food?" He sat up. "Let's have a drink."

"Fine."

He got up and groped toward the coffee table, poured out two drinks and brought them back to the bed.

"Hell," he said. "Let's not talk about Germany any more."

"I only want to ask one more question," she said. "Do you know anybody special that I can talk to in Munich about food? I have to go to Munich day after tomorrow, and I want to talk to somebody down there about crops and things."

Holding both glasses, he sat down on the edge of the bed. For a few minutes he said nothing. Then finally: "You're leaving for Munich day after tomorrow?"

"That's right."

"I thought you were going to stay in Frankfurt."

"I was. Only now I've got to go to Munich. The office wants a couple of stories from Bavaria."

"How long you going to be gone?"

"Just a couple of days. No more."

"Well," he said. "I'll be here when you get back. I hate to see you go off again though, when you've only just arrived."

"I know. But it's for such a little while."

Thoughtfully he handed her a glass and got back in the bed. "Carla, have you ever thought of quitting all this running around and settling down somewhere to do some serious writing?"

"No, not yet. Why?"

"I think you should. This story over here—the story of America in Europe—is too big for the daily press. God knows," he said wearily, "it's too big for the wire service. If I had any dough, I'd quit tomorrow and sit down to some real writing. But of course, I can't do it. But you could."

"How?"

"By marrying someone."

"Who, for example?"

"Me, for example."

"And be Mrs. World Press?"

"God, no! Be Carla MacMurphy who just happens to be married to a World Press man named Somers, and who now turns out her deathless prose for serious readers instead of subway straphangers. Doesn't sound so bad, now does it?"

"O no, Bill, it sounds wonderful. Only——" She stopped. "I don't think very much of marriage."

"Why not? Lots of people do, you know."

"I guess because I don't think much of divorce. And if you don't get married, you don't have to get divorced."

"You're a funny kid," he said.

She rolled over on her stomach and pillowed her head on

her arms. "Look what happened to my mother and dad. Maybe they were happy enough back in the beginning, I don't know. I don't remember. All I know is they never could agree. All she wanted to do was go back to Washington where her family was, and dabble in politics and become a famous Washington hostess. Her father was Vice President Tully, you know. And all Dad wanted to do was stay in South Boston and run his fish-packing plants and make money. So——"

"So——?"

"So she divorced him. He never recognized it, of course. I was only about twelve years old at the time, so I don't remember much about it. Anyway, now she's doing what she wanted to do all along. She's now Mrs. Horace Gladstone— the old Virginia hunting family, you know—and they claim you can't even get an introduction to the President unless she arranges it for you. And you just aren't anybody in Washington at all until you've been invited to one of her parties."

"And what about your dad?"

"I don't know. Mother's never spoken to him since the divorce, and I haven't been up there since before the war, the year I graduated. I guess he just goes on making fish cakes and drinking beer and getting richer and richer." She sighed. "I was nuts about him when I was little, but later on it got pretty awful. All the girls in prep school used to tease me about being the fishcake queen, and then I'd write home begging him not to meet the train because I was always so embarrassed at the way he looked and talked, and I didn't want the rest of the girls to see him. With mother it was different. She was terrifically impressive."

"But what's that got to do with you and me?"

"I don't know. I don't even know why I'm telling you all this. I guess I'm kind of tired."

He ran his finger down the velvety curve of her shoulder and back. "But that doesn't have to happen to us. After all, we're in the same business, we have the same interests. There's no reason why you and I should disagree on anything."

"Maybe not. Oh, I don't know. Bill, darling, let me do some thinking about it for awhile. I guess I do have a silly prejudice about marriage, but maybe after awhile I'll get over it."

"All right, honey. Only don't expect me to stop asking you."

"My darling," she said.

She reached across him to set her empty glass on the night-table, and in doing so her breast, her incredibly white breast in the shadowed room, brushed against his shoulder. He caught her in his arms.

20

She lay very still, her face turned toward him.

Deliberately, he leaned over and kissed her, a long tender kiss. "Carla," very low, "would you mind very much if I made love to you again?"

For answer she reached for his hand and placed it on her thigh.

By now, she thought, it must certainly be two or three in the morning. She was lying on her back completely naked, listening to his breathing. "Bill," she said.

There was no answer.

"Bill," a little louder.

She put her hand on his arm but he made no move. His breathing was deep and regular. Cautiously, she raised herself to a sitting position and started working herself down toward the foot of the bed, proceeding a few inches at a time. Her heart pounding, she slid off the edge of the bed and tiptoed to the window and looked at her watch. Twenty minutes after one.

On the table near the window lay the story on the Saar.

Quietly, she opened the closet door, took out a dark coat, put it on and buttoned it all the way up so no one would know she had nothing on underneath it. She found a pair of shoes.

"Timmy," she said softly.

The dog stretched and yawned, and in the quiet of the room it sounded like the roar of a lion.

"Sh-h-h," she said. "Come on."

Obediently, he climbed down from his chair and came to the door. Moving stealthily and almost without breathing she picked up the story and a pack of cigarettes from the table and let the dog and herself out, closing the door gently behind her.
· Once outside, she walked to the nearest corridor light, and standing underneath it began to read. "Good lead," she said, half-aloud. She read on a few paragraphs, then folded the story carefully and made for the stairwell and down the two flights to the lobby. The sergeant at the cable desk was fast asleep and snoring a little, his chin sagging on his chest.

"Hey!" she said. "Wake up!"

"Huh?"

"Copy to go out. Come on, Sergeant, get on your feet."

Squinting at her, he got up, took the story and began marking it for transmission. *"Washington Globe-Dispatch.* Press rate. MacMurphy. That right?"

"That's right."

"M-A-C-M-U-R-P-H-Y," writing it in.

"And could you please get it on the wire right away? Otherwise I'll miss the first edition."

"O.K., Miss MacMurphy. I'll get it out right away. Say, you look kinda tired."

She smiled wanly. "I am."

"You newspaper people work too hard. Know what time it is? Almost two A.M."

"Oh, that's all right," she said gallantly. "I'm used to it."

She started moving toward the door. "Get that story out right away now, O.K.?"

"Sure thing, Miss MacMurphy. Right away. Say," he added admiringly, "that dog is the exact same color your hair is."

"Really," not turning back.

"Yeah. Sure is beautiful to see the two of you together."

"Thank you."

"Say, don't go too far, Miss MacMurphy," he called after her. "It's not safe for a girl to be walking around this town alone this time of night."

"It's all right, Sergeant, we're only going a little way."

He watched her cross the lobby, then bent down and opened the transmission key.

Carla stepped out on the sidewalk into the moonlight.

God, how deathly still and cold the city was, as if at the bottom of a sea of stratospheric silence. As if, when you stamped your foot, all this pulverized rubble would rise in one slow dilating puff and burst like a bubble on some supernal surface a thousand light-years away. The feeling of living in an age long past came over her again.

There was something the mind could not accept about so much destruction, something that placed it either before the dawn of human civilization or after the twilight of its decline. Hairy-chested cavemen would be at home in this desolation, driving their placid mammoths around these piles of rubble; so would winged supermen riding radar-waves above it. But not an American girl reporter in a Fifth Avenue coat. In a Fifth Avenue coat and nothing else, she reminded herself sardonically, shoving her hands into her pockets to keep them warm.

The dog ran on ahead, stopping to wet on every heap of wreckage. She found a Kleenex in one of her pockets and meticulously wiped off the area of skin around her mouth. Probably smeared with lipstick all the time she was talking to the sergeant.

Footsteps came toward her around the corner; it was a German girl, a prostitute. You could tell by the long wavy hair, the

22

tightly pulled coat, the bare legs, the battered suitcase she was carrying, the defensive air of preoccupation. The country's full of them, she thought: Bund Deutscher Mädel offering GI's for chocolate and cigarettes what they used to offer Wehrmacht soldiers for Führer and Vaterland. State bitches without a state.

The girl passed her without a look, then stopped, set the suitcase down on the walk and said in hesitant English: "Hello. Miss."

Carla turned. "Yes?"

"Please, can you tell me where is the Bahnhof, the train nach Mannheim?"

In the pale moonlight she looked almost pretty, but very thin.

"Just at the end of this street, on the other side of the square." Carla pointed ahead. "But I don't believe there are any trains until morning. The trains stop at midnight, I think."

"Oh," said the girl, uncomprehendingly. It was evident her understanding of English was limited.

Carla looked down the rubbled street, silent and shadowless under the moon, and toward the spherical skeleton of the Hauptbahnhof. "I am walking in that direction," she said in German. "I will show you." She motioned to the girl to follow and started off toward the station.

"Oh, nicht doch, Sie dürfen doch . . . ist nicht nötig . . ." Her face anxious, protesting against the trouble she was causing, the girl picked up her suitcase and came along, walking just a little in back of Carla. The suitcase bumped awkwardly against her legs as she walked.

They crossed the street unspeaking, and were already in the bare moon-flattened Hauptbahnhof Platz before Carla explained again, this time in German, that the trains had probably stopped for the night.

"Oh, that doesn't matter," said the girl evenly. "I can wait. I have come all the way from Berlin to Frankfurt and it has taken me five days. I can afford another night." She stopped to shift her suitcase to the other hand. "Before the war it was only six hours from Berlin to Frankfurt. Now one is lucky to make it at all, even with papers."

"Your home is in Mannheim?"

"Oh, nein!" said the girl quickly. "We are Berliners, my family. We live in Berlin." There was a trace of pride in her voice and she began to walk faster.

Saying no more, they entered the station.

After the diffused moonlight outside, the Bahnhof seemed

an enormous dark cavern, walled in shadow and filled with an audible stagnant hush, the dead and smothering accumulation of all the sounds and smells that had filled it during the day.

It seemed as if every noise, their own footsteps as they fell, every smell, their own warm misty breath, was immediately snatched up by the silence and vaporized into a body of volatile human gases floating in its vaulted dome, as if the thousands of unwashed travellers who had passed through during the past twenty-four hours were still there breathing over their shoulders. Something of the station's size and its chill insatiable emptiness filled Carla with uneasiness, and she was only partially comforted to have Timmy so close to her side, walking quietly across the expansive, unlighted floor.

Rounding a corner into the main hall, she stumbled against the prostrate form of a man and drew back horrified. Timmy growled, and as the man slowly turned over on his side she realized that he was neither dead nor wounded but merely asleep on a blanket. Her eyes were more accustomed to the dark now, and suddenly she saw hundreds of faces looking out at her from the deeper shadows of the walls and corners, men, women and children huddled together in sleep or in wakefulness, on benches, on the floor, leaning against the walls or against bundles of baggage. Now, too, she could hear the heavy rhythmic breathing of hundreds of sleeping people, all the little noises of the waiting: a baby whimpered, an old man coughed, several men were quietly talking together, a child kept repeating petulantly "Ich habe Hunger, ich habe Hunger," and its mother's drowsy "ya-ya, ya-ya" was no more than a subconscious maternal response. Two ex-Wehrmacht soldiers walked past with packs on their backs and disappeared through a lightless doorway.

The girl from Berlin had moved ahead of her, still lugging her disreputable suitcase, and was making for a lighted bulletin board covered with pictures and notices. Curious, Carla followed and joined the four or five who stood before the board reading the signs: "Heimkehrer! Hast Du meinen Sohn gekannt? Heinrich Engstfeld, zum letsten Mal gesehen bei Stalingrad?" in neat amateurish handprinting above an army photograph of a blond Wehrmacht private. "Warst Du bei Metz?" asked another in crooked black letters over a faded snapshot of a captain.

The entire board was covered with them, hundreds of homemade signs, big and little, with or without photographs, all asking the same questions. "Homecomer! Were you at St. Lo? Kiev? Sevastopol? Warsaw? Salerno? Budapest? Have you seen

Sergeant, Lieutenant, Captain, Major Schmidt?"

Carla looked at the girl from Berlin, who was bending over her suitcase and pulling something out. When she straightened up, Carla saw that it was a similar card with a small military photo in one corner. Intently, her lips moving soundlessly as she worked, the girl found a free place amid the welter of notices and started tacking up her sign. In the overhead light of the bulletin board she looked younger than in the moonlight of the street. Her dark hair half obscured her face and she was shaking a little from tiredness or from cold. She was very thin, and her eyes, as she worked over the board, had a strange abstracted blankness.

Over her shoulder Carla read the sign: "Who knows my son Lieutenant Karl Lochmann, reported missing on the East Front?" and looked at young Karl Lochmann's impressive passport-photo face and impeccable Oberleutnant's uniform.

Finished with her work, the girl looked up and saw Carla watching her. She flushed slightly and turned away to pick up her suitcase, then came back and said earnestly: "Thank you very much, I am all right now."

"That is your brother?" asked Carla, motioning to the notice the girl had just tacked up. "The one named Lochmann?"

"Yes." The girl looked off into the darkness of the station. "I do not believe, myself. It is my mother who makes the signs and I put them up because she makes me promise. German women are all the same," she said listlessly. "They will not believe a man is dead unless they see him dead. And who ever sees the dead?" She took a few steps away. "So, thank you. I am going now to find a place to sleep." Without another word she walked off and disappeared in the shadows.

For a moment Carla stood irresolute in the center of the station, looking around at the huddled crowds of humanity lining the walls in all their attitudes of sleep or sleeplessness. Then, calling the dog, she started back.

As she came out into the clear moonlight of the street, she was mentally writing the lead on a story about German railroad stations and wondering where she could get a photographer to take a few shots of that bulletin board. The air was colder now, it must be just before dawn.

With Timmy running ahead, she entered the Park Hotel lobby and as she passed the desk left a call for eight in the morning. When she was halfway up the stairs she took her shoes off, and went the rest of the way in her bare feet.

That poor hopeless little girl from Berlin, she thought as she fitted the key stealthily in the lock. Too bad I couldn't have

25

done any more for her. But she wouldn't have accepted it if I had. Probably not a whore after all. Too proud and too skinny.

CHAPTER THREE

MUNICH looked worse than Frankfurt. Probably, thought Carla, wheeling the jeep easily around a devastated square, because it had originally been a more beautiful city.

The streets had been cleaned up, the rubble pushed back and heaped upon itself in vacant lots or neatly stacked in the window openings of hollow buildings. Yet somehow the new tidiness had only succeeded in making the destruction seem more extensive, the city emptier and more desolate.

As if perpetrating a coarse joke, the clearing away of the rubble had exaggerated into monstrosity one of prewar Munich's greatest charms, its spaciousness. What had been wide tree-shaded avenues were now flat serpentine tracks through deserts of waste. Under a pitiless southern sun, Munich lay naked and prostrate. All covering, all protection gone, the corpse boiled and rotted in the sizzling heat of summer, its population like ants crawling unceasingly in and out of its gaping, festering wounds.

The road in from the autobahn cut through an abandoned tenement district, past mile after mile of bleak architectural stubble that was nothing but fragments of wall and stumps of amputated chimneys. Stopping for crosswise traffic to pass, she watched crowds of Müncheners jamming themselves into a streetcar. No more bright Bavarian costumes, no more good-natured shouting and singing in the streets. Only a sullen, ragged people pushing and jostling their way onto an already densely packed rear-platform, latecomers hanging on the back like monkeys and those left behind waiting stolidly and unemotionally for the next trolley. All of them, those who got on, those who were forced off, those who waited, had the air of people who didn't know where they were coming from or where they were going, and didn't care much either way.

Traffic, mostly American jeeps and command cars, was heavy in the narrow street. She proceeded slowly, watching the pavement carefully for bomb holes. The devastation in this area was deep and extensive. The beautiful Acropolis-like National Theater was a surrealist wreck, its roof gone, the pediment fallen, its Doric columns reaching up in architectural

26

futility to support an empty blue sky. Block after block it continued, blackened gutted buildings, boarded-up shops, trees and lampposts uprooted, monuments and statues toppled like broken dolls.

Nowhere was there any sign of rebuilding. All that had been accomplished was simply a rearrangement of the rubble, sweeping it up from here and piling it there, shovelling it to one side as if one were clearing a driveway of snow and expected it to melt away in a few days.

Abruptly, she swung left through the Isar Tor of the ancient city wall, across the Isar and out of the center of the city toward the suburb of Grünwald, where she had been told she would find the press camp.

As she proceeded outward the devastation diminished, and as she entered Grünwald, she felt some of the atmosphere of the old Munich returning. Behind these heavy trees and luxuriant shrubs, she knew, were bombed houses, every bit as ugly in their destruction as the city buildings. But you had to peer through thick foliage to see them; if you drove fast you would think this was the Munich you had known before the war. With relief, she found the sign she was looking for: PRESS CAMP. A heavy iron gate, half-open, led down to a wide expanse of lawn.

The drive was newly limed white crushed stone, winding through beautifully landscaped gardens and around thick clumps of evergreens. At the end of the drive stood a rambling, heavily timbered Bavarian country house surrounded by tall Norway pines, its overhanging balconies and steep roofs scarcely visible. Behind towered the misty theatrical backdrop of the Bayrische Alpen, silently communing with the clouds.

She brought the jeep to a crunching stop in front of the house and got out to look around. The place was heavy with midsummer silence, with the droning of wasps and the sleepy murmuring of swallows under the eaves. There were no signs of habitation, except for a lone jeep parked under the pines a few hundred feet from the main door. She released Timmy, who ran immediately around the side of the house. At least if there's a kitchen, Timmy'll find it, she thought.

A corporal appeared at the door and walked slowly down the steps toward her. His walk was loose and indolent and he scowled against the sun as if it were a constant personal annoyance to him.

"Miss MacMurphy?" He held out his hand. "My name is Samsen, I'll take care of your bags and park your jeep for you.

27

You'd probably like to go in right away. The Colonel's been expecting you."

"Fine, Corporal. Thank you."

They walked up the steps to the door and into a cool tile-floored vestibule filled with potted linden trees. "Quite a press camp," she commented.

"I think you'll like it here," said Corporal Samsen. "It's a wonderful place to rest."

She glanced at him sharply, but he seemed quite serious.

"Used to belong to Robert Ley, the labor chief," he continued. "The old guy'd left by the time we latched onto it, but his family was still here. We kicked them out."

They started up a curving staircase. "You're the only correspondent we got here," he said, "outside of a French reporter who's writing a book. The Colonel's been kind of bored, nothing to do and nobody to entertain. He'll be glad to see you."

"What's the Colonel's name?" she asked.

"Oh, don't you know Colonel Kennebunk? I thought from the way he talked he'd known you in London. He used to be PRO in London, you know, ever since right after the invasion. I've been with him all the way," he said proudly. "Through here."

He led her into a bedroom littered with men's army clothing and through it to a sun-drenched balcony. "Colonel Kennebunk, this is Miss MacMurphy."

Colonel Kennebunk got up from the balcony floor where he had been sitting sunning himself. He was a huge bald man with an enormous hairy chest, and all he had on was a pair of khaki shorts. His back and shoulders were browned to the color and texture of shoe-leather, but his stomach, miraculously enough for such a prominent mound of flesh, showed no effects of the sun. It was white, like the belly of a frog, and it hung over his shorts like an enormous obscene breast with the navel where the nipple should have been.

"How do you do?" she said politely, holding out her hand.

The hand that took hers was soft in spite of its brownness, and surprisingly small. "Damned glad to see you. We thought maybe you'd fallen in a manhole somewhere." He laughed broadly, a laugh that cut across his red-brown face like the snap of a shark and then suddenly vanished. "Sit down, I'm just about to order up some martinis." He turned to the corporal. "See what you can do about some drinks, eh, Pete? This young lady looks dry."

The corporal vanished.

28

"Sit down, sit down," he said jovially, motioning to a couch. He sat down in a chair and leaned back with his arms crossed behind his head, his spindly brown legs spread wide apart. His armpits were as white as his stomach, and Carla thought of the frog again. "Or maybe you'd like to change into something more comfortable, some shorts or something, and get some of this Bavarian sun before it goes down. No? Well, tomorrow. Anyway, make yourself comfortable. One of the boys'll be up in a minute with the drinks."

"It's a little early for cocktails, isn't it?" asked Carla.

"Never too early for drinks around here. We start in the morning and end up the next morning. Oh, you'll like it here. Get a good rest. No better place in the world for a rest. You know Polly Wilson, she was here with us two weeks, didn't do a damned thing but lie in the sun and drink gin. Great girl for gin, Polly. How was your trip? That's a pretty good road, isn't it? Made it myself in four hours one day, going up to Frankfurt to see the General. You know General Blakely, wonderful fellow. Oh, here they are." He got up, nervous with anticipation. He almost wags his tail, Carla thought.

A pfc set a tray of glasses and bottles on a wicker table nearby. "Now, let's see," said the Colonel, hovering over the tray. "Gin, vermouth. Ice. Olives. Hey, is that all the olives we got in this fu——" He recovered himself. Then to the pfc sharply: "Get me some more olives."

"Yes, sir." The pfc vanished.

The joviality returned. "Yes, this is quite a place. Used to belong to Robert Ley, you know, the labor chief? We kicked him out though. Guy's up at Nuremberg now, being tried." He measured out the gin and vermouth. "Where in Christ's name are those olives? Yeah, those Nazis sure put it on, took all the best spots in Germany, lived like country squires lording it all over everybody else. You want to have Pete show you around later, see how this guy Ley lived. Boy!" He handed her a martini. "There now, try that."

The corporal stuck his head out the door. "How's everything going?"

"Oh, Pete. Come on in, grab yourself a martini. Carla here is just telling me about her trip. Here, take mine, I'll make another." He fixed himself a martini and settled back in the deck chair. "Where's that Frenchman? Ought to get him in here to meet Carla and have a drink before dinner. Handsome fellow. Damned handsome, I'd say, wouldn't you say, Pete? I suppose I ought to keep him and Carla apart." The smile slashed ruthlessly across his face. "Against my own interest.

Should keep the pretty girls to myself and let these handsome fellows make time with the Fräuleins. That right, Pete?"

The corporal grinned. "That's right, sir."

"Well, here I go, getting soft again. Go get the Frenchman, Pete. Ask him to come up for a drink."

"He's gone into town, sir. He had an appointment with some Military Government people. He told me he'd be back around six."

"Oh, well, you'll meet him at dinner," the Colonel reassured her.

"Perhaps I know him," she said casually. "What's his name?"

"Poignon, Charles Poignon," said Kennebunk. He pronounced it Poy-gi-nun. "He's a queer duck. Was a prisoner somewhere in Germany during the war. Now he's writing a book about postwar Europe. Pretty intelligent fellow, though. Seems to know a lot about economics and politics and things like that." Unconsciously, the tiny brown hands were patting and caressing his stomach, moving intimately and tenderly along the folds of flesh, the tips of his fingers proceeding lasciviously across that soft white mound to the armpits, then sliding back to begin again their delicate caressing movement. Carla looked away.

She finished her martini and turned to Samsen. "Could you tell me which room I have? I'd like to go in and get cleaned up a bit."

The corporal looked inquiringly at Kennebunk.

"One more," urged the Colonel. "Can't fly on one wing." And as if running through a familiar routine, the corporal jumped up for the cocktail mixer and refilled Carla's glass.

The corporal's hands were as freckled as his face and covered with fine red hair. She liked his looks, easy-going but alert, obviously the Colonel's pet, otherwise a pretty typical GI who'd seen enough of war to know his way around but not so much that he'd become bitter. Probably a good guy to talk to when she wanted the GI attitude on something.

The Colonel had settled back in his deckchair again. "What did you drive down in?" he asked Carla.

"Jeep." The corporal answered for her.

"A jeep? Haven't you got a car yet?" The Colonel was astounded. "You better hurry up, girl. First thing you know the Army's going to put an end to all this. Already it's damned hard to get a car registered, unless of course it's legal, and they won't let you buy gas unless the car's registered."

"I thought I might be able to get a car down here, but I didn't quite know how I'd go about it." Her voice was sweet

30

and childish. "Maybe you and Corporal Samsen could help me a little bit."

"Well——" His wink was as subtle as the click of a camera shutter. "If it's just a question of a legalized bill of sale, little thing like that, maybe our bright young Pete here could help you out. Eh, Pete?"

"Now, sir!" chidingly. "You know it isn't so damned easy any more." Still grinning at the Colonel, he got up and filled the glasses again. "Let's put it this way—I'll do what I can. How's that, sir?"

"That'll do for a start," said the Colonel with mock gruffness. "Anyway, get to work on it. Can't let a beautiful chick like this run around in a jeep all her life, can we, Pete?"

The sun was beginning to set. Behind the Colonel's head the pinnacles of the Bavarian Alps were outlined with red, the pines pompous and aloof against an apricot sky. Carla picked up her WAC purse and beret and prepared to leave.

"Gee, if you could——" she said, smiling appealingly at both of them. She let the sentence hang unfinished and stood up.

"Not leaving, are you, Carla?"

She explained that she had to bathe and dress for dinner, and Pete said he'd show her to her room, which was the corner room with the big balconies. "Best room in the house," boomed Kennebunk. "Now don't take too long, Carla. We'll meet you in the dining room at half-past seven."

How I'd love to get hold of a car, she thought as she unbuttoned her tunic and pulled off her skirt. Something really lush, too, like a Horch or a Mercedes-Benz. Maybe if I pushed the colonel a little bit more. . . . She decided to wear a simple, demure little yellow dress, and shook it out and laid it on the bed while she went in to bathe.

After her bath, she walked out on the balcony to brush her hair. What a spot for a press camp! More of a health resort or a country estate than a billet and communications center for reporters. She wondered what you did with your copy when it was written. Maybe you sent it into Munich by pony express, Corporal Samsen galloping the entire distance in his indomitable little jeep.

The mountains were already darkening, purple peaks that seemed hundreds of miles farther away than they had seemed an hour ago, the pines shrouded in a Götterdämmerung mist that drifted cool against her face. Under the last sheets of sunlight, the press camp grounds lay snugly bedded down for the night. Near a dark clump of pines, a group of men stood talking. She recognized Pete Samsen, the other three she didn't know: two army officers in pinks and a stocky dark-haired man in a French uniform. Poignon. She stepped back quickly into the shadow of the eaves and buttoned her housecoat carefully up to her throat. Then she leaned forward and looked again.

He seemed very broad, medium height, well-uniformed. She heard his voice in answer to one of the others; it was deep and resonant, with only a slight accent. So he spoke English. From the corner of the balcony she watched them turn slowly and disappear behind the pines.

Charles Poignon. He was probably a bore, just another thick-lipped silver-tongued Frenchman who happened to be writing a book on Europe. Certainly not very important as a journalist or she'd have met him in Paris.

She turned and walked back into the room and started collecting from the two bags the various items she needed to make up her face. The dressing-table was poorly lighted, but it was a beautiful piece of furniture, a Louis Quinze in rich mahogany with a five-paneled mirror. In the dim overhead light her hair was like polished copper, it fell straight and silky to her shoulders and in the back almost a third of the way to her waist, curled up only at the ends. Should remember to call Bill in Frankfurt sometime tonight, I promised to call him as soon as I arrived, by now he might be worried about me. If it hadn't been for that patronizing frog-bellied colonel and his dry martinis, I wouldn't have forgotten. Well, I'll be sure to call him before dinner. Bill is an angel, really. It's too bad he's Jewish.

In the middle of her dressing, she changed her mind and put on a low-necked black dress. Frenchmen like sophisticated clothes. From a second-story balcony, and with the lawn so shrouded in mist, you couldn't tell whether he was good looking or not. But he did have a wonderfully rich deep masculine voice.

She was a little later to dinner than she had expected to be, and when she came in they were all seated at a long, candle-lit table in front of French windows that opened onto the lawn. The colonel was at the far end of the table; the place at the foot had been left for her. Gracious and smiling, she acknowledged Kennebunk's introductions, shaking hands with each one in turn: a tall blond, vacuous-looking Major Post; two captains, whose names she missed; a thick swarthy sergeant named Pitterino; Corporal Samsen; and finally, at her right, Charles Poignon.

He was taller than she had thought, with very broad shoulders, curly dark hair. He didn't kiss her hand, but said simply "How do you do?" and even let the major pull her chair out for her.

"Well," said Kennebunk heartily, when they were all re-seated. "Here she is, just like I promised you. Now you wolves can go ahead and eat your chow. They've been sitting around here with their tongues hanging out," he explained down the length of the table to Carla, "and not for food either."

Carla unfolded her napkin and turned to say something to Poignon, but he was already engrossed in conversation with the captain at his right. At her left, Major Post started listing people he thought she should see while she was in Munich. "I know the newspaper game all right," he informed her. "Before the war I was in the advertising department of the Jacksonville *Blade*." She listened politely, at the same time trying to catch what Poignon and the captain were talking about.

"Now of course you'll want to go down to Berchtesgaden," said the major. "Just let me know when you want a jeep or a driver and I'll fix you up. I take care of all transportation for the correspondents."

"Oh," said Carla. "Thank you."

"What time do you want to leave?"

Poignon and the captain were talking about tank warfare. "For all his faults," Poignon was saying, in that deep under-toned voice, "de Gaulle knew the importance mobile armor would have in this war. I'm not pretending that he could have saved the French Army, but——"

"Oh, excuse me," said Carla. "What time do I want to leave? About eight, I think."

The major put his hand over hers and assured her gravely that he would have a driver waiting for her at eight. "I'd drive you myself," he said, "except that I've got to go in to Head-quarters tomorrow." He was a pleasant young man, self-confident and dumb. Must have got his commission through the mail, she thought.

Dinner was served by two young girls in full-skirted Ba-varian Dirndl-Kleider with white aprons. It was better-than-average army food—a heavily gravied steak, French fried potatoes and canned green beans—and the Colonel ordered a bottle of wine from the cellar. "It isn't often we have such a beautiful guest."

As soon as the glasses were full, Carla lifted hers and laughingly proposed a toast in French: "A ma mère, à la Vierge, au Général Bonaparte."

"Tiens!" said Poignon, surprised, turning away from his discussion of tanks. "You speak French?"

"Sometimes." She smiled and held up her glass. "Will you drink with me?"

Their glasses clicked.

"Carla, what the hell does that toast mean?" bellowed the colonel.

Carla looked helplessly to Poignon, and he answered at once, his voice easy and clear. "It means 'To my mother, to the Virgin Mary, to General Bonaparte.' "

He turned back to Carla. "You are an admirer of Napoléon?"

"Not really," smiling. "Except that Napoléon conquered Germany too, but was smart enough not to try to occupy it on a quadripartite basis."

His reaction was quick and appreciative. "But Napoléon too proceeded from a victory over Germany into a catastrophic war with Russia."

"You think we are doing the same thing?"

He shrugged his shoulders. "Perhaps not. But from the way things are going———. Certainly, one has no business today being optimistic."

The candle flames flickered and brightened in the wind that blew from the gardens. Conscious that she had worn the low-cut dress, she leaned forward over the table.

"How long are you staying in Munich?" he asked.

"Only a few days this time. I was here with the American armies during the last year of the war, but after V-E day I went back to France. Now I've come back again to do a series of pieces on the occupation."

"You are with an American newspaper?"

"The *Washington Globe-Dispatch*. Then I also write a column called 'Look Here, America!' which is syndicated to 120 newspapers."

He didn't seem very impressed. He was looking at her throat and the curve of her breasts, but unlike Major Post, whose eyes had been moist with admiration, his glance seemed cool and absent-minded.

"And what do you think of the occupation?" It was more polite than interested.

She smiled a full sweet smile. "I think—I think that at the present moment the most important political factor in Germany is food." She hesitated to see how he was taking it, then continued. "After all, you can't teach people democracy when their stomachs are howling for food. Certainly the Germans

34

deserve a good hard lesson in how to behave in a civilized world, but starvation is not the way to do it. Starvation has never taught anyone anything, except perhaps the value of bread."

His eyes now were alight with interest. He wasn't handsome, she decided, he was simply big and well-built, with a magnificent broad forehead and, under thick black eyebrows, startlingly clear blue eyes. There was a powerful masculinity to him, a kind of suspended violence that you caught immediately, either from the latent vitality of that broad stocky figure or the mature resonant depth of his voice. She wondered where he had learned English.

She asked about his book, and he seemed pleased that she was interested. It was a study of postwar Germany, he said, an analysis of the occupation. Or, rather, he corrected himself, the occupations. On the whole, he said, he preferred the British one. The British had no illusions, as the Americans had, that underneath those crumpled swastikas beat an automatically democratic heart. On the other hand, they had none of the proselytizing fervor of the Russians, who were spreading the faith with Tommy-guns and clubs.

"I'd like to talk to you about that, some time," said Carla. "Perhaps when there isn't quite so much noise around."

Dinner was now finished, the plates taken away, and one of the waitresses was serving coffee. Conversation at the other end of the table had grown enormously in volume. Kennebunk and the little Italian sergeant were holding a loud, mock-serious argument on U.S. bombing. "To hell with the Ninth Air Force!" bellowed Kennebunk.

"To hell with the Eighth!" shouted Pitterino, grinning. The rest of the table were laughing like farmhands at a burlesque show.

In the middle of the shouting, the Colonel got up to get a bottle of brandy and started around the table filling brandy-glasses. When he passed Pitterino's chair, he whacked him soundly on the side of the head. "I'll have you courtmartialed, you little wop sonofabitch!" he roared.

The officers were convulsed with laughter. "O Christ! O Christ!" said the major softly at her left, wiping his eyes with his napkin.

"One should finish one's wine," Poignon advised her gently. "It is not the worst, even if it is German."

At that moment there was a crash just behind Corporal Samsen's chair. The waitress who had been serving coffee had fallen; tray, cups, saucers, coffeepot smashed to the floor. The

35

Italian sergeant and Samsen jumped up immediately and before Carla could offer help had lifted the girl and carried her out of the room. Uncomprehending, she turned to Major Post.

"It's nothing to worry about," he explained. "She's been ailing for some time. She does that every once in awhile. She's leaving here day after tomorrow."

A middle-aged woman in a Mother Hubbard apron came in and quickly swept up the debris, and Kennebunk, who had not spoken a word during the entire scene, continued his way around the table, pouring brandy. Sergeant Pitterino and Pete came back to their places announcing that more coffee would be coming up in a minute.

"How about a brandy for Carla?" Kennebunk leaned suggestively over her shoulder. "Have to finish this meal up right. How'd you like your dinner? That's a wonderful cook we got, eh, Carla? Used to be an art critic in Boston, but he sure can cook. Hey, Pete, run in and get Otis to come out here and meet Carla and have a cognac with us." He stood back away from the table with the bottle in his hand and started to sing. "Off we go, into the wide blue yonder———" in a deep lusty baritone.

They all joined in.

"Do they do this for every guest?" she asked Poignon through the singing.

"I don't know. They've done it for me only four times."

"Why don't you join in the singing?" asked the major.

She shook her head.

He leaned over confidentially. "Don't worry about that gal. She's all right. She's going back to the DP camp Tuesday."

"What's the matter with her, though? Does she faint like that often?"

"Oh, she just gets a little sick once in awhile. Nothing serious." He hesitated a moment. "The Colonel's got her knocked up, that's all. Or at least, that's what she claims. The Colonel says it's Pete. Anyway, she's leaving."

"Oh," said Carla. "I see. What nationality is she?"

"Jug."

"Yugoslav?"

"Yeah."

"Carla, my pet." Kennebunk was around in back of her chair again, leaning over her shoulder. "I'd like you to meet our cook, Otis." His words were a little foggy.

She turned around to say hello to a pfc who must have been forty or forty-five years old and who was obviously very drunk.

"Hello, Miss MacMurphy," said the pfc slowly. "Pleased to meet ya."

"Hello, Otis," she said cordially.

Kennebunk helped Otis to a chair, where he sat swaying unevenly from side to side. He poured him a drink, and then started around the table again, pouring brandy with varying accuracy into one glass after another.

As soon as he passed and was moving back up toward the head of the table, Carla touched Poignon's arm. "Would you like to take a short walk around the garden with me? I think I'd like to get outside."

His eyes shone. Without a word, he got up and pulled out her chair.

"We're going for a little walk," she whispered to the major. "We'll be back in a few minutes."

The major nodded and watched them leave.

Outside, the air was cool and dark, the pines still and secretive. They walked slowly away from the house, not talking, listening to the sounds of revelry diminishing as they walked.

"Who told you I was writing a book on Germany?"

"Colonel Kennebunk."

"Der Gutsherr, der Oberst Kennebunk, the new lord of the manor. He is an old friend of yours?"

"No, not at all. I just met him a few hours ago."

"But he calls you by your prénom."

"It means nothing. It's just an American way of being friendly."

"Carla? Is that your name? It's an Italian name."

"Yes." She was delighted that he had asked. For a moment, she thought of explaining to him how she had acquired the name Carla, but thought better of it and said nothing.

"I think I am against all occupations," he said thoughtfully. "Particularly the kind that produce that," motioning back toward the lights of the house, the sounds of shouting and laughter that drifted to them across the patterned lawn. "That is the way the Germans acted when they were occupying France."

"But the Americans aren't the only ones who behave like that."

"No. But they are the noisiest and the most noticeable. They are the richest, they have the most to eat and drink, and they are completely unconscious of how they look to others. Like children, innocent and destructive."

She stood quietly beside him, shivering a little in the cold. From the other side of the garden came the steady pulsating singing of crickets, undaunted and optimistic.

He looked down at her. "It is difficult to believe that you

37

are a serious reporter, interested in what happens now to Europe."

"Why?"

He touched her cheek softly with one finger. "This," he said. "You are so dernière mode. You look as though you should be dancing at Les Ambassadeurs, instead of covering Germany for a daily newspaper."

He'll kiss me now, she thought.

But instead he started walking again, and she had to hurry to catch up with him.

At the edge of the rock-garden he stopped. The crickets were quiet now, only one, way to the right, with the courage to keep up his cheerful chirping. "Which would be all right. The world must have its children. Except that in this case the children have as a plaything the most destructive force ever known, the atom bomb." He shook his head. In the half light his face seemed angular, almost tragic. "You are cold," looking down at her again. "I think I' had better take you inside." From the house came a sudden burst of male laughter, the sound of singing: "Roll me over, roll me over——"

They stood still for a moment, listening, then started around toward the front entrance. The gardens were quiet, the grass wet under their feet, the sound of the crickets regular and unceasing as the roll of the sea. I've ruined a pair of shoes, she thought, but it doesn't matter.

"Will you be here tomorrow?" she asked, as they let themselves in the front door.

"Tomorrow I am going out to Dachau."

"Oh, how strange. So am I. Perhaps we could go together."

"Bon!" he said. "What time?"

"At eight?"

"Fine."

They mounted the stairs in silence. When they reached the door of her room, he bowed slightly, said goodnight, and turned to go. He was halfway down the corridor when she called after him. "At eight, then, at the front door."

"D'accord." Without even pausing, he rounded the curve of the staircase and continued down the stairs.

Slowly she closed the door, and for a long moment stood there inside, leaning against it. Below, like an intestinal rumbling, she could hear the noisy drunken singing of Kennebunk and his staff, still at the table.

She walked over to the Louis Quinze dressing-table and looked at her face in the mirror, the pointed baby-chin, the wide grey-green eyes, the frame of burnished red hair. You are so dernière mode, you look like someone who should be dancing at Les Ambassadeurs.

She wished she had worn the demure little yellow dress.

CHAPTER FOUR

THE MORNING was moist and cool, but with a heavy unremitting brightness that promised a blisteringly hot day ahead. Carla walked slowly, gracefully, down the steps of the press camp, confident that Poignon was already there waiting.

He wasn't.

Her jeep had been pulled out of the parking place onto the drive and a stocky little German in a khaki shirt and a pair of ill-fitting black trousers was working on it. Head and shoulders buried behind the hood of the jeep, he was moving back and forth with a rag and some tools, whistling as he worked. Otherwise, the place was deserted.

Hearing her step on the crushed stone, the driver stuck his head out from under the hood, grinned, and said politely: "Morgen, Miss MacMurphy."

His hair was lightbrown, like that of most Germans, and a shock of it hung down over his sun-browned face. She wondered that a German driver hired just for the day had gone to all the trouble to find out her name and learn how to pronounce it. Anything for cigarettes. "Morgen," she answered.

She stood for a few minutes watching him work, then walked around the side of the house into the garden where she and Poignon had been together the night before. She tried to remember what he looked like but it escaped her, all she could recall was his voice and a kind of bulkiness he had, the curly blackness of his hair and the breadth of his shoulders. The garden was covered with dew, lawn and flowers glistened in the early sunlight, thick with the quiet fragrant impersonal business of pollination. It would be a hot day. It was a good thing she had put her hair up and worn the little yellow dress. Slowly, she wandered back toward the jeep. The one time in months she had been on time. What could be keeping him?

The driver was still working industriously under the hood, whistling tunelessly but with considerable volume. He had the average German's love of work for work's sake, a seeming happy devotion to the job itself, which she knew from experience was not always accompanied by an understanding of what was to be accomplished. She hoped he knew what he was doing, and wasn't simply taking the jeep apart out of curiosity.

"It's a pretty good jeep," she ventured in German.

"Ja-ja," he said, not bothering to look up. He continued with his tinkering.

"Is there something wrong?"

"Nay," preoccupiedly, over his shoulder.

She was beginning to get a little irritated. "What are you doing then?"

"Filter."

Aware of her momentary impotence she stood in the bright sunlight staring at his broad back, the dark circles of perspiration under his armpits, the clipped brown hair of his thick neck. She could have kicked him. She looked back at the house to see if Charles was in sight, turned around furious, then thought better of it. A long day ahead, and Charles would be sure to sense any unpleasantness. If she were alone, in her slacks and tunic, she'd get rid of this nervy kraut and take over the jeep herself. Looking down at the folds of her yellow skirt and the childishly chic sandals on her feet, she tried again in as pleasant tone as she could manage: "In the Army we always used to say that the jeep won the war."

His head bobbed suddenly up from under the hood. "Nein," he answered shortly. "Ist nicht wahr. The American Panzer won the war, the Sherman, you call it." With his sleeve he tried to rub away a smear of grease that streaked his face. He squinted at her under his rumpled hair, good-natured but positive. "In May of 1942 we who were on the Eastern Front knew the war was lost when we met the first American Sherman tanks. There was one full Russian division against us, all in these American tanks, wave after wave of them. At that moment we knew Germany was beaten, no matter what the officers said. In the Stari Crim, that was."

"Where?"

"In the Crimea."

"You were in the Wehrmacht?"

"Ja-ja," grinning. "All German men my age were in the army." His teeth were even and white, his face a healthy brown. He put down his wrench. "I was in the 24th Panzer Division."

"On the Eastern Front?"

"On all fronts," proudly and unequivocally. "Belgium, France, Italy, then in Russia, Hungary, Bulgaria, everywhere. All the way through to the end. 1945—the end."

"You were a mechanic?" motioning to the jeep.

40

"Mechanic and tank-driver—and fighter. A Panzer Grena-
dier." Then, with no attempt at modesty: "That's why I can
fix anything. This is a good jeep, but you don't give it enough
attention." He reached down around the filter, made some
expert adjustment, wiped his hands off on an oil-soaked rag
and started around toward the other side of the jeep.

"I would like to get an auto," she said tentatively.

He put down the rag and came back. "An automobile? Miss
MacMurphy, you are an American, with cigarettes, it is the
easiest thing in the world to get a car. A schöner Wagen, so!"
He curved the forefinger of his right hand in a circle with his
thumb and held it up as if blowing a kiss. "So! Horch, Merce-
des, Opel, Adler, even a Czechoslovak Tatra. You want a wonderful car, Miss MacMurphy? You have cigarettes?"

"Yes."

"So! You leave it to Kripke. I know these Bayrischen, they
are crazy to get cigarettes, particularly for an automobile that
maybe doesn't belong to them anyway. What Spiessbürger!
Ha!" He waved the Bavarians aside, shaking his head in dis-
missal of the entire province. "How many cartons do you
have, Miss MacMurphy? Thirty, maybe?"

"That depends on what kind of car it is."

"For thirty cartons, a twelve-cylinder Horch, almost completely legal——"

"Sh-h!" She caught sight of Poignon coming down the steps.
She took a step away. "What did you say your name was?"

"Kripke," he said, smiling broadly. "Ernst Kripke." He
bowed from the waist, made a crisp military turn and before
she knew it was back under the hood whistling the same un-
recognizable tune, this time with a loud, deliberate innocence.

"Good morning!" she called, watching Poignon cross the
drive. Her voice was sweetly cordial.

"Good morning!" He was in uniform, as last night, but with
his shirt-collar open at the neck and revealing a heavy growth
of dark chest-hair. He looked younger than she had thought,
perhaps in his mid-thirties, and she had another quick intuitive
sense of his easy, confident masculinity.

"Well," he said pleasantly. "You are up earlier than I expected. I always suppose that a beautiful woman will be at least
thirty minutes late. This is your jeep?"

"Yes."

"Bon!" Without more ado, he unbuckled his camera and
put it on the seat. "We are ready, then?"

Kripke noisily slammed down the hood and fastened it first

41

at one side and then the other. With alacrity, but limping a little, he appeared at Carla's elbow to help her in.

She stepped as gracefully as she could into the jeep. Next time she would keep him waiting an hour.

In a moment they were settled and Kripke with a great roar of gas had the jeep underway, clattering across the gravel toward the gate. At the exit to the road he braked. "To Berchtesgaden?" he asked with routine politeness.

"Nein," she said sharply. "Dachau."

"But the Major said you wanted———"

"Never mind what the Major said. To Dachau."

"Yes, Miss MacMurphy," meekly. He turned left.

She threw Poignon a glance of secret amusement. "They're always so positive," she said. "They were even positive they'd win the war."

Poignon said nothing. She wondered how much German he understood, and had a moment's uncomfortable suspicion that both men had seen through her change of plan but were too gentlemanly, in Poignon's case, and too mercenary, in Kripke's case, to betray their knowledge. She glanced sharply at both of them, but Kripke was engrossed in watching the road and dodging holes, Poignon gazing fascinated at the block-on-block monotony of ruins, half-ruins, ruins.

For a long time they bounced along in silence. Both men seemed closed away in some secret area of thought, walled around by an imperturbability to anything but the immediate job, the driving of a jeep from Grünwald to Dachau. It was one thing the war had taught soldiers on both sides of every battleline, she thought: total immersion in the task at hand. To the exclusion of everything not immediately relevant, like the girl you are riding with, who also just happens to own the jeep and to have made the whole trip possible. She was beginning to get angry at Poignon's silence.

At last he turned to her. "Terrible road," he said.

Terrible! It was a washboard of hardened mud, furrowed and ribbed like a frozen field, and the jeep was a lame jackrabbit nosediving its way across muck and mud and dusty gravel, throwing up a bombardment of each as it hobbled along.

"Yes, isn't it?" she said sweetly, hanging onto the hard iron seat and doing her best to maintain some kind of physical and emotional equilibrium in the rattling, jumping jeep. She clenched her teeth and hung on, as if by clamping her jaws very tight together she could hold down the flood of irritation rising inside of her.

Another long period of hot dusty clattering, with not a word exchanged between them. She wondered if he was always this rude, or was he really thinking of something.

"We are almost there," said Kripke, slowing down for a paved crossroad. "Links oder rechts?"

"You have not been here before?" asked Poignon.

"Nein," said Kripke flatly.

Poignon nodded gravely and said nothing.

Carla saw a sign. "Hier rechts," she directed, and they turned right through a neighborhood of neatly tended middle-class bungalows, like an average American small town. The road proceeded straight and flat between a small single-track railroad on the left and a line of identical small houses on the right. Tiny squares of lawn edged with shrubs and picket-fences, ivy growing over red brick walls—everything but sprinklers and baby carriages to make it Main Street, U.S.A.

"Well, here we are," said Poignon.

They were halted by a U.S. sentry who popped out of a red-white-and-blue sentry-box with the precision of a cuckoo-clock figurine and said expressionlessly: "AGO cards." Behind the sentry-box they could see the main gate of the camp, a wide concrete arch mounted with an enormous Nazi eagle in bronze.

The MP hesitated over Kripke. "He German?" he asked.

"Yes," said Poignon politely. "He's our driver."

The soldier pursed his lips and looked speculatively at Kripke, whose face under the rumpled brown hair was a wordless picture of urgent boyish appeal.

"Well, O.K.," he said reluctantly, and Kripke broke into a wide grin. "But see to it he stays in the jeep all the time he's inside."

Kripke started up with a lurch that almost threw them out of their seats, and they were inside the gates, curving recklessly around circles brilliant with geraniums and asters, a white flag-pole flying the Stars and Stripes.

"What did he say?" Kripke asked Carla, jerking his thumb back in the direction of the sentry.

"He said you weren't to leave the jeep."

"Ha!" he bent excitedly over the wheel.

They sped down a dirt road and came face-to-face with another gate, this one a heavy triple-set iron one between two guard-towers. "The inner camp," said Carla, ordering Kripke to stop. Two steel-helmeted American corporals with Tommy-guns stood on guard.

Poignon seemed not to have heard her. He was looking

intently at the gate, reading an inscription in large iron letters: ARBEIT MACHT FREI. "Work makes free," he read aloud, musingly. "The same in all of them, the last great lie." He shook his head as if unable to comprehend.

The two corporals were gazing at them with the mild interest of guards who know beforehand that nothing is going to happen.

"Hi!" called Carla.

"Hi," said one, unenthusiastically. He was very young and he wore his helmet rakishly on the side of his head.

"What have you got in here?"

"SS."

"What for?"

"Waiting for trial. Screening."

"This was the concentration camp before?" she asked.

The other corporal spoke up in a mid-western accent. "That's what they tell us, ma'am. We wasn't here then."

"What do you mean by 'screening'?" she asked.

"Oh, every so often we run 'em around the compound with a bunch of former prisoners watching, like a police line-up. Usually some former inmate starts babbling an' shrieking, pointing to one of 'em and yelling what he seen 'im doing back in the old days. After a couple of times that happens, the legal boys write up charges, and then the guy is held for war crimes. Crimes against humanity, we call 'em." Now that he had moved into the conversation, the mid-westerner warmed to the subject. "You oughta stop in one of them buildings over there," he said, pointing to a cluster of buildings behind the jeep, "and see our guys giving some of the tough ones a working over. Boy, when our guys start on 'em they ain't supermen any more. They yell and scream just like anybody else."

"Which building?" asked Carla, suddenly interested.

"I don't think she can get in," said the younger one.

The other gave him a silencing stare and continued pointing. "Right over there, on the right."

"And that's where the SS troops get interrogated?"

"I guess that's as good a word as any," said the mid-westerner amusedly. "But I think he's right, you can't get in there. Security," he added, as if that one word explained everything.

"Oh," Carla nodded.

A lieutenant came out from behind the gate, a sober, well-scrubbed-looking young officer with a pink and freckled face. "What seems to be the trouble?" he asked.

"No trouble at all, sir," said the younger corporal. "Just giving directions."

The lieutenant walked over to the jeep. "Where do you want to go?"

Carla gave him a slow, deliberate smile. "I'm Carla·Mac-Murphy of the *Washington Globe-Dispatch*, Lieutenant, and this is Mr. Poignon. We'd just like to drive around back where the crematory was and look around a little."

"Pleased to meet you," he said, shaking their hands, manly and correct. "Well, there's no rule against you doing that, if you want to. Know where it is? You take this road, keep right along the canal here, then when you get to—— Well, look, if you've got some extra room I'll be glad to go along and show you around."

"Fine, Lieutenant," said Carla warmly. Poignon moved over and the lieutenant jumped into the seat beside him.

He immediately assumed command. "Straight ahead," he told Kripke.

"Geradeaus," translated Carla.

Kripke started up without a word.

"Now this," said the lieutenant, indicating a serried row of sheds behind a double electric fence, "was of course the camp for political prisoners. There were about 30,000 in there when we came in, most of them half-dead. That big building over there was the administrative building, and behind that was the women's building."

"Der Sonderbau?" asked Poignon.

"I beg your pardon?" said the lieutenant.

"The whorehouse, do you mean?" Poignon repeated in English.

"Charles!" said Carla, shocked.

He seemed surprised at her attitude. "But it probably was. Most concentration camps had whorehouses, I thought you knew that."

"I know nothing of the sort." Her voice was as shrill and severe as that of a schoolma'am.

Undisturbed, the lieutenant went on with his guide talk. "On this side was the extermination center. You can drive in here," he told Kripke.

"Hier links herein," translated Carla stonily.

They turned left through a high stone fence, along a drive edged with grass and arched by tall shade-trees. It was a cool and lovely green area, entirely surrounded by the thick stone fence, and in its center stood a modern red brick building that looked like a country school-house, except that it had a large chimney where the belfry would have been.

"The crematory," said the lieutenant. "Park the jeep here."

45

"Und hier rechts parken," echoed Carla.

Kripke spun the jeep to a stop and turned excitedly to look at the red brick building. "Ist das hier das Krematorium?" he asked Carla.

"Ja, Kripke," curtly.

They jumped out of the jeep.

"What a setting!" said Poignon, looking around him at the trees and vine-covered walls.

Carla threw him another infuriated look. They started across the grass.

"Miss MacMurphy," called Kripke hesitantly.

"Yes?"

"Could I please go with you, just to see the inside? The jeep is safe here."

Carla looked at his serious, pleading face. For some reason it seemed tremendously important to him to be allowed to come along. "All right, Kripke, you can come. But lock the jeep securely."

"Yes, Miss MacMurphy." He positively beamed.

She turned to join the others, and Kripke bustled happily back to the jeep, limping with anticipation.

The inside of the building was bare as a hospital and smelled strongly of disinfectant. Just inside the front door were the furnaces, as empty and meticulously clean as in an illustrated ad for heating equipment. Along the sides were cement ramps, along which, the lieutenant said, the SS guards had wheeled carts loaded with carcasses for disposal.

"What did he say?" asked Kripke.

She translated, and he listened with widened eyes. Then he limped over to the furnaces and got down and stuck his head inside and peered with intense and obvious interest behind the grilles, up the chimney, down into the firing chambers, like a puppy sniffing out a smell.

"Kripke!" said Carla.

He pulled his head out, surprised, and scrambled to his feet.

They moved around in back of the furnaces into a large cement-walled room, which the lieutenant said had been one of the gas chambers. Over the airtight steel door leading to the room was lettered: "Brauseraum" or shower-room, and in the ceiling of the room were fifteen to twenty perforated brass fixtures like showerheads or sprays. The lieutenant explained that prisoners brought up for execution were herded into the room for a "shower-bath." Since most of them had been months or years without a bath of any kind, they generally walked in quite docilely, even willingly, until so many of

46

them were crowded in that it became evident this was execution. Then pandemonium broke out, the doors were clamped shut, and the gas-emitting shower-jets opened. Carla translated and Kripke listened, his eyes moving from Carla's face to the lieutenant's.

The lieutenant then took them around into a corridor in back to show them the gas pipes and the levers and wheels with which they were operated, and the glass peephole through which the operator watched to ascertain how much gas was needed for how long. "They were very economical," said the lieutenant. "They had strict orders not to waste gas."

Poignon had moved off alone and sauntered out of the building. He seemed disinterested, absent-minded almost, and Carla, disgusted by his flippant cynicism at a time and place like this, let him go, and set to work to charm the lieutenant just in case she could get a line on that building back by the gates where the MP's were "roughening up" their SS prisoners. That, obviously, was the story. She could almost see the headlines: "GI'S BEAT UP NAZIS."

The lieutenant's name was Hogg, he came from Ottawa, Illinois, he'd been in Dachau from the time the Seventh Army took it, he had come in as an MP and he liked it here. His girl lived in town, her father owned Dachau's main garage, the old man liked him, had even fixed him up with a '38 Opel, and he was all set to get married as soon as the Army changed this goddam rule that you can't marry Fräuleins, maybe then he'd re-enlist and stay around in the occupation a year or two.

Carla showed a heart-felt and lively interest in his story, particularly in the prospective father-in-law who owned the garage and could fix one up with a '38 Opel.

"It's a funny thing," said Lieutenant Hogg. "I think they were all Nazis, the old man was one of those block leaders, you know, but they seem like awfully nice folks. They knew the SS had a camp out here, they said, but they thought it was a penitentiary for ordinary criminals. What about the stench, I said, because the day we came in here the stink was all over the damned town, like the stockyards in Chicago, but the old man said——"

"What did you say his name was?" Carla interrupted.

"Schaeffer. He said the townspeople thought——"

"And this garage is here in Dachau? Is it called Schaeffer's Garage?"

"That's right. Just at the top of the hill, on the main street. But let me tell you what the old man said. He said he thought they were burning garbage, meat bones and stuff. He never

47

imagined it was anything like a concentration camp. Now what I'd like to know is——"

"Do you suppose he could get me a car?" asked Carla. "I'm so tired of that old jeep."

"Well, sure, I think so, he's got a lot of them around. Matter of fact he's got a Czech Tatra there that's a honey, but it was too expensive for me, you can't pick up German marks here in Dachau the way the fellows can in Munich, and then I figured my C.O. would get suspicious seeing me sporting around in a de luxe job like that. If you want to stop up there, just tell him I sent you, and he'll take care of you all right."

"Schaeffer's Garage, on the main street at the top of the hill," Carla repeated to herself. She bent down to look through the glass peephole that the gas operator had used to watch the progress of his operation.

"But what mystifies me," continued Lieutenant Hogg, "is whether people could really live that near a place like this and never know——"

Carla was only half listening. She was engrossed in what she could see through the peephole. And what she could see through the peephole was Kripke, standing, a solitary and somehow pitiful little figure, in the center of the empty gas chamber. His arms were pressed tight to his sides, and he swayed stumbling a little from side to side as if he were being pushed and shoved by a crowd of people. He turned and spat in the direction of the door in an exaggerated pantomime of contempt, then stood for a long moment taut and still, and while Carla watched, threw his head back and stared at the shower-jet fixtures, and raised his fist and shook it savagely at the ceiling. Now he began to weaken, his face assumed a look of intense anguish and he closed his eyes and began to slump, knees giving way underneath him, and fell in a limp motionless heap on the cement floor.

"Now I don't know what to think," the lieutenant was saying. "But the way I got it figured, it doesn't much matter. After all, I'm not marrying the entire family, only Luisa, and what difference——" Then, seeing Carla preoccupied with the peephole: "What's the matter?"

"Nothing," she said, straightening up. "It's just the driver. He's gone now. He was in there getting gassed to death."

"What! Why that's impossible! We've cut off all the——"

"Nothing, I was only joking. Look, Lieutenant, how do you know your Herr Schaeffer hasn't already sold this Tatra to someone else?"

"Well, it was there this morning. And besides, it's too ex-

48

pensive for anyone but an American. I think he wants thirty to forty thousand marks for it, and only Americans would have that kind of dough."

"Yes, I suppose you're right." She looked at her watch. "Let's move on outside, shall we? I want to catch up with my driver and get started back to Munich." She bent down again to look through the peephole but the room was empty now, Kripke had already left. "Oh, and Lieutenant, do be an angel and tell me one other little thing. Do I have to have any special kind of authorization to get into those buildings back there where the MP's are interrogating the SS?" She smiled up at him, a sweet coaxing smile. "I suppose it's silly of me. There's probably no story in it at all. But gee, I would like to get in just for a minute or two—just for the fun of it."

He stepped back deferentially to let her pass in front of him. "I'm afraid that would be pretty near impossible. That's all security, you see. Nobody but authorized personnel allowed inside except by special authorization from General Potter, which I'm pretty sure you couldn't get."

At the doorway she stopped and faced him. "But couldn't I just talk to some of the guards who're doing the interrogating? Some of them who have been inside and seen what's going on?"

He looked doubtful. "Well, maybe if I could get hold of a couple of the boys for you——"

She caught his arm. "Oh, could you, Lieutenant? Gee, if you could——" She stopped, let some of the enthusiasm drain out of her voice. "I don't know why I'm so interested, really. Just plain old feminine curiosity, I guess. But please do what you can. You've been so wonderful to me——"

He seemed acutely embarrassed, and blushed all over his freckles, but when they emerged from the building he held her arm tightly to help her down the steps.

As they rounded the corner of the building they saw Poignon in back near the fence, walking meditatively up and down in front of a wide grassy bank. Besides the jeep Kripke stood respectfully waiting.

The moment he saw her, Kripke came limping over to ask if they were going now, and then before she could answer said excitedly: "I wouldn't have believed it, Miss MacMurphy! I wouldn't have believed it!" His face was serious, almost tearful. "I heard the stories, but I never believed them. How many were killed here?"

"About 300,000," she said.

"Communists," he added helpfully.

"No, all kinds of people, Kripke. Jews and Russians, and Poles, and Socialists and Communists. Mostly Jews."

"Ah, Juden, the poor Juden." He shook his head sadly. Then at once he brightened. "I saw the strangling hooks, Miss MacMurphy, over there, in a long room on the left."

"Strangling hooks?" Carla asked the lieutenant in English.

There weren't any at Dachau, Lieutenant Hogg said, although there had been at most concentration camps.

"Nein, Kripke," she said. "There weren't any here."

"Ja-ja," he insisted stoutly. "In the wall, Miss MacMurphy. Big ones." He made a hook of his forefinger and stuck it under his outstretched chin. "Like this, Miss MacMurphy."

"Kripke," she told him, "I think you'd better go back to the jeep. The MP said you weren't to leave it, you know."

Disappointed but obedient, he made a half-salute and went back to the jeep. As if acting on the same cue, the lieutenant said he'd better be getting back too if he was going to get hold of some MP's for her to talk to. "Wonderful," she said softly, laying her hand on his sleeve. "You're an angel, lieutenant, you really are. I'll be right along in about two minutes."

She walked off toward where she had seen Poignon pacing back and forth. She was excited and happy, her mind whirling around the prospect of getting that Tatra and the triumph of getting that story, rehearsing the questions she would ask the MP's and debating whether it would be better to stop at Schaeffer's garage with Charles along or make a special trip back later in the afternoon without him. The latter would undoubtedly be better but my God! How then would she get time to write her story and still be able to have dinner with Charles?

He seemed absorbed in thought.

"Are you ready to go?" she called. "I have to go back to the gate to talk to some MP's."

"Right away. I was just listening to a guide over here. Come, you'll be interested in this."

Reluctantly she let him take her hand and lead her back toward the wall where nine or ten GI's stood in a rapt circle listening to someone talk. As they came nearer, Carla saw that the speaker was an ex-inmate, wearing the familiar striped worksuit of the prisoner. His head was completely bald and he was cadaverously thin. "Then the prisoners would be compelled to kneel here in front of this bank," he was saying in a high monotonous voice, "then they shot them through the back of the head." He was tense and unsure of himself, and he talked in such a shrill rapid singsong that the soldiers had trouble understanding him and kept asking him to repeat. His thin bony hands shaking, his dark eyes fixed hypnotically on the distance, he would go over it again, using exactly the same words, like a child bolting through a memorized "piece."

Charles was looking intently at the man's face. It was like a gargoyle mask covered with human skin, the upperlip drawn back from his teeth in a nervous smirk, the eyes hollow and unblinking.

"Let's go," she said softly, tugging at his arm.

The high mechanical voice raced on: "This bank was for distinguished prisoners, the next was for ordinary prisoners. Over here——"

They walked slowly along under the trees. "A shock case," said Charles, taking her arm, "who can't remember anything so they can't send him back. I doubt if he understands a word of what he's saying." His voice was as compassionate as a benediction. "There were so many of those."

"Here?"

"Everywhere. At my camp too."

"Your camp? What do you mean 'your camp'?"

He answered her question directly but without emphasis. "I thought you knew. I was at Buchenwald for awhile."

She pulled away from him. "How could I know? You never told me."

He patted her hand. "I thought I had. Or perhaps I thought Colonel Kennebunk had told you. And besides, it was not so bad for me. After awhile one forgets, or rather one stops always remembering, and it becomes like another life. The tragedy is not for those like me, but for those like that." He jerked his head in the direction of the lecturing guide. "Because for me it is something I once lived but no longer live, but they live it all the time, like a madness. Now he cannot step out of it, because although it was madness, it was the most important thing that ever happened to him. He was murdered in the camp but he doesn't know it."

"Then that's why——"

"Why——"

"Nothing. I was only thinking, then that's why you made that remark about whorehouses in concentration camps. Was there a whorehouse in Buchenwald, really?"

"Young lady," he said, in mock severity. "I do not like to talk about such things with you. You are too gentille for these things. So, let us find the jeep and leave this depressing place. Even existing in this place is like dancing on a grave."

"But I only wanted to ask——"

"Yes. You have the curiosité of the young, and you have

51

a great sympathy for human beings. But this is a bad, immoral subject, and we have much better things to discuss." Putting his arm around her shoulders he led her towards the jeep.

She was quiet as she got in and settled herself on the tiny iron seat, quiet and thoughtful, thinking that since Charles wasn't competition she wouldn't have to make him wait in the jeep while she interviewed the MP's, she could let him come with her. Thinking also that it was obvious she couldn't stop at the garage with Charles along, she would have to come back later, just she and Kripke, with the thirty cartons she had in her suitcase at the Munich press camp. Thirty to forty thousand Marks, it was steep, but if the Tatra were reasonably new and in decent condition—— Besides, what were thirty cartons of cigarettes? About fifteen dollars.

Seeing her so thoughtful, Poignon leaned forward and took her hand and kissed it, and his eyes were warm and filled with admiration. "You are so émue by the misfortunes of others. Please do not be unhappy. There are thousands of people like us who will fight all the life to see that such things as this can never again exist in the world."

Her reply to his words was a tremulous smile, wordless and infinitely sad.

The jeep started down the drive, sputtering a little, and she could not look at him any more because of the bouncing, but he continued to hold her hand tightly in his.

"Miss MacMurphy," said Kripke.

"Yes, Kripke?"

"I did bestimmt see the strangling hooks. They were right there on the walls, where they used to hang the Jews up by the chin, like a cow or pig. Big hooks, so big." With his right hand he made an inverted question mark in the air. "So big. And pointed, so."

"All right, Kripke. You saw the hooks. Now to Munich, bitte."

CHAPTER FIVE

CARLA was sitting on an army blanket on a brassy mound high above the Walchensee, looking down at the incredibly blue waters of the lake and thinking today is the day, today is the day, it's a beautiful day, a beautiful warm day, he's in a wonderful humor, talkative but not too serious, and the way he looks at me means today is the day. She had fixed her hair very jeune fille, curled a little above her forehead and then clasped together at the nape of the neck and the rest cascading down her back in a shower of red-gold curls, and she was wearing a short full peasant skirt and a thin black sweater, and she pulled the skirt up just a little bit above her round brown knees, and watched a sailboat emerge from a harbor across the lake and proceed slowly toward the point. There was no denying the excitement she felt piling up inside her, all she could do was hold it back for awhile, deliciously, it was like when you were being made love to and you held back and held back because you knew that when you gave in it would be more wonderful, and so you sat very still in the hot leaf-patterned sunlight and looked poised and cool, knowing all the time that today was the day.

Through the languid branches of a big willowtree to the right she could see the gleaming silver bullet-body of the Tatra and heard Charles cheerfully talking in French to Timmy as he walked around the car with the dog following him. Timmy was already very fond of Charles, he's terribly fond of you, Charles, she said over again to herself, he, too, is terribly fond of you, and then she tilted back her head and looked meltingly, her lips parted in an alluring half-smile, at a certain small branch of the tree overhead.

"Mon Dieu, that is a wonderful car," said Charles, coming across the grass with the picnic basket. "I was just looking at the tablier, I don't know the name in English, it's the thing in front that has all the buttons on it——"

"The dashboard," she said.

"The dashboard, all silver and shining with all those thousands of things to push and pull. The Tatra is also a rocket, isn't it? A V-1 or one of those things that takes off into the air when you pull the right thing?"

She was pleased. "No, as far as I know it just flies on the ground, up to about 120 miles an hour. But you like it?"

"Like it? It is absolutely formidable. Coming from Munich this noon I sat there all the time wondering what it was likely to do with us if it made up its mind to revolt and try the stratosphere." It was difficult to tell whether or not he was serious, he spoke with such earnest enthusiasm. "We may end up in a better world yet, with the Tatra our appareil de sauvet-age."

"Or in a worse one."

"Impossible," he said. "Even the Tatra couldn't do that." He was smiling at her now. "It's a wonderful car, I am serious.

You are very lucky, young lady. The only trouble is I begin to suspect that you are also énormément riche."

"Nonsense!" She spoke soberly. "It was entirely luck, nothing more. I told you, Charles. A young major was being redeployed back to the States. And he was in such a hurry to get rid of it he let me have it for almost nothing. Really, Charles, almost nothing." She pronounced his name in the French manner, Sharl, rolling both the r and the l, and the lisping undertone of tenderness was sibilant and soft.

He set the luncheon basket on the edge of the blanket and stood looking down at her approvingly. "Well," he said, "I'm glad to know that. I like you to be lucky, and I like you to be so atrociously beautiful as you are, but I must admit, I wouldn't like you to be rich."

"Why not?"

"Because money is for people who love things, not for people who love ideas. You are too sensitive. You would be uncomfortable being rich."

Thoughtfully, she unhooked the top of the basket and started unpacking sandwiches.

"How did you know that?" she said slowly, her shining head bent over the basket. "Yes, I would hate to be wealthy, because —because it would be like a wall separating me from the rest of the people." A mental picture of the house in Chevy Chase and her mother's famous cocktail parties popped into her mind but she tossed it out as quickly as a hot coal. "Some of my friends used to think I was crazy because when I was in Paris, and the Parisians would shout 'A pieds, comme les autres!' I would be ashamed to be riding in a shiny big sedan and would insist on getting out and walking in the streets with the people."

She lifted her head and looked directly into his eyes, and the look on his face was one of awe, as if her pronouncement were the testament of an angel that heaven did indeed exist. For a long, serious, heart-felt moment he looked at her, then he took her hand and kissed it.

"Never, until I met you, did I believe that one so young and beautiful could have such understanding," he said. His words were low and blurred a little against her hand.

Silent, she looked down at this thick, curly black hair, thinking how easy it would be to pull his head down into her lap, how easy and how tempting, but thinking also that he was shy and whatever was done today would have to be done with delicacy and gentleness.

Delicately, gently, she disengaged her hand and went back to unpacking sandwiches.

"I don't know how good these will be," she said, in a tone of forced levity. "When I went out to the kitchen to ask for a box lunch, Otis—you remember the drunken cook who came to the table the other night?—was staggering all over the place and muttering to himself about Puvis de Chavannes and the Geist of defeat and screaming at the German help. These don't look inedible, though. And there's some French wine to go with them." With light fingers she touched his cheek.

Embarrassed at his own emotion, he lifted his head and together they set about unrolling the sandwiches from their wax-paper wrappings.

As she unpacked each one, she pried open the slices of bread and peered inside and recited off the contents. "Egg. Bacon-and-tomato. Another sliced egg. Ham-and-pickle. Spam. Imagine, Spam! Chicken. Where is the wine, I wonder?" She dug around in the basket for the wine, found it and handed it to Poignon to uncork, and then, settling herself comfortably back against the tree, her knees crossed under her like a tailor, she looked over the array of sandwiches spread out on the blanket. As gravely as a child choosing between strawberry and vanilla icecream, she looked from the bacon-and-tomato to the chicken and then, deliberately, selected a chicken and started to eat, absently watching him struggling with the corkscrew.

"Do you know, you speak English marvelously," she said. "I've been wondering where you learned it."

He held the bottle firmly between his knees. "In Buchenwald. There was a professor there, in the same block with me, a Pole who had taught languages at the University of Cracow, and when we had nothing else to do he taught me German and English. German I knew a little before the war, English not at all, and I think I was a very bad student, because I always wanted to read the languages more than to speak them. But we didn't have any books, and no paper and pencil, so he taught me with a new method, just by sound, you know. I don't think today I could write a letter in English that anyone could read, it would be all misspelled. So would my German, although not quite so much."

The cork popped, and he wiped off the bottle with a paper napkin and handed it to Carla. "Do you know, I never agreed with him, and one of the best kinds of exercise we had was arguing in our various languages. He was tremendously nationalist. He hated the Russians equally with the Germans, he hated everyone but Poles. Frenchmen he didn't mind, he said, because they were so far away from Poland they didn't really matter."

"But he was in a concentration camp, he must have been anti-Nazi," said Carla.

"Ah, yes," he said, leaning forward, "but, you see, to have been against the Nazis meant almost nothing. We who lived in the KZ's knew that better than any others, because we knew how many different points of view we represented. Some, for example, were against the Nazis because they believed the Nazi theories were an insult to mankind. Some were anti-Hitler because he had bought them and then sold them out. Some of the Jews, for example, were simple little people of no political thought; all they knew was that Hitler was beating them and murdering them and trying to wipe them out as a race. Some others were against him on purely ideological grounds. But there were still others who were against him the way pickpockets on one side of a street are against the pickpockets on the other—because he was moving in on them and driving them out of business."

She took a long drink of wine out of the bottle. "But wasn't there any comradeship in the camps?"

"Naturally there was. We, for example, I mean our political crowd, were in pretty close cooperation with the Communists in the KZ, we worked together in almost everything, and it was only when the common disaster was over that the real separation between us became open. But you have no idea how the Nazis worked to separate us. Every trick that they had they used: bribery, terrorism, everything. Sometimes it succeeded. And sometimes not."

His voice was deep and very masculine but melodious as well, like a bass viol, and she sat very still in the semicircle of half-opened sandwiches, listening as much to the sound of his voice as to his words. Timmy came back from beating the grass and crawled into her lap.

"Not that they really needed to," he continued. "Any ordinary criminal can tell you what the atmosphere of a prison is like, how it drives you to a kind of claustrophobic fury. Do you know, one day I almost murdered my best friend in Leipzig-Thekla—that was one of the so-called 'Aussenläger.' A French socialist like me, a friend of mine since I was eighteen, and I nearly killed him one day because he sucked his teeth. Because for months and months I had lain awake in the bunk and listened to him all through the nighttime sucking his teeth, and smelled the smell of rotting human bodies, unable to sleep because of the hunger and the smell, and listened to him sucking, sucking, sucking at his teeth. It almost drove me crazy, and one time I tried to strangle him—right in the work lineup —but some of the others grabbed me and knocked me out. They understood, and so did he, and for weeks he tried to stop it, but it was no good, he was too nervous and he couldn't help it."

This time she selected a bacon-and-tomato and bit into it crunchingly with her sharp white teeth, and gave Timmy the other half. "What finally happened?"

"Later he was shot for attempting to escape. Without consulting any of the rest of us he bribed a kapo to get him out and the kapo reported him. I go to see his wife now, when I am in the south of France, just to help her once in awhile with a little money and to tell her stories of what a hero her husband was—which he wasn't. Nobody could be a hero in a concentration camp; not and live through it for more than a week. It is a kind of expiation for me, for the murderous intention I had that day in the work lineup. None of us had anything but contempt for the kapos, but in my own heart I know that if I had been a kapo that day I would have turned him in —for sucking his teeth."

"Oh, Charles, you wouldn't!"

"Yes," he said. One knee pulled up in front of him, his pipe sticking straight out of his mouth, he looked contemplatively out over the lake. "Here, of course, such things are almost unimaginable." He held the bottle of wine in his hand ready to drink. "And yet it is always there, inside all of us—a kind of potential brutishness—in every man of no matter what nationality. That's what makes it so hard to judge the guilt of the Germans."

"Then you don't think the Germans are guilty?"

"I think all those who were Nazis are guilty. But even the fact that the Nazis are guilty means very little now. What matters now is how guilty they are as individuals, and for what reasons. There were many, for example, who organized and supported the Nazi party for their own aggrandizement, or ran the concentration camps as outlets for their own sadism. But there were thousands more who joined the Nazi party just in order to keep their jobs or to please their fathers-in-law. I am not a man of action, I am a writer, so perhaps I minimize the value of action, but I think no act can be evaluated until one knows the reasons why that act was committed."

"And you who were in Buchenwald don't think they were criminals?"

He did not answer her. Still staring out over the lake, he

continued: "It is the same for good action as for bad. Morality is in the intention. That too I learned in the camp: that only those who had reasons, ethical reasons, could win out over the force of Hitler's system. One fought Hitler to the death because he was wrong. Perhaps because the SS had murdered one's brother or kidnapped one's daughter or defiled one's synagogue, but also because he was wrong. That was the only thing one could hold to, the principles, because only principles remain."

Carla began neatly folding up the sandwich wrappings and napkins and putting the leftovers back into the basket.

"Look what happens in the world now," he went on. "So many nations who fought so courageously against Hitler are occupied today in developing militant nationalisms themselves. Particularly the two biggest—the United States and Russia. Have they forgotten that what they fought was German nationalism? Or do they think that all nationalisms in the world are wrong and dangerous except their own? They have forgotten the reasons, and so now, although they were victorious, they cannot quite remember what it was they won."

She listened intently, sitting back on her heels. Between the sound of his voice, resonant and strong, and the fierce intellectual sincerity of his words, she felt somehow lulled, as if she had at last gotten her feet on secure ground, the positive ground of masculine sureness.

"Why are you so against nationalism?" she asked.

"Because it is the stuff that wars are made of, and I am against war. Particularly the next one. Because nationalism is old-fashioned, and I am a man who likes new things. No," he said, more seriously, "I am what your editor would call 'an old European Marxist,' a socialist all the way back to my political adolescence."

"At the age of fourteen or fifteen?"

"Unfortunately, it takes longer for the head than for the genitals. That is one of the tragedies of life, that one's glands come to maturity before one's ideas." His smile was so naive and he spoke so naturally that she didn't have time to take offense. "For example, when I was young I was against everything and the Communists were against everything. So I was communist until I was about twenty-one. Since then I have been socialist."

He seemed to be thinking over something he had said, so she sat quietly next to him, listening to the peaceful ticking of the afternoon. From where she sat, everything within the range of her sight—the jeweled lake, the thick shrubbery that

58

covered the hill, the blond birches and swarthy evergreens—seemed glossy and wet, as though nature herself lay bathed in the somnolent perspiration of a summer afternoon nap. She was delighted that everything was going so beautifully, and over the lazy intimacy of their lunch a warm golden ambience of anticipation, knowing, yet not quite knowing, that it would all come out right, naturally and without apparent effort, like a rabbit out of a stovepipe hat—the pure spontaneity that comes of careful arrangement.

"Would you like to walk down to the water?" she asked.

"From here?"

She pointed to a path that led down, winding through birch trees and tall grasses, from a spot just to their left. "There. We could go down that way."

"Certainly we can try it." He got to his feet and walked down toward the ledge and looked over. A little surprised, she stood up by herself, brushed herself off and followed him, wondering if she had offended him. But when she and Timmy came up, he stepped back politely and helped her onto the path.

The grasses brushed suggestively against her bare legs as she walked; they were warm and sticky and sweet-smelling. She had a pleasurable perception, as she walked down just ahead of him, of her own smallness, a tiny female figure in a monumental framework of mountains and forest.

"What a beautiful country!" he said, coming up in back of her and stopping to survey the lake and the dark hills that ran abruptly down into it. "Do you call these hills or mountains?"

"Up there, mountains," she said, pointing to the snow-capped peaks that circled the lake and were mirrored on its turquoise surface. "Down here, hills—or rather foothills, when they are forested like that and run up into mountains."

"Do you know," he said, "when I look at Germany—Bavaria and the Rhineland and the great cities of the north and east as they were a few years ago—I wonder how a people with a land like this could ever have been persuaded to go to war. That's when I begin to mistrust my own profession, when I see what some other members of it—people like Goebbels and Dietrich—have been able to do using the same instruments we use: words." The look on his face was one of quizzical humor, the black eyebrows as pointed as arrowheads. "Of course, you, as a woman, are more accustomed to such a situation than I am, because for a woman sex presents almost the same problem. Every woman has it, it's just a question of how she uses it."

She blushed—something she hadn't thought she could do—and turned her face away, restraining herself from making the obvious remark that some women have more than others.

He reached for her hand, and they continued down the path.

At the water's edge, Carla bent down to test the water with her fingers. "Cold!" she said, wide-eyed. "Feel."

He bent down beside her. "It's not bad. If we had costumes de bain, I would not mind swimming in it. Do you swim?"

"Yes."

She took off one sandal and dipped her toes in and without looking at him said hesitantly: "We could swim anyway. Without costumes de bain, I mean."

She was glad that he had been so enthusiastic, racing back up the slope to get towels from the car and lock the Tatra against possible passersby, and while she undressed she thought how boyish he was, the contradiction of his emotional immaturity and that clear, disciplined mature mind.

As she slipped off her brassière, she looked along the bank and caught a glimpse of him pulling his shirt off behind a group of trees about fifty yards away. She waited a moment in a tension of excitement before tiptoeing to the edge of the bank and diving in. When she came up, spluttering and pushing her hair out of her face, she saw him standing on the bank looking into the water.

He was very well built, there was no denying that even from this distance. His shoulders were broad, his chest wide and hairy, his legs sturdy as a six-day bicycle rider's. Naked, he looked less tall than when he was fully dressed, and his skin, except for a whiter strip around the groin which his bathing-trunks had obviously covered, was a rich, almost tropical brown. Seeing her already in the water, he called across to her, "How is it?"

"Much warmer than I thought!"

He pointed down to the water in front of him. "Rocks!"

"Not bad!" she called. "They're fairly deep."

"All right, here I come!" he said and dove in, a shallow racing-dive that brought him almost within reach of her.

He was a fairly good swimmer and seemed to enjoy the water immensely. Instead of swimming up to her, however, he streaked past toward the center of the lake, swam some hundred yards out and then, breathing evenly, came back. Swimming slowly while he approached, she had that same feeling of compactness, of being deliciously outlined and contained by the silken rapture of cool green water.

He swam up to within a few feet of her and, treading water, looked frankly at her figure. "You are like a sirène in the water," he said. "How do you say sirène in English?"

"Mermaid," she said, breathing heavily.

"Mermaid," he repeated. "Meermädchen, in German." He continued to tread water, facing her.

"Haven't we had enough?" she asked nervously. "Shall we get out now?"

"Would you like to?" he asked, not raising his eyes from her figure.

"Please!"

With his arm he indicated a stony but more gradually sloping part of the bank, and together, side-by-side, they swam toward it. Seeing them coming, Timmy began running excitedly up and down the lake's edge, barking. From the water, with the sun almost down, the hill looked steeper, as if no human without mountain-climbing equipment could possibly scale it, and the trees seemed a thicker, darker green and more impenetrable, Timmy a lost speck of animal energy dancing up and down in red-brown fury.

Unsure of what would happen now and a little short of breath, she swam more slowly, and Poignon moved powerfully out across the water to reach the bank before her. When she was within a few feet, he was standing waist-deep, his legs apart in a firm wide stance on the rocky bottom. "Here," he said, and with a tentative shyness she approached and reached out her hand to him. For only a fraction of a moment he hesitated, holding her hand, and then suddenly she was in his arms and he was lifting her, carrying her up the steep stony beach toward the bank, a naked dripping sirène, dripping not seaweed or shells but clear Bavarian lake-water, shivering a little and goose-pimply from the cold.

Sitting on the khaki blanket drying herself with a khaki towel, she eyed him warily. For the first time in her life, she was at a loss to know how to play it. Until their swim together he had been so shy, she had recognized her cues and played it ingénue, all modesty and feminine tenderness, listening in rapt attention to his monologues on concentration camps and nationalism. But the water had transformed him, like Proteus, into something elemental and unrefined. Now he was a happy pagan, bold, self-confident, unintellectual and unabashed. She looked at him, standing in front of her in the grass, still completely naked, energetically rubbing the water out of his crisp black hair with a towel. Another man, she thought, would have tied the towel around his middle and let his hair dry in the sun.

Her clothes were lying in a heap fifty yards down the shore. What was she expected to do after she had dried herself she didn't know. Rise dignifiedly and walk down and get them? He hadn't said a word. He seemed oblivious to her presence, shaking his head like a bull, the towel eclipsing everything but his magnificent torso and legs, and he hadn't even looked at her since he had carried her out of the water.

She didn't have long to wait. Smiling at her, his eyes as blue as the Walchensee and twice as sparkling, he finished drying his shoulders and arms, hung his towel carefully on a nearby bush, and came over to the blanket and dropped to his knees beside her. Then gently, without a word, he took her towel away and knelt there looking at her.

It had all happened so fast, she thought, bending over to cup the brassière to her breasts and then leaning back to fasten it behind her. There had been no time for "O, Charles! you mustn't!" or "Charles, my dearest, I've wanted you so long!" or any of the other phrases that she continually assured herself were not stock reactions but only the spontaneous expressions of her libido. She wished she could go into the water again, but it was almost dark now and quite cold and she knew he was waiting for her to return. So she picked up her skirt and hooked it around her waist and looked around for her sweater. Everything had gone wrong. Or maybe everything had gone right. She didn't know. When she suggested their swimming together without suits, had he decided that she was a common trollop, to be laid on an army blanket like any Fräulein? Or—and she looked pensively out over the deepening purple of the lake—had he been compelled to make love to her out of the intimacy of the day and the sight of her body? A roaring excitement was going on in her nervous system, an unbearable suspense to hear his next words, to take from them some clew as to how he felt about her, and she noticed almost objectively how her hands quivered as she picked up her sweater and turned it right side out, ready to put on. Three things she knew: he was very male, very French, and he wasn't immature. But the fourth thing, equally important, she didn't know.

He was waiting for her halfway up the hill, and he took her hand and they walked silently to the car together. He was helpful and pleasant in the business of stowing everything back in, and made quite a fuss about spreading the blanket—the same blanket—on the back seat for Timmy, but the only words they exchanged were things like: "Did you get the basket?" or "It belongs in the back" or "Did we forget anything?" In a display of resentful efficiency she opened the door and got behind the wheel and started playing with the lights. After a final look around he climbed in beside her without a word and they started off.

A little lemon moon rode beside them in the mist, and as the Tatra dipped and climbed on the turns of the highway she could see the line of his profile in the half-light. What was the matter with him? Why didn't he say something? Obviously, she had loused the whole thing up by going swimming with him, she had lost her timing and let the offensive slip into his hands and now, thanks to him, the whole affair was over. Except that the way he had made love to her, she couldn't believe—— And that was exactly the difference, like those reconnaissance photographs of war damage showing the same scene before and after a raid. That was a man for you, an emotional before-and-after exhibit, particularly these damned intellectual ones. But at least he could say something! Whatever it was he was brooding over, he was as guilty as she. A fragment of his earlier conversation fell into place: it's the reasons behind an act that count, morality is in the intention. And what intention did she have that he hadn't had? So there he sat, wrapped in Hegelian silence, analyzing dialectically the reasons why he had made love to her and, she had no doubt, the reasons why she had let him; rationalizing the determinism of the sex act. Shivering with cold and with the tenseness of her disappointment, she felt a dangerous high-tide of tears ebbing in her throat.

"Are you warm enough?" he asked. His voice was quiet and deep.

"I—I don't know."

"If you can find a place to park, I'll get your coat for you. You can't be warm enough in that little pullover."

She pulled the Tatra off onto a shoulder, and he reached back and got her coat and helped her put it on. "Thank you," she said formally, in a thin baby voice, and the tears nearly spilled into her throat. Her fingers trembling, she buttoned the coat around her.

"All right?" he said.

"Yes." Almost blinded by tears, she fumbled for the ignition key. Suddenly she turned to him and her voice rose almost to a wail. "If I've done something so terrible, why can't you tell me about it instead of sitting there like a—like a stump, brooding over it!" Tears streaming down her face, she flounced back and went on groping for the ignition.

"Terrible?" he said, incredulously. "Terrible?" He reached over and put his arms around her and held her struggling against his coat. "Carla, Carla. O chérie, ma chérie, Carla." With one hand he reached into his pocket for a handkerchief, but with the other he held her tightly. The struggling stopped. "Carla, don't cry. Chérie, don't cry. I have so much to say to you, and it's my fault, I should have told you before, instead of waiting until—instead of waiting. Carla, ma petite." His words were soft and contrite.

Her sobs began to lessen and she held still to hear what he was about to say. She took the handkerchief and dried her face and eyes under cover of his lapel.

"Look," he said. "Carla, look at me."

She lifted her head.

"No, like this. I want to see your face." He turned her face toward the moonlight and holding her in his arms began to talk. "Carla, chérie, do you know that today was the most important day in the life for me? The happiest day I have ever had. Because today for the first time I see that it can all come together, the work and the need for love. Today, for the first time in the life, a woman means all to me."

She was looking at him intently, her eyes shining with tears, her angelic face upturned to his in the moonlight, thinking *O Christ, O Christ, and I thought I'd ruined it, I thought he was despising me, and this is what he was thinking all the time.* Shyly she tried to turn her face away from him, but he held her head firmly in his hands.

"I have to be modest with you, chérie. I have nothing to offer you of material things. I am a man who makes money and throws it away. All I have is a life of work for the things you and I believe in, and a life of so much love together. I have never asked a woman to marry me, because I have never wanted to be married. And even now it isn't important, we will be married if you want, or not married if you do not want. What I am asking is if you will live with me, from now on, always."

O Christ, O Christ, and I thought I had ruined it.

"I am an old man, chérie, I have forty years, almost forty-one, and I have had many—how do you say?—amours, many women. And they have come and gone, and I have loved them in a certain way. But they were without meaning, a procession of women without faces, that a man must love because he is healthy. Until now, my love has had no face.

64

Until now. Because now my love has a face, this face, so beautiful and wise. This face." He held her face in his hands and kissed it: the eyes, still wet with tears, the lips, the hollows behind her chin, the wide temples where the curve of red hair began.

In a rapture of submission she lay quiet in his arms, and the pain, the wonderful pain in her heart, was so great that his kisses seemed far away, a repeated invitation to some warm masculine paradise that her heart, being big with emotion, could not enter.

"Charles," she said softly, interrupting his kisses. "Charles ——"

"Do not try to answer now, chérie. It is a serious thing to decide to live the entire life with another. You must think what it means——"

"Oh, but I want to! I want to! I want to come with you and live with you. Oh, Charles, believe me! All I want is—to be with you——" Unaccountably the tears started again, and again he held her tightly in his arms, murmuring to her wonderful words which she only half understood, in French, German and, she thought, Spanish.

Again he put his hands on either side of her face. "Are you sure, chérie? You are sure?" His eyes, grave, almost tragic, were searching hers.

"Oh yes. Yes, I am sure."

"For always, Carla?"

"For always, Charles."

After some moments, she disentangled herself and smiling at him through her tears said tremulously: "I think I had better drive us back to Munich now."

Gently he released her. He fumbled around in his pockets for cigarettes and offered her one. Just as she had accepted the light and was letting out the clutch-pedal, an insubordinate thought intruded into her bliss: *Damn! I forgot to call Bill Somers, Frankfurt 33351.*

With a roar of its motor, the Tatra was away, floating over the hills under the Bavarian moon, and now, over the soft breathing of the engine, Charles began to talk. Not as he had talked that afternoon—of Marxism and of the political and moral problems of Germany and Europe—but of himself and her, of how they would live together and work together in his studio apartment in Paris.

The moment they pulled up to the door of the presscamp, Pete, the Colonel's corporal, came running out to tell her that Colonel Kennebunk wanted to see her urgently. "He's got the

65

papers on your car," he said in a stage whisper, "and they've got to be signed right away and sent down to the Provost Marshal's office tonight."

Excited, she turned to Poignon. "Charles, do you mind? I've really got to run in and see Colonel Kennebunk on something very important. Can I meet you in a few minutes somewhere?"

"I'll get dressed for dinner," he said, "and come to your room for you in about an hour."

At the door to the Colonel's office, he stopped, took her in his arms and kissed her, and the sight of his handsome unshaven face, his dark hair in unruly curls on his forehead, his dancing eyes, told her with a shock of delight how happy he was. "Oh, how I love you!" he said, and bolted up the stairs.

Am I that happy? she asked herself as she waited for the Colonel in the anteroom of his office. I guess I am, I guess I'm pretty terribly happy, and walked elatedly around the room in her dirty trenchcoat, looking absent-mindedly at the books that lined the walls.

"The Colonel will see you now," said Pete, sticking his head out the door of the office.

"Thank you, Pete."

Just as she was whipping into the Colonel's office, she saw the book she wanted: *The Origins of Marxism*. She pulled it out of the shelf and tucked it under her arm as she went in.

CHAPTER SIX

ON THE top of a heap of rubble a little boy stood urinating. With the rigid attention of a machinegunner, oblivious of passersby, his thin brown legs stalwartly astride the debris, he held the arc of his fire steadily spattering a rusty steel girder four feet below.

From the other side of the street Carla watched with the perfunctory interest of one who has seen the same play too many times: the backdrop a line of jagged snaggle-tooth ruins, torn roofs and empty windows like broken picture frames and the tattered blue canvas of the universe showing through; the performers a bunch of uninspired and aimless bit-players—men in patched Lederhosen, women in faded Dirndl-Kleidern and wooden shoes, skinny barefooted children plodding along under a sun as shadowless and harsh as a thousand kleig lights.

Even the star was commonplace—a ragged seven-year-old juvenile engrossed in the act of piddling against a broken steel girder.

Altogether a dull monotonous scene, smothered by the sun and by that peculiarly acrid odor that hung over all German cities now, the dusty burnt smell of destruction and decay. A scene so completely irrelevant to her own emotions that she felt like an actress who had stumbled by mistake onto the wrong set and now, for some unknown reason, had to stay there.

Because I can't go with him, she thought miserably. I can't. I want to, I want to more than anything else in the world. But I can't. He's so wonderfully unrealistic, he thinks all you have to do is just drop everything and go running off to Paris like a college girl on a lark. He has no idea what a mess it would be. My God, I couldn't walk out on the *Globe* like that, without any notice or anything; a trick like that and I'd be killed dead with every newspaper in the United States. And I can't give up my column. I've worked too damned hard on it to let it go down the drain now. He doesn't see how important it is. He doesn't know what a by-line means.

Morosely she wandered down the street, picking her way between piles of rubble, peering disinterestedly into the tiny isinglass windows of patched-up shops. The vacuous weariness of the faces she passed depressed her; the impudent curiosity with which the young men stared at her chartreuse slacks was equally irritating. She wished she could find some place to sit down and have a beer and wait for Charles, but of course there was no beer in Germany any more and all the little Gaststuben were either bombed-up or boarded up. Feeling as oddly hostile as a goddess sentenced to exile on a despised and dusty earth, she turned and started back toward the Tatra.

Already a kind of perverse excitement filled her, the delicious sadness of bereavement creeping over her mind and body. I should be going with him, she thought. If I hadn't made such a mess of things in France, I would. And now here I am in Germany with the most marvelous chance to make up for all that. But he doesn't understand. I know what he's hoping right this minute—that by the time he meets me here I'll have changed my mind and be all ready to get on that plane and fly off to Paris with him.

And leave the Tatra here besides! My God, he's so wonderful, he doesn't take anything seriously except me and his work. Something like the Tatra doesn't mean anything to him. Even if it did, I could never explain to him why I couldn't take

67

it to France on these phony papers. In three or four weeks I'm positive I can get it out by way of Austria and Italy, just a few weeks to get organized.

And where on earth is he? If he doesn't come pretty soon he's going to miss his plane, and there isn't another one to Paris until Thursday. But he won't miss it, she thought pessimistically, kicking at a stone with her feet; people that you want to have stay never miss·their planes or get weathered in or anything good like that. He'll make it all right. Within an hour he'll be gone and I won't see him again for almost a month.

Up ahead the Tatra waited, its long rocket-shaped body glinted metallically in the hot sun, its tousle-headed little driver strutting back and forth beside it in full view of his envious countrymen. She walked up.

"Kripke, what do you think could have happened to Mr. Poignon? Do you think something's gone wrong?"

"Nay-nay, Miss MacMurphy," positively. "Keine Angst. There is still plenty of time. Mister Poy-nong comes surely any minute now." His chest pushed out like a pigeon's, he regarded the Bavarians trudging by in the rubble. "Ach, these Bavarians!" he said disgustedly. "They are like pigs, like Dreckschweine. I will be glad when we leave here to go to Frankfurt and Berlin.

"Raus!" he yelled, raising his arm threateningly at a passing dog. "Du Mistköter! Keep away from my beautiful automobile!"

"Kripke, I am speaking to you!" Then, when she had his attention again: "I think you had better drive up to the French Consulate and see what happened to him. Here it is twenty minutes past two———"

"Miss MacMurphy, det is' nutzlos," he argued. "Mister Poy-nong comes any minute now. Ha! What did I tell you?"—as pleased as if he had conjured up Charles himself—"There he comes!"

Something inside of her made a quick dizzying twist and she looked up to see Charles threading his way down the street toward her. He was carrying his typewriter and two small suitcases which impeded his progress along the broken sidewalk. But he wore his cap pushed back on his curly hair and on his face a look of such open good-nature that he looked as carefree and ready-for-anything as a GI on a three-day pass. How young he looks, she thought. He looks ten years younger than when I first met him at that drunken dinner a month ago. On an impulse she ran to meet him.

In full sight of passing Germans he dumped his bags down

in the dust, put his arms around her and kissed her. "I must apologize to be so late, chérie," he said breathlessly after a long passionate kiss. "You know how these diplomats are. Half an hour to take a paper from the right hand and put it in the left hand. Mon Dieu! But you are beautiful!" The Germans scarcely noticed; carrying their peeling briefcases and satchels they walked apathetically past while she and Charles, their arms around each other, proceeded happily toward the Tatra.

Charles looked contemplatively at Kripke. "There is something that I have forgotten——" he started. "Kripke, my bags!" And Kripke, grinning, bustled back to get them where they still stood on the sidewalk.

Once rid of Kripke, he took her in his arms again. "You are all ready to leave for Paris?"

"Oh, Charles, no," she said miserably. "Charles, I can't. I have to stay in Germany another few weeks, really I do. I told you this morning, my darling——"

"But you are all packed?"

"For Frankfurt and Berlin, chéri. Not for Paris. Oh, Charles, please understand! After making such a fuss for them to send me here, I can't just turn around and go back without giving them *something* out of Germany. Don't you see, Charles?"

He held her a little way from him so he could see her face.

"Don't you see? And it's for such a little time! Only a few weeks——" Her eyes, pleading, moved from one to the other of his.

"What I see is that I am not very talented as a seducer," he said, his blue eyes dancing with humor. "I see also that you have a very strong will. Perhaps later these will both turn out to be very good things. Now do not be sad, chérie. I understand." He patted her cheek. "Come, we will take me to the airport. My bags are in the car, Kripke?"

"Ganz fahrbereit, Mister Poy-nong," said Kripke, bowing.

They climbed into the backseat and Charles pulled her over next to him. "Perhaps you are right, chérie. You are more sage than I. I always want to do everything right away, right away while I think of it, so as to keep my mauvais génie from telling me that something will go wrong. So you see you must not be sad. When you tell me that you cannot come with me right now, then I accept. And do you know that I am even happy?" His lips were against her hair. "Even today when I must leave you I am happy, because I cannot wait to get back to Paris to tell all my friends about you and to make everything ready."

Kripke was handling the Tatra beautifully, with the easy

hand of one completely accustomed to such a heavy powerful car, so she and Charles leaned indolently back—"like two prewar capitalists," he said—and laughed and held hands and talked. His mother, said Charles, would not believe that he was at last settled down "avec ma femme," but she would be overjoyed. "We had a wonderful house during the résistance, my mother and I," he said, his voice warm with the pleasure of reminiscence. "It had so many doors, it was wonderful for revolutionaries because if the Gestapo came in one door, there were six or seven other doors by which we could escape. My mother used to shake her head when we had meetings there, like a Cassandre predicting doom, but really she loved it." He laughed softly. "I think I must have inherited a great deal from her."

Cushioned comfortably against the red leather seat, listening to his deep confident voice, Carla thought with elation of the life that lay before her, a life of selfless devotion to Charles and to the social and economic betterment of mankind. And a series of visions, so real as to assume some of the revelational quality of a religious experience, flickered before her eyes. A vision of herself in dirty but well-tailored slacks storming barricades at his side, screaming defiance to the forces of capitalistic reaction. Another, of their daily life together in simple but emotionally charged poverty, their artistic left-bank apartment the center of a new circle of brilliant leftist intellectuals. Long serious political discussions around their fireside which would not break up until almost dawn, until the last coffee-cup had been emptied, the last inspired guest had gone, when she and Charles alone in the shadowed studio would put aside one passion for another, the quiet intellectual passion of the day for the fierce sexual passion of the night. And through it all she saw the soft radiant flame of her new self, keeping up her own writing reputation, of course, but otherwise submerging her personality—or at least a great part of it—in the romantic job of helping him achieve all that he was destined to achieve.

The last vision, apocalyptic, much hazier than the others, was of herself at the age of sixty being interviewed by reverent young journalists as the life-long mistress and companion of the great Poignon. Her hair by now was silver-white, her face lined by the struggle of the years but translucently beautiful in its composure, and it was with a tired gentleness that she would dismiss these curious upstarts to go back to the autobiography she was now writing, *Poignon and I*. "She won't live long," one journalist, who looked disconcertingly like a younger Bill Somers, whispered to the others as they tiptoed out.

"She must have been a fabulous beauty when she was young," said another in awed tones.

With a little start she came out of her dream to hear Kripke swearing at the pedestrians who crossed his route. In the middle of the road an old woman was stooping over horse droppings and packing them away in a big gunnysack. "Alte Zicke!" he yelled contemptuously and spun around the curve, narrowly missing her.

"Kripke!" said Carla. "Slow down!"

"Ach, Miss MacMurphy," said Kripke in his husky German. "You don't want to waste your time worrying about these Mistbauern."

"Slow down, Kripke," repeated Carla firmly, and the Tatra, which had been swerving recklessly over the cobblestones, around carts and stray chickens, slowed down. Satisfied, she nestled back in Charles' arms.

Over her head Charles began to talk. "You are not Bavarian, Kripke?"

"Gott im Himmel, nein!" said Kripke fervently, squirming a little in the front seat but keeping his eyes fixed on the road. "One of these Grüss-Gott cheese-eaters? Not me! All the time bragging about themselves, and in the war they couldn't even fight. We had hundreds of them in our division, and there wasn't a Draufgänger among them." The contempt in his voice thickened his words. "Now, in the peace-time, when all the rest of Germany is starving, what do they do? Sit around swilling their eggs and butter and Schinken, and what do they care for Germany? Do you think, Mister Poy-nong, I could buy one of those chickens there?" The right front wheel of the Tatra narrowly missed a squawking chicken. "Last week I asked, how many marks for a chicken? 'Oh,' said the farmer, a fat Tucker with three gold teeth, 'they are not for sale for Reichsmarks, but if you have a pair of new shoes, size 11——' And where, I ask you, where in all of Germany can one get a pair of new shoes?" The question was not only rhetorical but triumphant. The Tatra began picking up speed again.

"Where do you come from then?"

"I am a Berliner, Mister Poy-nong," said Kripke proudly. "Ein waschechter Berliner. I am only in Bavaria because I was here in the Wehrmacht hospital when the war ended. They sent me back from the eastern front, from Hungary, to have the slugs taken out of my belly and legs and while they were getting ready to operate on me the Americans came. So the Americans have been here ever since, and so have I."

"You like the Americans?"

"Ja, natürlich. With the Americans one can earn a living. Here in the U.S. Zone all a man has to do to get along is get a job working for the Americans, then everything goes O.K."

"Better than with the Russians?"

"Ach, Mister Poy-nong, die Russen have nothing, they are poorer than the Germans. The Americans have chocolate and cigarettes and coffee. They have everything—food and liquor, all kinds of automobiles and jeeps, plenty of gasoline——" He shook his head. "Those Russians! Such Dummköpfe! I still don't know why we didn't beat them, except that there were so many of them. They just kept coming at us till we ran out of ammunition."

Cuddled in the curve of his strong arm, Carla knew with certainty how right her decision was. And yet she had that feeling of bereavement, as if something that she wanted were slipping like water through her fingers. Within a few minutes he would be gone, his physical presence not here beside her but in a plane somewhere, his arms, his lips, the wonderful comforting warmth of him——

"So now you are going back to Berlin with Miss MacMurphy, as her personal driver. And you like that?" The words were spoken so close to her ear that they reverberated inside her head.

"Ja-ja," said Kripke evenly. "That pleases me."

"You will see your wife again, eh, Kripke?"

"Ach, Mister Poy-nong, that plays no role with me. I can see my old woman any time. But I have a son there I have never seen, maybe he is mine, maybe not——"

"Now, Kripke," said Charles, amused.

"Ja-ja. Two are mine, I know it absolutely, but the third——? I have been gone a long time, Mister Poy-nong. I had my last furlough in Berlin three years ago next month, right after we lost Kharkov, and the youngest is not yet two years old. A friend of mine, a guy who runs black market over the border to Berlin, he saw the boy himself. He used to be in my company in Italy, he is ein guter Lump, he would not lie to me. If he lied to me I would kill him and he knows it, so why would he take such chances? Nay-nay, all German women became very gefällig in the war, everything was Fatalismus because Hitler said so, and maybe my Anna did it too. We will see when I get home," he concluded, not unhappily.

Carla's arms suddenly tightened and she pressed her head hard against his chest.

He looked down. "Mais Carla! Qu'est-ce qu'i'y a, ma petite?" His arms locked around her. "What is it, chérie?"

Unshed tears ached in her eyes, a constriction of loneliness pulled like a rubber hose around her throat. "Nothing," she said, her voice almost lost against the wool of his jacket. "Nothing, Charles, nothing."

David Hawks had been drinking too much. He knew it, and so did everyone else in the Park Hotel bar.

Slouched in an overstuffed chair—one of the inheritances from the days when this had been a second-class commercial hotel for west German businessmen—Hawks watched the entrances and exits of his fellow journalists and their guests with an ironic and bloodshot eye. He was a handsome young American with thick brown hair and a strong square jaw which at the moment badly needed a shave. With fixed regularity of alternation he looked at his watch and ordered a drink, downed it, looked at his watch and ordered another. "What's the time got to do with it, Hawks?" somebody asked. "Rationing," he answered, draping one long leg over the arm of his chair. "Gotta go slow so there'll be enough to go around among all these newly arrived American wives and kiddies. Only one drink every five minutes."

"Hi, Dave!" called Polly Wilson, her sweet pink-and-white face smiling at him over the shoulder of a British correspondent. "We'll be over in a minute. Just going to have one drink at the bar." "Hi, Dave!" echoed her husband Mike, pulling out a bar-stool for her. "Be over in a minute."

He waved back at them and ordered another drink. "So now it ends," he said to the two other reporters, Ed Jones and Bentley Cross, sitting around the table with him. "The golden era. Gone. Now the real postwar era begins, when the carpetbaggers—that's us—are joined by their wives and families, and the little woman gets a chance to get her itchy housewifely fingers on the occupation. Boy, I can hardly wait to see us get tidied up, the fräuleins kicked out of the bars, napkins and candles on the tables over the usual army hash, the feminine touch in the cigarette market, and everyone in bed by midnight—with an American woman, if you please. Hey, Eric! Noch eins, bitte!"

"What's eating you, Hawks?"

"Nothing. I'm just a traditionalist, that's all. I hate to see the end of an era, particularly when I know a worse one is going to follow it. From honest immorality we will now proceed to dishonest immorality, where we'll go on doing the same things we've been doing all along—only with the little helpmeet at our side to make it respectable." He looked down

73

the bar, squinting. "Who's the dame down there with the green hat and the fake bosoms?"

"That?" answered Jones. "That's Ray Traunstein's wife. Just came in on the boat yesterday with five cases of cigarettes. Five *cases*, I said. Five hundred cartons. Enough to buy out the whole U.S. Zone. The dyed blonde is Colonel Brown's wife."

"Yeah, I know," said Hawks. "Met her last night at General Blakely's, little brawl he tossed to introduce Mrs. Blakely to the field-grade nobility of her husband's four-star kingdom. No Germans, of course. The loyal subjects were outside in the alley waiting for the garbage pails. No Russians either. Russians are all too busy spying for important information to bother with our generals." He looked at his watch. "How about another drink?"

Bill Somers came in, looked around the bar, and went out.

"Hey, Bill!" yelled Hawks. But he was already gone. Hawks turned back to the table. "Jesus, that guy Somers sure is fast on his feet these days. What do you suppose he's working on that's that important?"

A smile on his freckled face, Jones looked across the table at Bentley. "A dame by the name of MacMurphy, I'd say."

"Really!" said Bentley, half-surprised. "Is he the new incumbent? Only I was under the impression that she was down in Munich."

"She is," said Jones. "Or was, rather. She's due in here tonight."

The British correspondent left the bar and Polly and Mike Wilson came over to the table carrying their drinks. "Who's due in here tonight?" asked Polly, spreading out her skirt as she sat down.

"Carla MacMurphy."

Hawks was ordering drinks. "What'll you have, Polly? Gin? Mike? Okay, Eric. Three whiskies, two gins." Dropping cigarettes all over the table, he offered Polly one and with his big awkward hands tried to light it for her. "Carla MacMurphy," he repeated. "You know I've never met her?"

"Oh, oh!" said Jones. "Here we go again."

"You haven't?" asked Polly, accepting a light from her husband. "Why, she was around here all during the war."

"You forget, Mrs. Wilson," Hawks reminded her, "that in those days not everybody was lucky enough to be a war correspondent. In those days there was a small secondary organization around here known to its intimates as the United States Armed Forces——"

74

"All right, all right," said Polly good-naturedly. "So you never met her. Well, you will before long. I understand she's going to Berlin tomorrow too."

"Which I'll never reach," he said morosely, "unless somebody does something pretty soon about getting me a drink."

The waiter came with the drinks.

Bentley Cross picked up his whisky. "Did I hear you say, David?" he said in his slow deliberate Bostonian English, "that you have never met Carla MacMurphy? David, you have missed an important—ah—psychological experience without which you cannot really understand postwar journalism. Jones and I will not soon forget the memorable night that we had the pleasure of meeting the young lady."

"Okay, Bentley," said Jones. "Tell it. Only keep it to one column."

Cross took a big swig of his whisky, looked around the table to make sure everyone was listening. "This was in Algiers in 1943," he began, "one night when we had been out to dinner at the Auberge with some Red Cross girls. After dinner the girls invited us up to their apartment for some American coffee, and when we got up there the place was completely dark —black-out, you know—with all the windows opened to the warm romantic night air. We thought there was nobody there and one of the girls snapped the lights on. And there, on the daybed, in what one might call the most compromising of all positions, were MacMurphy and the local PRO colonel— stark naked."

"Go on, Bentley," said Jones. "I'll attest to your accuracy."

"Well," continued Cross, leaning confidentially over the table. "We gave them time to run off and get dressed, the lady in the kitchen, the colonel in the bedroom, and then we sat down and waited for the coffee. When MacMurphy and the colonel came back in, we were all introduced as formally as if this were a dinner at the British Embassy. The colonel looked as if a lecherous thought had never entered his orderly military mind. He took a cup of coffee, stirred it with care, smiled at everyone, and then he looked across the coffee-table at Mac-Murphy and said: 'About that wheat now——' "

"What?" said Polly, her plain round face flushed to the roots of her greying hair.

"That's right," said Jones. "Okay, Bentley, about that wheat now."

"Well, then—as any conscientious public relations officer would do—he proceeded to 'clarify' for us the entire North African wheat situation. Number of bushels, where grown, acreage planted, type of grain, suitability of soil, comparative production pre-war and present."

Cross' small lined face was alive with delight. Hawks wasn't listening. "Polly," he said, tapping her on the shoulder. "Polly, I'm getting drunk."

"That's a terrible story," said Polly, trying to keep from laughing.

"It was a nightmare," said Cross. "Particularly for anyone with a healthy imagination. Half an hour we sat around drinking coffee out of little cups and talking about wheat. Until finally the colonel—just to prove he was made of armor plate —gave us all a glassy smile, grabbed his cap and said goodnight. All of us had bad dreams for several nights after that. Jones—can I quote you, Ed?—Jones said that for eight nights in a row he dreamed he was making violent love to a loaf of bread."

"Bentley, stop it!" said Polly.

"But it's true!" remonstrated Jones. "Within a week it was all over the Mediterranean Theater. It damned near destroyed our war effort."

Hawks had finished his drink and was looking around for the waiter. "Outside of that, what's she like?"

"Outside of that, I don't know," said Cross. "I never got to know her as well as some of the—ah—younger correspondents did. She seems to do all right as a reporter. I'll say this for her, she really works."

"Yeah," said Jones, "she works everybody. She's the gal that broke D-day, you know. Got it from some other colonel she was sleeping with then, a G-2 at SHAEF. Poor bastard got busted for a security leak. As for our Carla, she was severely disciplined by having her copy double-censored for the next four days. Tough break for the kid, wasn't it, after so much hard night work!"

"I'm going to leave this table," said Polly severely, "if you boys don't stop talking like that."

"Hi!" said an unusually tall young man, coming down the bar with the woman in the green hat. "Mind if we join you?"

"Not at all, Ray. Sit in."

"I'd like you all to meet my wife, Mrs. Traunstein. Just got in last night all the way from Cedar Rapids. Ida, this is Mr. and Mrs. Wilson of World Photos, David Hawks of the *New York Press*, Ed Jones, INS, and Bentley Cross."

"How do you do, Mrs. Traunstein?" Hawks lifted himself clumsily out of his hair and knocked over a glass. "Sorry," he

76

said, slumping back in his chair. "Hey, Eric! Schnell mit einem Handtuch!"

Mrs. Traunstein sat down carefully in the chair next to Hawks and examined the front of her dress minutely for possible stains. Her fingernails were as long as bird-claws.

Ed Jones paid little attention. "Actually, she wouldn't be so bad if she could only *feel* something. She's the kind of reporter who if she were sent to cover the Crucifixion would interview the Good Thief."

"And how do you like our little civilization, Mrs. Traunstein?" asked Hawks politely. "Watch out for that puddle there."

"Oh, fine." Mrs. Traunstein's voice was both nasal and grating, as if she were recovering from a bad head cold. "I'll have a bourbon and gingerale, please," to the waiter.

"I think you boys are mean!" said Polly. "At least she gets what she's after. During the war she was practically a legend. One time when I was at Ninth Army Headquarters, I went out to the outhouse and on one of the planks in back of the hole in bright red letters it said: CARLA MACMURPHY SAT HERE."

"One thing you will notice, Mrs. Traunstein," said Hawks, leaning perilously over the table, "is we have the finest waiters in Germany right here in the Park Hotel bar. Wonderful waiters, absolutely first-class. All of them Nazis."

"Nazis?" repeated Mrs. Traunstein, horrified. She looked at her drink as if it were poisoned, then up at Eric who was now serving the others at the table.

"Certainly," said Hawks. "Make the best waiters and bartenders in the world, devoted to their work and to the kind Americans who give them a cigarette once in awhile. Ask Eric here. Eric!" loudly. "Komm hier, Eric. Eric, tell the pretty American lady. Were you a member of the NSDAP?"

"Yes, sir, Mr. Hawks," said Eric politely, with no change of expression.

"And what did you do before the war?"

"I had an automobile garage, Mr. Hawks. In Kassel."

"Thank you, Eric. You may go. You see what I mean, Mrs. Traunstein? Garage owner. Finest kind of preparatory training for a waiter, gives them that technical skill that is so necessary in an important job like this."

Puzzled, she looked at him. "But I thought they were all being denazified."

"Oh, Mrs. Traunstein, have no fear. They *are* all being denazified. People like Eric, for example, are denazified out of their garages and made into waiters. All the waiters are being denazified into cleaning streets. Then we denazify the streetcleaners and put them to work running garages." He smiled at her warmly. "That is why denazification is so very, very important, Mrs. Traunstein, so very, very, *very* important. To keep labor over here from getting too frightfully stale. You wouldn't want German labor to become stale, now would you, Mrs. Traunstein?"

"No," she said dubiously, moving her glass out of his reach.

His pauses were oratorical. Each time he lifted his head and gazed sadly, soulfully, into her eyes. "But tell me about yourself, Mrs. Traunstein. You've scarcely said a word since you sat down. How do you like your new home in Frankfurt?"

"Oh, fine," she said without enthusiasm. "It's a beautiful house, just like Hollywood. Eighteen rooms and three bathrooms, and all those balconies and terraces—— I just don't know how I'm going to take care of it all, not speaking German or anything. And then there's no silverware. You know, knives and forks. We had to come over here for dinner tonight because we didn't have anything to eat off of."

"How dreadful!" said Hawks, shaking his head. "How terribly, terribly——" He spotted Bill Somers standing alone again at the bar. "Hey, Bill! Come on over have a drink."

Somers strolled over and sat down. "You waiting for that Bizonia announcement, Dave? I just saw Blakely's PRO outside and he said he'd have it over here in ten minutes."

"Thanks," said Hawks thickly. Conversation among the others at the table eddied dizzily around him. Mrs. Traunstein was now engaged in powdering her long sensitive nose, describing, meantime, the furniture in their new house, which she thought was very nice, especially a writing-desk that she hoped she could take back to the States with her when she went. "Ray says all you have to do is just go out and buy another one, a cheap one, and then when you leave you exchange them and take the good one with you, and nobody's any the wiser." From a very great distance he heard the name "MacMurphy" again and looked up.

"Carla MacMurphy?" said Traunstein. "Who's she sleeping with these days?"

The table rocked and righted itself as Somers got to his feet. Without a word, he reached his left arm across the table for Traunstein's lapel.

"Ray!" screamed Mrs. Traunstein.

A hush fell over the entire table.

"I oughta bash your goddamned face in!" said Somers.

Every word was staccato larghetto, pushed forcibly out of his mouth in a spasm of slow emphasis.

Hawks stumbled to his feet and knocked over another glass. "Aw, come on, Bill. He didn't mean anything. Let's all sit down, have another drink."

Somers' face was a vivid red.

"Look, Bill," said Traunstein, pulling away from his grip. "For Christ's sake, you know I didn't mean anything."

"Come on, Bill. Be reasonable," added Jones.

With studied hostility Somers looked around the table. "Oh, go to hell!" He let go of Traunstein's lapel with a push and made his way toward the door.

Jones turned to Traunstein. "He's been waiting for her for three weeks, you dumb fool. Does that answer your question?"

"Oh," said Traunstein, unconsciously stroking his jaw. "Oh, sure. Jesus, I had no idea."

Mrs. Traunstein put her compact carefully back in her bag. "Well, if you ask me, I didn't even know what it was all about. Ray, what did you say that made him so mad? Ray. Ray! What did you say that made him so mad?"

"Nothing, Ida, nothing."

Hawks put one of his big knuckly hands on Polly's sleeve. "Sounds like quite a gal," he said, his glazed grey eyes widened with humor.

Outside, Somers stood leaning against the frame of the Park Hotel doorway, watching the American jeeps and cars splash up in the rain. Those goddamned bastards. He had half a mind to go back to the bar and beat up the whole damned bunch of them single-handed.

A colonel came up in a command car, jumped out with the exaggerated agility of the middle-aged, and the car moved on. A jeep stopped at the corner, but it was only a Stars-and-Stripes jeep dumping some papers. That bastard Traunstein! Couldn't cover a fire if it exploded under his can.

Disinterested, he watched a magnificent Czechoslovak Tatra sidle slowly into the curb, and its driver, a tough-looking little German with a decided limp, dash out from behind the wheel and throw open the rear door as if he were a Teutonic Sir Walter Raleigh with a velvet cloak. For a moment the door hung open. Then a shining red head appeared over a pair of chartreuse slacks, and out stepped Carla.

"Carla!" yelled Somers, darting across the pavement.

She kissed him with affection.

"Wait just a minute, Bill, while I tell Kripke where to put everything." She turned back to the driver. "All the baggage here in the hotel and then take the car around back into the parking lot. Timmy can sleep in the car."

Somers picked up one of the bags. "Where in Christ's name did you get that snazzy car? I was looking all the time for the jeep. You borrow it somewhere?"

"I'll tell you later," she said, smiling. "Everything all right, Kripke?"

"Ja-ja, Miss MacMurphy. Alles in Ordnung."

Somers took her arm in his and they made their way into the hotel. "Never mind about registering," he said, heading past the desk toward the elevator. "I've already taken care of everything. We've got Room 205 again, same as last time. And wait'll you see the terrific story I've got for you besides. Terrific!"

She looked at him for a moment with a blank stare.

Then she stepped into the elevator. "Wonderful," she said.

He got in beside her and the German porter began stacking the luggage around them, one piece on top of another. The doors closed, the elevator started up.

"Second floor?" asked the elevator boy.

"Please," said Somers.

CHAPTER SEVEN

"Where are we, Kripke?" asked Carla, waking up in the wide back seat and looking around her.

"Just coming onto the Berliner Ring, Miss MacMurphy," said Kripke. "In twenty minutes we should be in Berlin."

She peered out the window at the thick pine forests through which the autobahn cut its swift shining scythe. Over dark hills to the left the sunset sky was a thunderous circusy pink with heavy rain-clouds hanging fullbellied and threatening above. She rolled down the window, and a dank smell of wet pine needles and rotting leaves swept into the car, a refreshing coolness after the intense heat of the day. Around the black boles of the trees curled a thick grey mist, grey gauze wound around the posts of a church aisle, grey tulle ballet-skirts over black tights.

Timmy, who had been sleeping on the floor, raised his head and looked at her. "Nothing at all, Timmy, mon vieux," she said. "Go back to sleep." The dog yawned, stretched, and put his head back down on his forepaws.

She lit a cigarette to wake herself up, and leaned her head close to the car window to catch the most of that refreshing cool mist. Beyond the convex curving rim of the black pines was space and a far-away cerise glory.

The autobahn wound off into a cloverleaf turn and then banked onto a narrower highway. At the cross-over stood an enormous monument of a Russian tank, the base of the monument piled with flowers and wreaths like a mausoleum. "Ha!" said Kripke. "The Bolsheviki and their Stalin-Panzer!" His voice rang with amused contempt. "Maybe the Russians are afraid we'll forget what a tank looks like."

They turned off the highway into a long, tree-shaded avenue. "We are already in Zehlendorf," said Kripke. "Welche Nummer, Miss MacMurphy?"

"Friedrichstrasse 18," she said, lighting another cigarette.

Prepared for ruins, for a city leveled to the ground and reduced to one enormous heap of granulated debris, Carla looked with amazement at the graceful uncluttered streets, so neatly in keeping with financially and socially secure suburbia. Then, looking more closely, she began to see. Behind the carefully planted shrubs, the fences and lawns, landscaped gardens and flag-stone walks, were yawning holes and the collapsed ivy-covered walls of former residences. About one house in four was destroyed or half-destroyed, hanging crazily open and empty behind its discreet curtains of vines and shrubbery.

Yet for the rest, this might have been Larchmont or Chevy Chase, the dignified quiet of tree-arched avenues enclosing a society sure of itself and of the tranquil morality of its intentions. Sprinklers curled their wet fingers over the lawns; here and there one could hear the interrupted whine of a lawnmower. Beyond the closed contentment of the streets, evergreens and poplars reached long protective arms into that cerise sky.

She noticed that all the undamaged houses had red placards tacked to their doors, and when Kripke slowed down for a turn she made out a few words: EINTRITT VERBOTEN. REQUISITIONED BY THE U.S. ARMY FOR AMERICAN PERSONNEL.

Down a long, curving avenue they rolled and came to a stop before just such an undamaged house, a square hospitable-looking residence with a tall iron fence and an imposing sign just to the left of the gate: THE WASHINGTON GLOBE DISPATCH.

Kripke pulled the emergency brake and shut off the motor. Peering up at the house, she stepped out. The smell was wonderful: freshly-cut grass, rose bushes in bloom, the damp semi-coolness of a summer evening after rain.

The door of the house opened above her and a dumpy little blonde stuck her head out, pulled it back and disappeared. Welcome home, thought Carla. Who was that, I wonder? A moment later, the door opened again and there was Norman, a small thin corduroy-jacketed figure in the wide white doorway.

He strolled down the walk, holding his coat together. "Well, Fräulein MacMurphy! I expected you to tumble up in a jeep," he said, with that deliberately sly humor she remembered. "In a minute the entire street will be out to titter over that monstrous thingumagummy you've got there." His eyes were bright. His crooked yellow teeth poked timidly out of his smiling mouth.

"Hello, Norman," said Carla.

Kripke was unloading the luggage from the nose of the Tatra. "And who's this German teep you've picked up?" asked Norman, regarding Kripke as if he were a performing animal. "Something you won in a crap game?"

"He's a Berliner I found in Bavaria to drive for me," said Carla. Then in German: "Kripke, I want you to meet Mr. Norman Brant, who is European Chef de Bureau of my newspaper."

Kripke took his cue well. He put down the bags, came around the side of the car, clicked his heels and stood rigidly at attention. "Kripke," he said with dignity.

With Timmy running circles around them, she and Norman started up the steps toward the door. "But I've already got a chauffeur," protested Norman.

"And now so have I," said Carla.

They were on the top step. The crown of his head with its untidy greying cowlicks was just even with her shoulder; like a small, bright-eyed grey squirrel, he stopped short and looked at her. "Meaning, Fräulein MacM, that you are willing to pay his salary?"

"Of course."

"Oh well," he said, his voice dropping with reassurance. "Then that's your Sache, as we German teeps say. I wash my paddies of it." The crooked yellow smile flickered over his face. He opened the door. "I'm afraid, however, that this is something we will have to discuss. I had told all our domestics that when I went to Nuremberg you would take over the house exactly as it is, and each one could be assured of keeping his little Arbeitsstelle. I scarcely expected you to come in with a fleet of faithful retainers, you know."

Carla smiled one of her most disarming smiles. "Let's talk about it tomorrow or the day after, Norman, after I've gotten settled a little bit."

"Right you are," he said, nodding. "Right you are."

They walked through the cool darkness of a large hall and toward some doors at the other end, crossed a wide, nicely finished livingroom and emerged on a small terrace. There were two white tables and some little white garden chairs, and one of the tables had been set for tea. Beyond the terrace was a vegetable garden edged with small evergreens and over at the left a man worked on his knees tying up some plants.

This was their "defeat garden," explained Norman, motioning her to a chair at the tea table. He had thought for awhile of having it plowed back into lawn, now that he was getting plenty of fresh fruits and vegetables from the army. But the owner of the house, Graf von Etwas, he went on, had got himself into such a "tizzy" about it, he had let it remain as a vegetable garden. The Graf lived several hours' subway ride from there but came every evening to "piddle around" with the plants and "commit gluttony" on whatever bits of fruit or vegetable he could find.

"But I must say I'm titillated to see you, Fräulein MacM," he said, sitting down and unfolding his napkin. "Partially because I'm in such a fussety to get to Nuremberg, partially because your presence is always a matter for increased glandular activity. Now tell me," smiling with a secret delight at what he was about to put into words, "what you've been doing these past three months and with whom. Whoever he was, he must have been what we German characters call 'herrlich' to hold up a woman of your caliber for three long months."

She did not answer.

"Come, come," he said, smiling his slow yellow smile. "Every journalistic wood-pussy in Berlin has been questioning me about your arrival and the current repository of your affections. There have been ugly rumors of the *Globe Dispatch* being linked, in some intimate personal way, with the WP. Is this true?"

About half of Norman's conversation was in subquotation marks; when he spoke you could almost hear the punctuation dropping into place. His vocabulary was like a store of acorns which he had hidden away in his thin brown cheeks. Appreciatively, he would roll forward a saliva-coated cliché, hold it out in his discolored teeth and then, slyly, roll it back to its accustomed place where it would be easily accessible for future use.

"I wouldn't really know," said Carla sweetly.

"Come now, Fräulein MacM," he cajoled. "What am I to report to these characters? Surely you know what they're interested in. Women always have a subtle uterine sense of these matters. Until now, I have guarded your interest by replying that this is just some more of your fabulous coping. But now, of course, they're in a tizzy to discover how long the option runs and who is in the best position to pick it up from here."

A perfect opening, she thought, for telling him that in three weeks she was going to give up her job, leave Berlin, and go to Parris and marry Charles. Yet, somehow, just because of his surreptitiously sensual delight in the anticipation of her answer, she could say nothing. To explain to him now about Charles would be to open herself to the gentle devisceration of his questions.

While tea was being served, he ran quickly and with relish through an intimate description of the members of the household, several chiding and intentionally provocative theories on why she was so late in getting to Berlin, plus the latest press club gossip about himself which he related with lascivious enjoyment. From his conversation life in post-war Berlin emerged as a subtle and slightly obscene joke, an insular 19th-Century colonial civilization amid 20th-Century ruins, in which "the Hauptsache, as we German teeps say" was who slept with whom and for what price.

While he talked, the pasty little blonde who had opened the front door served sliced chicken sandwiches and little cakes. This was Inge, Norman said. The entire press colony was convinced that he was "taking his pleasure" of her, but this wasn't true.

"We colonial teeps," said Norman, carefully pouring the tea, "have to exercise great care as to which of these natives we take up with. It can be dangerous. All the army posters say so. Even with such sweet young things as Inge. The exact figures escape me, but our ever-watchful MP's just announced that about seventy-five percent of the fourteen- and fifteen-year-old girls they pick up have VD. Imagine! It gives me a willy every time I think about it. One night last week I woke up in a cold tizzy, determined to fire every one of the servants under 60. The next morning, looking at their bright dishonest faces, I decided against it, having no inclination for being tended by a bevy of crones and cripples." His sharp eyes were

84

looking past her. "Speaking of cripples, your man Kripke seems to want conference with you."

Holding his cap in his hand, Kripke asked was it all right for him to put the Tatra away in Herr Brant's garage and go home. "Verzeihung, Miss MacMurphy," he blurted miserably. "But, if it would be possible—I haven't seen my family for three years."

"What did he say?" asked Norman, and when she had explained, "why not let him go? I've invited a tableful of people in tonight to wolf my food and likker and launch you into military government society. Let him run home to his three-years-repressed Frau. You won't need him till tomorrow."

"All right, Kripke," said Carla reluctantly. "You can put the car away and go. But be sure to be back here in the morning before nine." What was it that Kripke had said about his sons on that ride to the airport with Charles? That he wasn't sure about the paternity of one of them? "And give my best to Frau Kripke," she added pleasantly.

Grinning and bowing, Kripke limped off.

The guests for tonight, said Norman, were to be a young State Department attaché named Willstrom, a military government colonel, a German politician and his wife, and two journalistic "teeps" whom she undoubtedly knew: Tom Adcock, an editor who was just in from Washington, and David Hawks. The German, he said, was a certain Herr Geisler, a "saintly character" who was head of the Catholic Party in the Soviet Zone.

"This is the first time I've ever invited a German teep here," he explained, "and I must admit I'm in something of a perspiration about it. Ordinarily I wouldn't do it. But Connell asked me to do a personality piece on the sanctimonious old boy for the Sunday edition and I've got to dredge up all the color I can on his personal life—whether or not he beats his kids, deceives his wife, seduces young Fräuleins under the frock and so forth. I'm afraid it's going to be boring for the rest of us, but it just can't be helped."

"Hawks," said Carla, her soft baby voice both casual and reflective. "He's the *New York Press,* isn't he? Somebody told me he's the best reporter in Germany."

Norman leaned back frowning, all chef-de-bureau again. "Well—just between the two of us, and I wouldn't admit this to anyone else—he is. Of course, he's got everything on his side. He's young and energetic, speaks the language almost like a native and knows Germany like the palm of his hand. On top of that, he can write. That's one reason why I was in such a tizzy for you to get here. Not being a regular German correspondent, I'm not equipped to keep up with him. I would say, objectively, that except when he's drinking he's good, so good that even you are going to have your troubles. Even you, my proud beauty. Of course," he paused to glance archly at her, "of course, if worst comes to worst, you can always take him into camp. I understand his wife in the States is divorcing him and he's in a nice ripe state of bitter young disillusionment."

"I'll do all right," said Carla quietly. "No one's ever beaten me yet. And no one's going to start now."

"As for this evening," he concluded, "all I'll ask of you, Fräulein MacM, is to behave with seemly decorum toward the saintly Geisler and keep a firm hand on the behavior as regards these young and naive boys like Bob Willstrom and David Hawks. I warn you, I'll not have any laying of intrigues in this house until I'm safely off to Nuremberg. After that, you can take any steps you deem efficacious to out-file and out-frontpage the *New York Press* and set up a snuggery here with whomever you please. But until I've gone, no incidents, please."

He really means that, thought Carla. Behind that smirking waggishness was a real anxiety at what she might do, whom she might drag in in the dead of night. As if she were an alley cat. Her green eyes narrowed, she watched him finish the last drop of his tea, meticulously fold his napkin into a neat square and tuck it under the flange of his plate.

"So, Fräulein MacM." He pushed back his chair. "Watch the behavior."

The house, Carla decided as Norman took her from room to room, was comfortable enough but was hopelessly mismanaged and far from clean. On one bookshelf the dust lay so thick that she could have written her name in it. Simpering and blinking her pale blue eyes, the serving-girl named Inge accompanied them on their tour, stuffing things out of sight and chiding Norman with such familiarity that Carla began to revise her earlier estimate of Norman's sex-life. In the kitchen the cook, a buxom laughing woman named Luisa, wiped her hands on her apron and shook hands with Carla as if they were equals, and then hospitably invited her to sit down on one of the kitchen stools. That makes two I'll get rid of, thought Carla, coolly declining the proffered stool.

If Norman thought—she was taking off her dusty dress and pinning up her hair for her bath—that she would tolerate a situation like that, he was crazy. He had no right to promise the servants that they could all stay on. Even for the three or four short weeks that she would be here, she would still run this household the way she saw fit. Kripke of course she would keep; unscrupulous rascal that he was, he would be useful for an infinite number of purposes. The secretary too could stay on. A serious-looking German-Jewess named Gerda, she seemed both pleasant and efficient; her office downstairs was the only clean, well-ordered room in the house. But my God, that Luisa! And that creeping venereal disease, Inge!

Her cheekbones tightened as she touched them with a slight film of vaseline to emphasize the shape of her face. The dames men would pick up with when there was no one around to watch them!

The first guest to arrive was a man with a heavy booming voice that shook the walls of the house and resounded all the way upstairs to the bathroom in which she was finishing her eyelashes. When she came down in a full-skirted black linen dress and with her shining hair curled on the top of her head, he was introduced to her as Colonel Townsend, head of one of the political divisions of American Military Government. He was an exceptionally short fat man with a figure like a basketball. He said he had heard a lot about her, had read her column, and then before she knew it he was off on a long interminably detailed account of a conversation he had just had with someone named Keife, who it seems was a Social Democratic leader in Bavaria.

From his remarks she gathered that he was on intimate and friendly terms with all present-day German politicians and knew by an infallible personal slide-rule what their chances of leadership were. Schumacher, he said, was "through." Adenauer was "too autocratic," and would soon be deserted by his party. Kaiser was "a good old boy" but had been co-operating too closely with the Communists. "None of them have got any real power," he said loftily. "If it wasn't for us and the British they'd all be has-beens." Yet when Herr Geisler and his wife arrived he lifted his huge bulk from his chair and said how-do-you-do with the cordial formality of a first introduction.

Herr Geisler was a tall, saintly-looking, completely bald man with deep-set dark eyes. His manners were courtly. With feet together and arms held restrainedly at his sides, he bowed to her, to Norman and to Colonel Townsend and introduced his wife, a sweet little middle-aged woman who sank wordlessly into one of Norman's big chairs.

"Well," said Norman, filling everyone's glass. "Well."

A chasm of silence yawned uncomfortably around them.

Carla waited politely for Norman or Colonel Townsend to open the conversation, but neither of them said a word. Finally Townsend inclined his rotund weight toward her and said in a loud whisper, "You speak German, don't you, Miss Mac-Murphy?"

"Yes, of course," surprised that he should ask.

Frau Geisler sat quietly back in her chair, looking with moderate interest around the room. Geisler fingered his martini glass but said nothing. Self-consciously, Norman picked up a plate of hors d'oeuvres and politely passed them around.

It occurred to Carla suddenly that in spite of all this talk of German "teeps" and detailed conversations with Bavarian politicians neither Norman nor Townsend spoke German. She leaned forward graciously. "You have just come from the Russian Zone, Herr Geisler?" she asked in German.

"Yes," he answered gravely. "I live there. I am just in Berlin for a few days away from my regular work in Weimar."

At this moment, raucous voices were heard in the hall, the door burst open and two very cheerful-looking young men stood in the doorway. "Hi!" said one, the thin one with spectacles. "Mind if we come in!"

"For some reason or other," Norman sighed, "I always seem to be visited by inebriates every time I throw a festivity. All right, Mr. Bob Willstrom, come in. And while the door's open, I suppose you may as well let the Hawks in with you."

Both of them bowed low over her hand with the exaggerated dignity of the nearly drunk. She rather liked Willstrom, he was young and pixyish-looking; behind his thick spectacles his dark eyes twinkled with humor. Hawks she instantly resented. There was something sardonic about him, a cool self-confident humor that marked him as invulnerable.

His first remark to her was a pleasant insolence. "Bob and I," he said, his strong handsome face adorned with a wicked smile, "have been so delighted with the prospect of meeting you, Miss MacMurphy, that we rather outdid our toasts to your singular combination of beauty and intelligence. I know you will forgive us." He gestured widely toward Willstrom. "You must get to know Bob well, Miss MacMurphy. He is an excellent source on all matters pertaining to German politics. One of my dearest friends too, but an exceptional chap just the same. Only liberal I've ever known who treats his own servants like human beings."

What a cynical remark, she thought. Obviously a reactionary.

All this time Herr Geisler had been standing waiting. As Hawks turned to accept a martini from Norman, he saw Geisler for the first time. "Und auch Herr Geisler," he said warmly. "Na, mein lieber Freund, wie gehts? Und wie ist die Lage in der Ostzone?"

The entire scene filled Carla with disgust. The German, his pale serious face alight with pleasure, turned to Hawks as if he were his sole friend in a land of hostile strangers. While Hawks, completely oblivious to his fellow-countrymen, acted as if no one had any importance to him save the German. Absent-mindedly accepting the drink that Norman put in his hand, he dropped into the chair next to Geisler and they were immediately lost in conversation.

When Tom Adcock strolled in, elegant in blue serge and a bow-tie, Carla made quite a fuss over him. "Tom!" she said, in a low lisping voice. "How long it's been since I've seen you!" Hearing her, Hawks looked up, nodded to Adcock and went back to his conversation. Sitting demurely on the divan, one slim leg curled under her skirt, one idly tapping the floor, she listened to Tom and Norman discussing tables. Tom, it seemed, wanted to pick up some eighteenth-century German tables for his Washington collection, and Norman was advising him on the number of cartons he should be prepared to spend and the best shops to spend them in.

She sat erect, her breasts lifted up and forward, her cheekbones tightened and her head tilted to one side, looking very attentive but hearing nothing. Her wide green eyes under their thickly blacked lashes were repeating their old trick, bringing each man in the room into their shining moist focus, considering him with feline empiricism, gently setting him out of focus again and proceeding to the next one.

She was watching Hawks' face as he talked, noticing the strong line of his jaw and the alert grey eyes under their heavy eyebrows and wondering that the *New York Press* would keep on as their German correspondent a man who was so obviously pro-German. His forehead was broad and well-formed; as he talked a lock of brown hair fell over his temple but he brushed it impatiently aside. His hands were big, with knotty knuckles and long squared-off fingers.

At dinner, she was amazed at the way everyone ate. Geisler and his wife, while preserving a dignified reserve, ate as if they had never seen food before. Willstrom and Dave Hawks stuffed themselves with the frank avidity of the drunk, and Norman, despite his involution with the role of host, kept nibbling surreptitiously at the hot breads and biscuits that

Inge was constantly replenishing. Most astonishing of all was Colonel Townsend, at her right, who kept pushing food into his broad mouth as if filling an insatiable cavity. She began to understand his great girth. He fell on the food with a concupiscence that was almost revolting, as if his whole existence depended on his ability to fill out his spherical shape from the platters that were offered him.

The meal was more than excellent, it was a work of art. The lobster bisque, the salad, the sliced cold turkey in aspic, the wines—Carla began to reconsider her earlier judgment of Luisa; perhaps a semi-autonomous kitchen kingdom was necessary in order to produce meals like this.

Tom Adcock, who sat at her left, was refusing each platter with melancholic restraint. "I've been dieting," he explained in that soft Groton drawl of his. "A horrible kind of self-imposed frustration at a time like this." His beautifully manicured hand indicated the platters of cold shrimp, crabmeat and flaked fish, the heaped-up baskets of hot buns.

He was, she agreed, a great deal plumper than when she had known him in Washington six years earlier. He had not lost his air of smiling Calvert distinction. It was only that his distinction had become heavier and more glossy, like polished hothouse fruit in an expensive delicatessen.

"You certainly don't look it," she said prettily. "I'd never know you'd gained an ounce."

Hawks, unbearable egoist that he was, was still engrossed in conversation with Herr Geisler. She began to suspect that Geisler was a more important German figure than Norman had implied, with perhaps a knowledge of conditions in the Russian Zone that one could not otherwise acquire. Otherwise Hawks wouldn't be wasting his time with him. Townsend she could murder. With that earthquake laugh and booming voice he was thundering away in English to poor little Frau Geisler who couldn't understand a word he was saying, and was so obscuring the conversation of the table that Herr Geisler's quiet German was completely drowned. Across the table from her, Hawks' young face and Geisler's lined patient older one were as placid and remote as two faces in a fifteenth-century religious painting. The master and the disciple, she thought scoffingly.

She took a scoop of potato soufflé from the dish Inge offered her. "What do you think of Germany, Tom?" she asked, well aware that he had arrived in Germany only an hour or two ago. And was pleased when Adcock started to give her one of his long editorial answers, heavily interlarded with quotes

90

from unnamed but "top-level" government "thinkers." As he continued, his soft honeyed voice gained in volume, until everyone was listening.

"Since the problem of tomorrow is war with Russia, everything we do from now until the outbreak of hostilities must be judged by one standard alone—will it help us defeat the Russians?" He paused. "I say this as much for Herr Geiler's— Geisler, is it?—Herr Geisler's benefit as for our own. America no longer has time for the ifs, ands and buts of Germany's so-called democratic politicians, nor for all this silly twaddle about building bridges between east and west. It's time for the Germans to stand up and be counted. Either they're on our side or they're not. Democracy in Germany is of secondary importance. The prime consideration now is: how fast can Germany get herself politically and industrially organized to carry her share of the coming war against Russia?"

There was a pause while Hawks translated for Herr Geisler, and the old man nodded gravely as he listened.

"He'd like to say something in reply, Tom, if that's all right with you," said Hawks. "But he has to say it in German. I'll translate for him."

Herr Geisler's voice was steady and clear, his German crisply enunciated and guttural in the accent of Brandenburg. While he was talking, Carla noticed Frau Geisler nervously twisting her wedding ring, her eyes never leaving her husband's face. As if afraid that he might say something wrong and incur the displeasure of his conqueror-hosts.

"He says," translated Hawks, "that that is exactly what she was under Hitler—politically and industrially organized for war, especially for war against the Soviets. Since it was in the name of democracy that the Allies knocked it all down, it seems strange to him to see them now setting it all back up with little or no thought to its democratization." Evidently Hawks thought old Geisler's rebuttal a shrewd one. He was grinning at Adcock as if he had caught him in a trap.

"Tell him," said Adcock smoothly, "that German democracy is his problem, not ours. He's a German political leader. If the Germans are so passionately fond of democracy, how come they've made so little progress in it since the end of the war?"

Geisler's slow steady voice recommenced again, and again Frau Geisler sat as if frozen with fear, her black eyes fixed on her husband's pale, deeply lined face.

Hawks leaned back. "Herr Geisler respectfully submits that Germany is—and bids fair to remain for some time—under military occupation, the most totalitarian form of government known to man, and the least likely to demonstrate to any nation the joys of democratic government. It is also devastated. Under such circumstances, he says, it is very difficult to preach democracy. He adds that it is hard for a man with a full belly to understand the psychology of a man with an empty one."

"That's exactly what I mean by their 'ifs, ands and buts,' " said Adcock. "All these German politicians have the same idea —that a democratic state can be developed only in an hermetically sealed container. *If* all the conditions were exactly right—plenty of bread and butter and Ruhr coal, no ruins, no unemployed—*if* there were no east-west conflict, et cetera, et cetera. Unfortunately, the real reason is that they don't care enough. Actually I'm very pro-German, but I must admit that they seem to *like* dictators. It makes them feel secure."

"Why you great big galloping liberal, you!" said Hawks suddenly. "While Herr Geisler and thousands of Germans like him were in concentration camps because they didn't 'care enough,' where were you swilling your Manhattans?"

Adcock shifted in his chair. "I have always deplored your rudeness, David," he said, without changing his expression of smiling tolerance. "However, in case your question is a serious one, I was with the Office of War Information during the entire war."

"Oh," said Hawks solemnly.

"But to continue," Adcock went on in his mellifluous voice. "It is unfortunate that conditions in Germany are not perfect. It is also unfortunate that the American taxpayer has neither limitless money nor limitless patience. However, Germany does have one chance left. And only one."

"Which is?"

"Was hat er gesagt?" Herr Geisler wanted to know, and Hawks whisperingly translated.

"Which is to get ready to do what she was always aching to do under Hitler—fight the Bolsheviks."

"A kind of paid buffer state," suggested Hawks.

"Exactly," said Adcock easily. "We will supply the money and they will do the fighting. Simple."

"What a wonderful visionary policy!" said Hawks sardonically. "For a nation that has indicted twenty-one men at Nuremberg for cynical manipulation of peoples and states, this is the new idealism!"

"It may not be idealistic, David, but really you must see that it's the best possible out for Germany. And for ourselves.

And I assure you, a good many Americans agree with me. Some extremely influential Americans, I might add."

"I'm sure," Hawks said meaningfully. "But if you don't mind, I don't think I'll translate that scintillatingly realistic solution of yours for Herr Geisler. It might interfere with his digestion. It's so seldom that he gets a chance to eat like this."

"I must say, David, that your attitude is something less than——"

"Never mind commenting on my attitude until you know what it is," said Hawks, his voice rising. "And by God, I'll outline it for you. Everyone at this table knows how anti-Communist and anti-Russian I am. So I don't need to go into that. I believe in American democracy and the American capitalist system. But I believe in defending them with the best means at our disposal, not the worst. You fly-by-night, Johnny-come-lately editors and columnists rush over here, take a quick look around and then go back to America to write columns about how the Russian soldier is being seduced away from Communism by the sight of western bathtubs and Swiss watches. When the truth is that you yourselves are being seduced away from democratic principles and procedures by watching the Communists operate. How much better than the Communist line is this Adcock line about organizing a continent to fight our wars for us? In essence isn't it the same goddamned policy, Washington version instead of Moscow version?"

"If I may be allowed to put a word in," said Bob Willstrom slowly, his glasses shining in the candlelight, "I'd like to say that I agree with Dave."

Adcock interrupted with an amused smile. "Where am I, anyway? At a sewing-bee for fellow-travelers?"

"Yeah," said Hawks. "We love the Russians. We're so indebted to them for outdoing us. Think of where American policy in Germany would be today if the Russians hadn't obliged us by behaving even worse than we have and following a policy of conquest even more cynical than our own! As a matter of fact, Tom, you could do a swell editorial on that. Entitled 'America's Debt to Russia,' and showing that the only thing that has saved us from complete disaster in postwar Europe is Russian imperialism. Make a swell editorial and give you a wonderful opportunity to demonstrate to all your devoted readers that Russian bad faith is as bad as your own."

Adcock pushed his chair back. "Look here, David, that's scarcely good form." He turned to Norman. "I'm terribly sorry, Norman. I've known David a very long time, and I know what he's like when he gets one of these streaks of rudeness. I think I'd give him a chance to cool down and do a little thinking."

Herr Geisler was listening with the attentiveness of a man who was with difficulty understanding about half of what was being said. Glancing at Frau Geisler's strained and nervous face, Carla had an almost irrepressible desire to yell "Boo!" at the unhappy little woman; anticipation of catastrophe had transferred her into a caricature of fear. Not understanding a word of English, she evidently thought her poor old husband had started all this and was about to be rushed off to prison as a result.

"Come, come," said Norman. "Don't let's all get into a fluff over a casual discussion." He folded his napkin thoughtfully and stood up. "We'll have our coffee and brandies in the livingroom and settle down to a discussion of something safe. Like sex, for example. What do you know about sex, Fräulein MacM?" he said, coming up and taking her arm. "All these dull teeps talking about politics all the time when they could be listening to an old master—mistress, rather," he smiled at his own witticism, "on a much more basic and entertaining subject."

The coffee was strong and hot, served in tiny gold cups carrying the heraldic seal of Mark Brandenburg, and the liqueurs were liberally poured in large green shot-glasses which Inge kept refilling. But the evening had been broken, and there was no putting it together again.

Norman started brightly off on a discussion of Freudian tendencies among the American press colony, but no one listened. Conversation was like a prairie summer-night storm, small disagreements flaring up on every side like heat lightning, disappearing, then flaring up again. One by one, the guests started to say their farewells and drift out. When Adcock got up to leave, Hawks lifted his head and said sardonically: "That's an excoriating column you've plotting, Tom. All I ask is that you keep my name out of it."

"Goodnight, David," said Adcock coolly.

When Colonel Townsend offered to drive Willstrom home, Hawks got up and helped his stumbling friend out of his chair and to the door. Herr and Frau Geisler he also took to the door, his arms around Geisler's thin erect shoulders. "I'm a little drunk," he told them in German as they moved across the room, "but don't let it disturb you. I can always lose my temper, drunk or sober." Frau Geisler's face was a contradiction in emotions. Seemingly she wanted to believe him, that all was well, but she couldn't.

Carla smiled conspiratorially at Norman: "Are they always so frightened?"

"I wouldn't know," he said. "As I informed you earlier, Fräulein Carla, this is my first experience. And I must say a rude breaking-in of my maidenhood of hospitality."

With graceful deliberation she half-stood, half-knelt at the divan until Hawks returned.

He dropped into a chair and poured himself another drink. "Well, Norman," he said tiredly. "Now that everyone has gone, let me tell you that I'm sorry I tangled with Adcock at your table. I'm afraid I wasn't very polite."

"Would you mind," said Norman, smiling his yellow smile, "pouring one of those for the lovely lady at your left and then one for your host?"

"Christ, Norman, I'm sorry." He poured two drinks, spilling an almost equal amount on the cocktail-table, gulped his drink down and eased himself out of his chair. "Norman," he said, "it was one of the best 'festivities' you've ever held. Up until the moment, of course, that I got teed-off at that elegant fake. For which I apologize. Excellent dinner, wonderful drinks, and affording us all the pleasure of meeting the fabulous Carla MacMurphy. For which I, above all men—or should I say, exactly like all men—am grateful." He bowed, imitating Herr Geisler. "Guten Abend, Gnädiges Fräulein."

Carla smiled up at him, her beautifully even white teeth gleaming against the moist red of her lipstick. "Oh, don't go," she coaxed. "Stay and have one more drink."

Norman, who had been moving around the room closing windows and doors and emptying ashtrays into a large oriental bowl, turned abruptly and looked at them. "I would suggest," he said, his bright eyes a little tired, "that we have one last drink and then Carla and I will walk the gentleman home. Bear in mind, dear kiddies, that the dawn is almost upon us."

"Dawn?" echoed Carla. "Why, it's only two-thirty."

Hawks picked up his drink and walked over to the window. "You know," he said ruminatively, "I can't tell you the number of times I've wanted to bash Adcock's face in. That great American liberal thinker! He's the kind of patriot who would be in favor of a concentration-camp if it had an American flag flying over it." He turned away from the window. "The sun's coming up," he said. "I think it's time I went home."

The street looked shadowless and pale with neither street-lights nor moon to enliven it, only that submarine green twilight-in-reverse nudging under trees and bushes. They turned left in the street and after several blocks entered a lane guarded by a large iron gate and walked down into a kind of woods. Except for the chittering of birds, the only sound was the crunch of their footsteps on the driveway.

"I apologize for my house," said Hawks, as they rounded a heavily overhung turn. "The army put six of us in here originally, three radiomen and three reporters. But one by one they've all moved out, and now I find myself living in a mansion-by-the-sea that's big enough to house twenty German families. In my defense, I want you to know that I'm handing it back to the army next week to move into a bachelor joint with Larry Harper."

The moment they turned the last bend in the drive, she drew in her breath in enchantment. It was a ranch-house, painted white brick with a sloping brown roof, a big, low rambling house with the most magnificent gardens and terraces she had ever seen, gardens that ran down among evergreens and willows to what appeared to be a lake. "How lovely!" she said, turning breathlessly toward him. "And so buried away from everything!"

He looked at her. "Yeah," he said. "A guy can sit here any night he wants and get good and stinking drunk. Wonderful, isn't it?"

The pale green of dawn was drifting into the grey of morning. In the tall trees that surrounded the house, birds were chirping like housewives in a tenement.

"Well, goodnight," said Hawks, moving toward the timbered door and the carriage-lamp that still burned irrelevantly outside. "A lovely evening, Norman." He hesitated, "and Carla."

They stood for a moment near the door.

"My God, those birds!" said Norman. "What a lot of clattering!"

Hawks' hand was on the handle of the door. "Well," he said, "I'll admit they're kraut birds. But do you really think they make any more noise than any other kind of birds?"

CHAPTER EIGHT

NORMAN stood on the top step, his trenchcoat cinched tightly around his waist, his suitcases and portable typewriter piled neatly at his feet.

"Well, that takes care of about everything. If you need any help from me you can always reach me at the Nuremberg press camp. Gerda's got the number in her little black book." He glanced at his watch and rocked up and down on his heels. "That car ought to have been here five minutes ago." His sharp bright eyes peered apprehensively up and down the street, but there was no car in sight. A middle-aged woman in a neat business suit was carefully picking things out of the garbage pail that stood in front of the gate and packing them away in a small satchel.

"As for you, Fräulein MacMurphy," he said, turning his back to the street, "watch the behavior. Do what you can to keep our friend Connell happy in his glassed-in cubby-hole in Washington. Beat the *New York Press* whenever and however you can. But don't throw away your virtue for it. I assure you, the *Globe* wouldn't pay you an extra dime. They wouldn't even know what column to enter it in."

Carla smiled vaguely, leaning against the doorpost and looking up at the fuzzy greyness of the sky. It will rain, she thought. That moist heavy stillness to the air, and the sky so low it seemed to be resting on the treetops.

"And another thing, Fräulein Carla," he said, looking slyly up at her. "Let's hear no more of this silly twiddle-twaddle of yours about quitting to run off with this Poignon teep. Let's just put aside our girlish fancies about French socialist love, douches and dialectic, and Marx and Freud in one handy volume, and face the facts of life. The MacMurphy as a Hausfrau would be one of the most ridiculous and unworkable pieces of casting ever perpetrated, even including some of Hollywood's more outstanding blunders. Consider for a moment what it would mean—no more headlines, no more glamorous streakings across two continents hot on the trail of a news beat, no more *Look Here, America!* by Carla MacMurphy, no more taxi-drivers and airplane pilots falling at your feet. Nothing but housekeeping and sex. And with the same man all the time, at that!"

"I'm still going to do it," she said stubbornly.

"Nonsense. You just stay on here in Germany for awhile and get yourself involved with some nice virile young man with a big bankroll of American scrip, and I'll call you from Nuremberg in a few weeks so you can tell me all about how you've changed your mind."

"But I haven't changed my mind and I'm not going to change it." She spoke slowly, with a childish earnestness. "You know how I feel about it, Norman. I've already told you. This is something so much more important. It's my duty toward society, to live according to the principles I believe in. And besides——"

An amused smile played over his yellow teeth. "And besides, he's good in the feathers, eh?" He patted her arm. "Now be a good girl and stop thinking like a heroine in a second-rate novel of social significance. Ah, here's my car at last." He picked up his suitcases and started toward the gate. Carrying the typewriter, Carla followed.

At the curb he stood back to watch his bags being stowed away in the trunk. "These Russian teeps! If they hadn't closed the highway, I could be in Nuremberg for dinner tonight. As it is, it'll take me the better part of two days. Annoying bastards, when you come to think about it. I'm certain they only do it to get us in a tizzy." He climbed into the car. "Well, Fräulein MacM, that's it. Don't forget my good fatherly advice on this proposed French elopement of yours. Settle down and forget about it. And watch the behavior now!"

The car pulled away and he was gone.

Carla stood for a moment looking down the street. The foliage of the trees, already parched and dusty from the late summer sun, hung limply on the warm grey air. Except for an old man pulling a cart full of dug-up stumps, the street was deserted. It would certainly rain before nightfall.

She felt relieved at Norman's anti-climactic departure, relieved and apathetic. She wondered if it was too early to call Hawks and ask him to dinner, or whether she shouldn't wait a day or two to keep it from being too obvious. Wearily, her head aching from last night's drinking, she turned and went back into the house and into the room that served as an office.

Seeing her at the door, Gerda looked up and stopped typing. Behind her spectacles her sallow face was serious but friendly. "I called up the Labor Office, Miss MacMurphy, and they're sending a girl over right away to take Inge's place. She should be here any minute. Then I have the office records ready too, if you'd like to go over them while you're waiting."

"Fine, Gerda." She sat down in an armchair and Gerda brought her the account-books, large fat loose-leafs which had been meticulously and exactly kept. The girl was obviously a conscientious and intelligent worker; her answers to Carla's questions were quiet and sure. Yet she rarely smiled, and when she did it was only a fleeting tribute to someone else's humor and altered not at all the somber composure of her face.

"How is it you speak English with an American accent?" Carla asked.

98

"I lived in Brooklyn for five years, Miss MacMurphy. From 1934 to 1939."

"And came back to Germany just as the war was beginning? Wasn't that kind of dangerous?"

"It wasn't so dangerous for me in those days, Miss MacMurphy, because I am only half Jew. And I thought that whatever happened, I should be here with my family." As if that were the most natural thing in the world. And as if, thought Carla, she wished to close the conversation.

Carla lit a cigarette and went back to the accounts.

The doorbell rang and Gerda went out to answer it. When she came back she had with her a dark-haired German girl who sat down in a chair near the door and waited, staring all the time at Carla as if in amazement.

Finished with the account-books, Carla turned to the little brunette, who had been waiting by the door. "You were sent by the Labor Office, Miss——"

"Lochmann," said the girl in a faint low voice. "Erika Lochmann."

Carla looked at her, frowning. Now where? She seemed somehow familiar. She was pretty but terribly thin, with round brown eyes like a kitten. Probably about seventeen, and with a sweet gazelle-like shyness that was pleasing after that insufferable Inge. Not unlike thousands of German girls, and yet puzzlingly like someone she had met before. "Have we met somewhere, Miss Lochmann?" she asked in German.

The girl nodded. "In the Frankfurter Hauptbahnhof, Miss ——" She looked down at the slip of paper she held in her hand and read the name off. "——Miss MacMurphy."

Oh, of course! That girl at the bulletin-board! On an impulse Carla got up and put her hand on the girl's shoulder. "Erika Lochmann," she repeated. "And do you think you would like to work here as my maid, Erika?" she asked kindly.

"Oh, Miss MacMurphy!" blushing and stammering. "That would be wonderful! I would do anything—you were so kind to me that night."

"You can sew? And press things with an iron?"

"Yes."

"And wait on table?"

"Yes."

"And you can start right now?"

"Yes," still blushing.

"Fine. I think you will do very well. Now, don't be frightened." She smiled at the girl and patted her again on the shoulder. "I think you will like it here. Gerda will take you out to the kitchen and introduce you to everyone, and Luisa will show you where your uniforms are and tell you what you are supposed to do. All right?"

"Oh, Miss MacMurphy, thank you a thousand times." Still flushing with gratitude and embarrassment, the girl went out with Gerda toward the kitchen.

Warmed by the inner glow of a good deed well done, Carla went back to the accounts. Erika would do very well, she was sure. Young, reasonably intelligent, and grateful for a chance to work. A stroke of luck, bumping into a girl like that again.

Restlessly, she got up and wandered around the room looking at the books that lined the walls. Bored, bored, bored. And what was she going to write about when nothing had happened? Another paraphrase of a *Tägliche Rundschau* editorial. She considered again calling up Hawks and inviting him to dinner, knowing all the time that she really should let a day or two go by in the interest of subtlety. But she was so bored, and after all who else was there? That bitch Polly Wilson and her photographer husband Mike, who couldn't talk about anything but lenses and apertures. Tom Adcock, Bentley Cross.

"Your lunch is served, Miss MacMurphy," said Erika, standing self-consciously in the doorway. She looked quite pretty in her neat black uniform, her dark hair curling softly around her shoulders, her thin young face fresh and pink above the white collar.

"Thank you, Erika," said Carla, rising.

She had her lunch in the dining-room, alone at the end of the long polished table, feeling like a dinner-for-one-please-James cartoon and listening to the talk that drifted in from the kitchen every time Erika opened the door. Her lunch was excellent and Erika's serving was a little shaky but otherwise perfect.

Drinking her coffee, she gazed absent-mindedly out the long windows of the dining-room at the oppressive grey sky and listless garden. She hated eating alone. Even Norman, with his moist and viscid humor, was better than no one at all.

She finished her lunch and went back to the office. "Get me Mr. David Hawks on the phone, Gerda, please. *New York Press.*"

He answered the phone himself.

"David," in a soft low voice. "This is Carla MacMurphy. I was just wondering if you'd like to come in to have dinner with me tonight."

There was a short silence at the other end of the wire. Then his voice, regretfully: "Gee, I'm sorry, Carla, but I just can't

100

make it. I'm supposed to have dinner with some students, and then I've got an appointment to see the Bishop of Berlin at eight-thirty. Could we make it some other night?"

"Of course," she said, understandingly. "But how about stopping in later tonight for a drink or two anyway?"

"Fine! I'd love to. Around nine-thirty or ten, is that all right?"

"Wonderful. Between nine-thirty and ten, then."

She put the phone down and sat for a moment tapping with her fingers on the top of the desk. "Gerda," she said slowly, "who is the Bishop of Berlin?"

"Cardinal von Flichter."

"Um. What does he have to do with students?"

"I don't know, Miss MacMurphy. I suppose he has something to do with the Catholic students, that's all."

"Um." Her green eyes lit up with a mischievous gleam. "Well, please get him on the phone and ask him if he can see me at seven o'clock tonight." Smiling to herself, she watched Gerda dial and then disappointedly listened to the busy signal buzzing along the wire.

"I'm sorry, Miss MacMurphy. It's busy."

"All right. Try again in a minute or two."

She wandered over to the window. A breeze had sprung up and was tormenting the dusty trees. Gusts of air that blew in were chilling and strong, sweeping down swarms of tiny yellow leaves to beat ineffectually against the glass.

"Will you try the Cardinal again, Gerda?"

This time the phone was answered. Yes, the Cardinal would be happy to see Miss MacMurphy at seven at his home. Gerda jotted the address down on a slip of paper and handed it to her.

"Fine," said Carla, taking the paper. "Then you'd better tell Kripke to have the Tatra out in front and ready to leave by quarter after six."

When she came out at half past six, the sky was overbearing and dark. Kripke was working on the car, giving it some last licks with a rag. "Ein Uberfall, Miss MacMurphy!" he sang out.

She walked around to see what he had. A new powerful spotlight, a set of wonderful woven straw slipcovers and a complete set of tools. "Good work, Kripke," she said, pleased. "But how much money?"

"Ach, cheap as carrots," grunted Kripke. With fatuous pride he unrolled the tool-kit and took out the jack, and before she knew it was on his knees jacking up the Tatra to show her how well it worked.

"Some other time, Kripke," she remonstrated. "Right now we're in a hurry."

Obedient but unperturbed, Kripke lowered the jack and rolled up the tools again. "For these," he said, grinning up at her, "two packs of cigarettes. For the slipcovers, one pack. For the Scheinwerfer," pointing to the spotlight, "two packs. The whole thing, one half a carton! Ein Geschenk!"

She got in and gave him the Cardinal's address. "You know how to get there, Kripke?"

"Miss MacMurphy," stepping on the starter. "I have Berlin in my vest-pocket."

They wheeled down Argentinische Allee under the overhanging trees and turned left at a cross-section where a white-gloved Schupo was directing traffic from a box in the middle of the street. On their right was a magnificent combine of modern buildings, pristine white with great slabs of glass for windows, American flags flying from several towering flagpoles and hundreds of men and women in U.S. army uniform walking leisurely to and fro across the billiard-table lawns. OMGUS, said a ten-foot sign. Office of Military Government, United States.

"That was the Luftwaffe Headquarters during the war," said Kripke, not even turning his head. "First one army, then another."

It began to rain, slowly at first, then with a rush of wind and a sudden blackening of the entire sky. "Ow-w!" cried Kripke, as if in pain. "My fine Putzen, all for nothing! Now the whole car will look like a Flitzer on the eastern front!"

Grunewald, she noticed, although heavily forested, was more badly bombed than Zehlendorf. Behind the swaying, rainpelted trees, every other house was a splintered pile of wreckage. That, of course, was the pattern. The nearer one came to the center of the city, the more desolate were the streets, the more interminable the ruins. Except for its suburbs, the city of Berlin had been leveled, as if by a scythe—by bombs, artillery, machinegun fire, tanks, bulldozers, incendiaries—and all that remained were fragments sticking up like broken stalks of wheat in a well-reaped field. Where the people of Berlin lived she couldn't imagine.

"Where do the people live, Kripke?" she asked.

"In the cellars, mostly," he answered matter-of-factly. "It's wet there, but in the winter it's warmer."

It was nearly dusk when they reached the center of the city

and the rain was coming down in steady dark sheets, slanting over the rubble-heaped sidewalks, the ruined shops, the burned and gutted buildings, racing in swollen streams down the ugly mutilated streets. People hurried by in the rain like characters out of some existentialist play—real people going nowhere, flesh-and-blood people walking nonexistent streets, turning up a stairway to enter a building that wasn't there, ducking under an archway that in pitiful perseverance supported nothing.

There were, as far as she could see, no street lights. Like an enormous dank cave, the city lay cold and dark, rotting in its own slime, its anonymous survivors scurrying from hole to hole like grey rats. Between sagging sky and crumpled skyline there was no distinguishable difference, only here and there, from some patched-up window, a faint glimmer of light.

The rain was coming in on her dress. She rolled up the window and lit a cigarette, peering out at the gaping, tottering walls that, laced and interlaced with rain, swam by as they proceeded up the streets.

"Aren't we getting somewhere near?" she asked.

"We are there, Miss MacMurphy," said Kripke, swerving in toward the curb.

They stopped in front of a dingy, lightless apartment building and Carla stared out at the doorway. A doorway like thousands of others they had passed on their way, a debris-piled hole propped up with what seemed to be a steel girder from some other building. Pleased as a child, Kripke started playing the new spotlight up and down the façade of the building like a long white finger exploring a series of wounds—broken windows, dilapidated stairways picked up, exposed and passed over.

"Kripke!" she said, half-laughing. "What will His Eminence say?"

"Ach, Miss MacMurphy, he'll be glad to get a little light. Look, there's no light in the building at all."

Buttoning her khaki raincoat around her, she got out and followed Kripke to the entrance-way. She didn't like the idea of going in; the whole building looked as if it might collapse on her at any moment. "You'll be all right, Miss MacMurphy?" asked Kripke anxiously.

"Ja, bestimmt." Taking the hand flashlight from his hand, she started courageously up the rickety steps to the third floor, and shivering with chill rapped on the door.

What a crazy mission, she thought, standing there in the darkness with the beam of her flashlight eating into the frayed carpeting of the floor. She wondered what she could ask him.

Having no lead whatsoever on what the story was about, except that perhaps it had something to do with students, she could only hope that he would come out with it himself.

At this moment the door was opened by the Cardinal himself in cassock and a sleeveless manteletta of some kind of wool. Holding a candle above his head, he made a strange medieval picture in the shadowed doorway, the light of the candle playing on his skull-cap and pale smooth forehead and the hem of his gown. "Miss MacMurphy, isn't it? Won't you come in?" he said in perfect English, taking her hand. "I'm sorry to have to offer you so cold a place and so little light."

His voice was deep and vibrant, reminding her fleetingly of Charles, and a strictly secular image popped up in her brain. He motioned to a chair. "If you will just sit down here, I will get you your copy of the speech."

She smiled warmly, "Oh, thank you," and sat down in a curved Queen Anne chair. The Cardinal disappeared, still carrying his candle.

Speech? she thought, looking about the quiet littered room and hearing his padding footsteps in a room behind her. What speech? The place was clammily cold from the rain. From a sky-light overhead water was dropping in loud conclusive plops into a bucket almost at her feet. In the corner, above the prie-Dieu, a candle struggled flickeringly against the draughts that blew in through cracks in the wall.

The sound of his returning was like the rustling of a brook. His garments flowing in the quiet room, he appeared in front of her.

"May I ask," he said gravely, "how you happened to hear about this?"

She felt a little bit the way she had felt on confirmation day and hoped she looked about the same. "From David Hawks of the *New York Press*."

"Ah, yes, David," he said, pleased. "A fine boy. A bit fallen-away, and going through an understandable skepticism, but a fine young man. The only American journalist who has ever taken the trouble to come and see me. Until now, of course," he added smiling. He handed her some typewritten sheets. "This is the exact text. It will be delivered at the twelve-thirty mass on Sunday." He stood back. "Now, if you will excuse me, I have so much to do——"

Hoping desperately that she had not been short-changed, but certain that there was nothing she could do about it if she had been, she moved toward the door, meanwhile folding the transcript he had given her and tucking it away in her purse.

"Thank you so much," she said graciously. "But what about the students?"

"You will see when you read the sermon," he said, kindly. "We are doing all that is possible under the circumstances."

She was standing in the door. "Has this been given out to the rest of the press?"

"Oh, no!" he said. "Only to you and in a few minutes to Mr. Hawks." He took her hand again. "Well, thank you for coming in this horrible storm. It is very kind of you. Let us pray that the Lord in His mercy will bring our children back to their homes."

"Yes, Father," she said, and stumbled down the dark musty stairwell.

In the car, as Kripke snaked through the ruinous and rubbly streets, she tried to read the Cardinal's speech, but the light was so poor she could only make out a few words. But what a story! According to this, eight Catholic students of the University of Berlin had been called up by the Russians for political questioning and had never returned. A "Studentenraub," the Cardinal called it. Excitedly lighting herself a cigarette, she saw the headline moving in front of her eyes like a neon strip in Times Square: BERLIN'S CARDINAL PROTESTS RUSSIAN KIDNAPPINGS. "Hurry up, Kripke," she said impatiently. "I've got work to do."

Kripke guided the Tatra slowly through a flooded crossing. "What time is Herr Hawks coming?" he asked innocently.

"Mr. Hawks? Who told you that?"

"Mr. Hawks' chauffeur," he answered comfortably.

"Oh." She thought that over for a minute. "Kripke," she said severely, "it is all right for you to listen to what the other chauffeurs and maids tell you. But if I ever catch you giving any information to them about me——"

Kripke waved his hand. "Ha, Miss MacMurphy! Keine Angst! Kripke is no blockhead. Kripke knows who he's working for."

He spoke with such fervor that she said no more.

The moment he pulled up in front of the house, she was out of the car and into the office, where she dumped her raincoat on the floor, rolled up her sleeves and sat down at her typewriter. She ate her dinner at the desk, turning the pages of the Cardinal's speech with one hand and eating with the other.

As a story it was a natural, a perfect front-pager. And she had just time to make the first edition and beat the *New York Press* on the streets by at least an hour. She grabbed up some carbon and paper, shoved the sheets in the roller and began to write:

P R E S S . . . WASHINGTON GLOBEDISPATCH . . . EX MAC-MURPHY . . . BERLIN AUGUST TWELVE . . . RUSSIAN KID-NAPPING OF EIGHT YOUNG CATHOLIC STUDENTS EXCLASSROOMS CLOISTERS BERLIN UNIVERSITY WILL BE DENOUNCED EXPULPIT SUNDAY VIABISHOP OF BERLIN CARDINAL VON FLICHTER IN STINGING SERMON DIRECTED AGAINST QUOTE NEW TERROR UN-QUOTE IN GERMANY STOP IN TWOTHOUSAND WORD STATEMENT RINGING WITH SUCH ACCUSATIONS AGAINST RUSSIANS AS QUOTE CHILD SNATCHERS UNQUOTE COMMA QUOTE TERRORISTS UN-QUOTE COMMA QUOTE NEW GESTAPO UNQUOTE COMMA SIXTY-TWO YEAROLD BISHOP INTENDS MAKE PUBLIC . . .

It was a long story. By the time she had it done it was nine-thirty. She called for a messenger-boy from the press camp, handed him her cable and raced upstairs to bathe and dress. From the bathroom she yelled down to Erika to set out a bottle of Scotch, two glasses and a bowl of ice, and to serve her coffee in the livingroom in fifteen minutes.

While Erika served the coffee, she arranged the lights and pulled the drapes closer over the French windows to muffle the sound of the rain. The wind was coming up strong, rattling the window-panes and whining at the corners of the house. She looked out into the rain-drenched garden but could see nothing but a wet patent-leather blackness, and she pulled the drape back into place and went to the gramophone to set aside a pile of records that she considered appropriate. He's late, she told herself, looking at her watch; he's later than he thinks. She giggled to herself at a mental picture of him sweating over the typewriter to finish a story that was beaten one hour ago.

She had just finished her coffee when the bell rang and Erika ushered him in, taking his wet raincoat and hat to dry in the kitchen.

He looked much tidier, somehow, than he had the night she met him. His brown hair was combed in place, showing off the high breadth of his forehead and the wide temples. Sober, his eyes seemed softer and more kind, his thick eyebrows less sardonic. He seemed ill-at-ease, but the look on his face was one of such pleasant humor that she was instantly disarmed.

"Come in," she called.

"I am in," he said, coming across the room toward her. "Whew! What a night! Theatrical as a Grade-B picture!"

"What would you like to drink?" she asked, smiling up at him. "We have Scotch."

"Then Scotch, of course. But why do you say 'we'? Hasn't Norman left?"

"He left this morning. In a veritable 'tizzy' over the damned Russians who won't let him use the direct highway."

He swung himself down into an armchair. "I don't blame him. Before the war you could get to Nuremberg in four hours. Now it takes two days. I sometimes think if the Russians would just confine themselves to being bastards on the big issues and let the little issues alone, the world wouldn't be shaping up the way it is."

"Have you had any dinner? Are you hungry?"

"As a matter of fact I am," he said candidly. "I had dinner with some German students, and you know how they eat. Or rather how they don't eat."

She poured him another Scotch and rang for Erika to bring a plate of roast beef sandwiches.

"Now," she said, wriggling back into the corner of the couch, "tell me more about the students."

"Oh, there's not much to tell. I thought I had my hands on a hell of a good story, and the whole thing fizzled out on me. I had to end up writing another piece on the Kommandatura."

"It fizzled?" she asked naively. "What kind of a story was it?"

Relaxed, drinking his Scotch, he told her about it. "Seems that seven or eight Catholic students from the University of Berlin turned up missing last week, and the general theory among the other students was that they'd been hauled up by the Russians for questioning and then tossed into jail. Anyway, the Bishop of Berlin got all het up about it and wrote himself a sizzling sermon on political terror which he was going to deliver Sunday at high mass. He promised me an advance on it, but when I went over to get it just now he said he'd changed his mind and called the whole thing off."

Carla's face whitened under her tan. "You mean," she said as lightly as possible, "that he isn't going to give it—the sermon, I mean?"

"Evidently not. When I talked to him he'd just had a phone call from General Ivanov absolutely forbidding him to mention the matter in public. So of course he had to cancel it." He helped himself to a sandwich. "That's the way it's been going for me for about three weeks. Every time I think I've socked one into right field, it goes foul."

She sat there staring at him. "But—but isn't that rather unusual?"

"Sure it is. But what can the old Cardinal do? Karlshorst puts the bite on him, and he's got to obey. That's all there is to it."

"I see," slowly.

"Well, so it goes," he said, leaning comfortably back in his chair. "No luck is bad luck. Speaking of Catholics, how did you like old Herr Geisler who had dinner with us last week?"

"Fine," unenthusiastically, looking at her watch.

"I'm sorry you didn't get more of a chance to talk to him. Wonderful old guy. Spent the last year of the war . . . Is anything wrong?"

"No-o. Why?"

"I just thought maybe I was boring you. You seemed to be thinking of something else." He took another sandwich. "Wonderful sandwiches."

"Look," she said, flashing a rather limp version of her brilliant smile. "To be frank, I was thinking of a wire I've still got to send off tonight. It's quite short. Would you mind if I excused myself for a minute or two to get it off?"

"Not at all, not at all." He stood politely while she left the room.

In the office she snapped on the light, shoved some paper into the typewriter and sat down. She was so nervous, and hurrying so, that her fingers kept missing the right keys and she had to pull the sheet out and start again.

PRESS . . . WASHINGTON GLOBEDISPATCH . . . EXMACMURPHY . . . PLEASE WITHHOLD BISHOP KIDNAPPING STORY UNTIL RECEIVE FURTHER CONFIRMATION FROM ME STOP DUE RUSSIAN PRESSURE SPEECH CANCELLED STOP WILL NOTIFY YOU DETAILS TOMORROW REGARDS MACMURPHY

She pulled the sheet from the typewriter, folded it thoughtfully, picked up the phone and called for a wireless messenger. For a few minutes she sat there staring into the desk-light and drumming with her fingers on the desk-top. Then she said aloud in the quiet office: "Damn! Damn! Damn!" re-read her wire, folded it up again and sent it off.

When she came back into the livingroom Hawks was standing at the window with the drape pulled back looking out into the rain. On the gramophone Jean Sablon was singing "J'attendrai."

"All done?" he asked pleasantly. "That didn't take long. How about a Scotch after all that work?"

He poured her a Scotch.

"Do you dance?" he asked.

"I think so," winsomely.

Competently, but holding her as if she were his mother-in-law, he moved her out onto the floor. He was an excellent dancer, but it was difficult going. She felt awkward and stiff, and once she tripped over his foot.

She smiled up at him appealingly. "Let's finish our drinks, and dance again later."

Back at the cocktail table, she curled up in the corner of the divan. "A big drink this time," she said, watching his large knuckly hands uncorking the bottle. She downed it fast and began to feel better. After all, it was still only six o'clock in Washington. Actually, Connell had until seven to pull the first edition and kill the story. She accepted a cigarette, looking up at him through her long black lashes as he lighted it for her.

"Tell me, are you really going to move out of that wonderful ranch-house of yours?"

"Next Tuesday."

"Then who's going to move in?"

"I haven't an idea. Probably some quartermaster colonel. They like those big places. They always have a lot of wives and daughters who go in for entertaining."

"You're not married?"

His handsome face flushed. "I was. I'm now in the midst of getting unmarried."

"You're divorcing her?"

"She's divorcing me."

"What for?"

"I don't know." He seemed embarrassed. "Cruelty, drunkenness, incompatibility, enlisting in the army, occupational insanity, desertion. Probably all of them."

"You didn't get along very well together?"

"Look here, young lady," he said, holding out his glass for another drink. "Enough of your Columbia School of Journalism questions. Let's try another record."

This time when they danced she did a little better. Still he held her in that gingerly gentlemanly way, his right hand firm but impersonal at her back. When the music stopped he brought her right back to the table, handed her onto the divan and then went back to his armchair.

She arranged the folds of her skirt around her. "Do you like Norman?"

"Very much. Don't you?"

-"Oh yes," she said slowly. "Only—only sometimes it embarrasses me, his talking about sex all the time." Her smile was sweet, her eyes modestly downcast, the lisp very pronounced. "Personally, I always think people ought to do more about sex and talk less. After all, it's a very important thing, probably the most important thing there is."

"By the way," he said, lighting another cigarette. "Now that Norman's gone, you'll be taking his place on the trip through the Russian Zone next month, won't you?"

"I think so."

"There ought to be some good stories in that trip. Reparations removals, the Bodenreform, the new SED organization, the Zeiss works, Buchenwald—all the things the Russians have been sitting so tight on. It'll be a good trip."

The storm was continuing outside, the drapes bellying like sails in a damp sweet breeze from the garden. But inside it was dry and softly lighted, and there was still plenty of Scotch in the bottle. Carla turned a little on the divan, and the bodice of her peasant dress fell carelessly off one rounded shoulder.

"Norman says I shouldn't go on that trip because it's almost all men and I might find my virtue compromised." She tilted her head to one side and looked at him with shining eyes. "Silly, isn't he?"

"Oh, I don't know."

"I think it's silly to talk about one's virtue being compromised," she said earnestly. "I think a really mature person knows exactly how he or she feels about sex and then just behaves accordingly. Don't you think so?"

"I don't think I ever thought about it."

"Sometimes a man doesn't have to think about it. Because for a man it's so much easier than for a woman." Her voice was soft and hesitant. "A man can always go out and get what he wants any time he wants it. A woman—well, she can go just so long too, and then, if she isn't in a position to do anything about it . . ."

He was listening carefully, looking at her down-turned face.

"That is to say, if she isn't married, or living regularly with someone——"

"Yes," he said. "I think I see what you mean."

"Of course," she went on, lifting her face and looking directly at him, "for nuns and widows and people like that it's no problem really. They're more or less inured to repression. But for a normally well-sexed woman—you know of course what the doctors say: that for a normal woman sex experience

110

is absolutely necessary every ten days. That's just simple hygiene."

He leaned intently forward, looking at the slow curve of her shoulder. He cleared his throat. "And how long has this 'normally well-sexed woman' been without sex experience?"

Innocently, she looked at him. "Oh, I don't want you to think I meant—I was just speaking generally, you know, about certain physiological facts." Then again she tilted her shining red head to the side and looking modestly downward said: "Of course, if you want to know—if you really want to know— nine days."

He got up out of his chair and walked over and sat down on the divan next to her. His kiss was so hard and forceful that it hurt her lips. She almost cried out with pain, and then, infuriated by the remorseless pressure of his mouth on hers, from anger. But already it was too late. She was pinioned on the couch, suffocated in his embrace, clawing and struggling to wriggle free. Through the clinging weight of his lips she spat out at him: "David! Let me go! Let—me—go!"

But it did no good. Frantic, she pushed with her body against his, struggling weakly under his immense powerful weight. In one frenzied twist she caught sight of his face and his expression sent her into panic. It was the face of a near-animal, a man out of control, emptied of every human consideration, of rationality, humor, tenderness, everything that had existed there before.

This wasn't at all the way she had planned it. Through the unbearable pounding of her heart and the stifling heat of his body-pressure came the cool mirage-like image of the bedroom as she had arranged it upstairs, the clean white sheets turned back over the satin coverlet, the black chiffon nightgown laid so prettily and casually at the side, gone, gone, impossible, vanished, only this turbulent and degrading struggle on a living-room divan with the lights burning screamingly on and the storm raging outside. In a sudden wrench, she tried to pull her hair free where it was pinned under his arm.

And then she lay still. As if from an immense distance she were looking down and watching a young woman being made love to on a divan by a fiercely determined young man with brown hair.

When she woke it was morning and she was in her own bed upstairs. Weak from exhaustion, her head spinning from the Scotch, she propped herself up in bed and looked around her. From the bathroom came the sound of the shower running and a masculine voice singing lustily under the rush of the water. Innocent and cheerful, the sunlight streamed in over the rumpled bed, a pair of trousers and shorts lying on the floor, the black chiffon nightie hanging untouched on the bed-post. Her own clothes, sopping wet, lay in a heap near the dressing-table.

Had they really gone walking in the garden in the storm, and had he made love to her on the grass with the lightning flashing over them? And finished the bottle and laughing unroariously tossed it in Graf von Etwas' tomato garden? And how then did they get upstairs? Her head reeled around the contradictions of memory. How fierce he was, fierce and unrelenting. Her legs tingled as she stretched them deliciously down under the sheet.

There was a discreet knock on the bedroom door and Erika came in with a tray of coffee, cream and sugar and two cups. How did these servants always know everything? she wondered idly, reaching for her nightie. On the tray was a telegram addressed to her, but she let it lie there a moment or two while she pulled the chiffon carefully over her aching shoulders and breasts. Then she reached into the drawer of the night-table for her hairbrush. Contentedly brushing out her hair, listening to his singing in the shower, she opened the wire.

PRESS . . . MACMURPHY US PRESSCAMP BERLIN . . . CANT UNDERSTAND YOUR WITHHOLD ON BISHOP KIDNAPPING STORY STOP PULLED FIRST EDITION OFF STREETS AND KILLED STORY ONLY TO FIND NEW YORK PRESS EARLY EDITION FRONTPAGING THREE COLUMNS DAVID HAWKS SAME STORY STOP PLEASE ADVISE IMMEDIATELY WHOS WRONG YOU OR HAWKS QUERY REGARDS CONNELL

The brush held in mid-air, she stared at the bathroom door.

CHAPTER NINE

SHE LOVED Berlin. To look at, it was nothing but an enormous bomb-crater, a 300-square-mile pit full of dust and devastation. But to live in and work in, it was the most exciting city in the world.

Of course—she picked up the clippers and started meticulously cutting away the cuticle from around the nails of her left hand—of course, she didn't exactly live in Berlin or work in it either. Since most of her work was covering American press conferences and interviewing American military government officers way out here in the American sector, it was only occasionally necessary to go down into Berlin, when there was a hunger riot or some Communist street-fighting or something special like that. And when there was, all she had to do was step into the Tatra in the ranch-house garage and within twenty minutes she could be in the center of the city.

Zehlendorf, thank God, wasn't Berlin. It was a peripheral suburb that had out-survived its mother city, a lush green American hillock from which she could see as much as she wanted of the ruined city and back to which she could always run the minute she had had enough. From here she could descend to talk to British, French, Germans, sometimes even Russians, to mingle from time to time with the natives to pick up "color" for her stories. And back here she could always come to wait for David on this very terrace with a jugful of martinis.

She moved her chair slightly to get back into the sun and started on the cuticle of her right hand. Five o'clock. That man with the drapes should be here.

Under these conditions an occasional trip through Berlin was fun. Poking around among the ruins was an adventure, like a tour of Chinatown or a night in Harlem. There was something bizarre and a little frightening about the life of the city, a silent watchful hatred in its lightless streets and in the hard humorless faces that the headlights of the car sometimes picked up as they rounded a corner or eased slowly over the ruts and cavities of a bombed-up alley. Behind these bleak boarded-up windows and in the dark cellars and passageways under the ruins, some kind of life went on. And just to imagine what kind of life it was, to pick up a clue from some bawling voice or the slam of a door, the sound of footsteps racing along a dark corridor, was as exciting as a treasure-hunt.

Yes, she admitted, each time they headed out of the debris and back toward the ranch-house in Zehlendorf she was relieved. Too long a time in such desolation depressed her.

"Berlin is all right to visit," she told David gravely after one of these trips around the city, leaning exhaustedly back in the Tatra like a Des Moines matron after a weekend in New York, "but I wouldn't want to live there."

"I couldn't agree more heartily!" he had answered mockingly. "The social life is so terribly strenuous. How *do* these Germans stand it? On the go from morning to night!"

113

But David didn't understand that that was exactly what made Berlin so enchanting—the strenuousness and uncertainty of the city's life. The same bombs and artillery that had turned Berlin into a desert of rubble had also made it the crossroads of world politics. With four great powers sitting here in tight squabbling occupation of a fifth, Berlin had acquired an internationalism like no other city since Vienna under the Hapsburgs, an internationalism as vulgar and quarrelsome as a street brawl. And just as exciting.

She opened the nailpolish and wiping the brush carefully on the edge of the bottle started lacquering the nails of her right hand. How blissfully quiet it was out here! With only the wet rustling of the poplars and the intermittent sound of demolitions in the background, one could almost hear the leaves falling. From inside the house came the sound of pans rattling in the kitchen, and from the office which she had set up for David and herself came the steady tick-tick of Gerda's typewriter copying that level-of-industry story for tomorrow's edition. If only that drape man would get here!

By six-thirty or so David ought to be home, and she didn't want him to bump into the drape man on his way in. David could get so temperamental about a thing like that. If the drapes were already up and the man gone, he'd never even notice.

Just like the battles over his tux. She wished to hell he'd get himself a dinner jacket, like all the other Americans and British had, and she knew damned well that if she could possibly get one for him ready-made and hang it in his closet, he'd put it on and absent-mindedly walk off in it and never even ask where it came from. But of course she couldn't. And every time she suggested that he do it, he got enraged. Last time they'd been invited to dinner at Colonel Horwich's house everyone but David had been in evening clothes. He not only hadn't minded, he hadn't even noticed, and when they got home and she had begged him, "Please, David, please send home for a tux," he had turned on her almost savagely.

"I'm trying to cover Germany, not a bunch of misplaced American hostesses. Where do you think we are? Westchester?"

Of course, there was no answer to that. Because whether David could see it or not, the truth was that Zehlendorf *was* a kind of Westchester. Now that so many American wives and dependents had come over to join their husbands, the whole American colony had gone festive. The commissaries were crammed with shrimp, lobster, chicken, anchovies, cocktail

114

onions, all the special luxury items you needed to entertain. The shelves of the army liquor stores were loaded with every conceivable liquor from Scotch to crème de menthe. Everyone was entertaining like mad, and the drinks and dancing would go on almost until dawn. Every night there were cocktail and dinner parties, every week there were receptions and garden parties thrown by the army for some visiting VIP. A riding club had been formed, and a country club and yacht club, and every week-end there were yachting races and regattas on the Wannsee.

"Revelry on the edge of disaster," David called it. But of course David missed the point altogether. The point wasn't whether it was moral or not to live like this when the Germans were starving or whatever. The point was that if everyone else was doing it, you had to do it too. When she had told him that, he had been furious with her, and she had dropped the subject. Yet here the Americans were, cooped up in this horribly mutilated city in the middle of the Russian Zone, surrounded by a population that was far from sympathetic, and certainly they had to do *something* to keep up their morale.

I should write that to Charles, she thought. He feels the way David does, that it's a psychological mistake to get too ostentatious when other people have nothing. But O my God, how can I write to Charles when I'm already three weeks late getting to Paris? And when everything's going so well that I don't see when I can leave? What on earth would I say?

She looked up to see Gerda coming across the terrace toward her, her sallow face businesslike but pleasant. "The man is here with the drapes, Miss MacMurphy. He's already got them up in the bedroom upstairs and he wants to know if you'd like to see them before he starts on the downstairs rooms."

Carla was just finishing her left hand. "No, tell him to go ahead with the downstairs and I'll see them in a minute. How long will it take him to finish? Oh damn!" She wiped the edge of a nail she had smeared.

"Just a few minutes, Miss MacMurphy. He works very fast."

"Fine. All right, tell him I'll be right in. Oh, look at that! I've ruined another."

Alone on the terrace, she removed the polish from the two damaged nails and carefully lacquered them over again. When she had finished, she stood for a moment in the cool autumn sunlight waiting for them to dry. She looked at her watch. A quarter to six.

She looked down toward the boathouse to where the red canoe was pulled up on the bank and remembered with a little flood of warmth the night she and David had gotten so drunk and had overturned the canoe and dumped themselves in the Waldsee. David had told the story to everyone in the press camp and with a great deal of detail had described how beautiful she had been with her hair all dripping and her clothes half off. David was an angel, really. She hoped he'd be in a good humor when he got home, so there'd be no trouble about her going off to dinner with Peter Rausch. Peter was such a marvelous informant, she *didn't* want to share him with David, she just didn't. And besides, who found Peter in the first place? She did. Let David get his stories from his *own* Germans.

Actually David *liked* competing with her. Ever since that morning when he had queered her Cardinal kidnapping scoop, and then had stood in the bathroom doorway laughing his head off, she had known that to him it was only a kind of friendly game. Even when she beat him—which was reasonably often—he got a kick out of it, the I-told-you-so delight of a racetrack tout watching his horse break out in front. And when she didn't—which was also reasonably often. . . . She dismissed the thought and with a delicate finger investigated her nails. Almost dry.

A pleasant contentment filled her, as warm as the sun on her bare arm, as bright as the sunlight through the falling leaves. I've come a long way, she thought, since that day back in 1940 when I decided that I could become as famous as mother in an entirely different field and succeed at it without anybody's help but my own. With all these contacts I've been making, with the name Carla MacMurphy known from New York to Santa Monica, I've come a long way, a long, long way. By the time I go back to Washington she'll be giving cocktail parties for *me,* making up lists of "interesting people" to present to her fabulously successful daughter instead of kicking me around from boarding school to boarding school in order to get me out of her way.

"But these people bore me," she would tell her mother sweetly but firmly. "After all, mother, what are they? Just a bunch of crusty old senators and business tycoons with no understanding whatsoever of the problems of today. If you don't mind I'd rather dine quietly at the Shoreham and get to bed." And she could just see the envy and rage on her mother's beautifully preserved face.

Through the window of the pantry she caught sight of Luisa's cheerful smile and the flash of one of her fat brown arms as she beat up some sauce or something in a big bowl. Tyrant or no, the wonderful thing about Luisa was that she

116

could really cook. Everything she concocted was always perfect. It was the same with Erika, who had developed into a wonderful maid. Erika was running around with an American captain and always had that delicately spiritual pre-Raphaelite look of a young woman in her first love-affair. But what the hell! Still a wonderful maid.

Contemplatively Carla looked down again toward the lake to the place where the Russian soldier was buried. Should have that dug up sometime. So obviously a grave, even without a headstone or cross, and the mound of it spoiled the sweep of the lawn. With that macabre humor of his, Kripke claimed it was the corpse of the Russian GI who had raped the old-maid owner of the ranch-house, Fräulein Klingel, and should be left there for the alte Tante to put flowers on when and if she were ever allowed back to take over her house. And David had agreed. "You don't understand German sentiment," he told her. "Leave the poor bastard there. If you dig him up the Russians will get him."

She examined her nails again. Dry. Then she pulled her housecoat closer, picked up all her manicuring equipment and entered the house.

The drapes looked wonderful. Green satin for the living-room, library and hall, which was lovely with ivory walls and the apricot-colored carpet. Pleased, she experimented with the trolley-pulls and pulled them together and apart several times.

"Schön, eh?" said Kripke, watching her from the doorway and grinning as proudly as if he had made them himself. It was an olive green, not as bluish as the green she would ordinarily have chosen. But after all, this was Germany and one couldn't have everything. Remembering that it was Kripke who had found the little drape man and had arranged the whole deal, she turned her head and smiled. "Ja, schön," she said.

The diningroom was even better: thick white linen against chocolate-colored walls, a perfect background for the pewter she had acquired last week in the Russian Zone. But what really delighted her was the bedroom: dark blue velvet for drapes and bedspread, with pull curtains of floor-length white tulle. With shining eyes she regarded the room: the really gigantic bed, the matching loveseats on either side, the big white cocktail table, and now the superb drama of those drapes only half-concealing the balconies outside. On the dressing-table lay Charles' latest letter, which she hadn't yet had time to read. I'll read it tomorrow, she promised herself. All that French, it takes time.

"Erika!" she called, walking out into the hall and leaning over the balustrade of the staircase. "Will you make some martinis immediately and bring them up here with two glasses?"

"Sofort, Miss MacMurphy," came the answer in Erika's clear, emotionless German.

Back in the bedroom, still admiring the new drapes, she took off her housecoat and began perfuming herself from head to foot. "Good, good," she said aloud, wriggling into her dress; the hem was exactly right, just mid-calf. And so daring, she thought, regarding in the mirror how it hugged her figure. Young Peter Rausch will spill the whole thing tonight about the C.D.U. He always does when I look at him right.

She was just clasping on her pearls when there was a knock at the door. "Miss MacMurphy," came Gerda's soft hesitant voice. "The drape man is finished and ready to leave."

"Wonderful."

"I think, Miss MacMurphy, that he expects to be paid now."

"Oh." She looked at her watch and a fierce panic seized her. Six-twenty. David might stroll in any minute. "Why does he have to be paid now? For Christ's sake, what's the matter with him? Can't he come back tomorrow?"

There was a short silence behind the door. "He says he has to be paid now, Miss MacMurphy, because tonight he's got to pay the man who sold him the material."

"My God, these crazy black-marketeers! Never even half a jump ahead of themselves! All right, tell him I'll pay him right this minute!" She darted over to the dressing table for her jewel-case, grabbed up the key, unlocked her private closet, and began unloading cartons of cigarettes from the top shelf. Pulled out from the bottom of the piles, the cartons began to tumble. An avalanche of cigarette packages and cartons rained around her shoulders and head and scattered over the floor. "Tell Kripke to come here immediately. Get Kripke!"

"Miss MacMurphy, if you like I can take them down for you myself," helpfully, from the other side of the door.

"Do as I tell you and shut up! Get Kripke!"

She knew she was screaming, but she couldn't help it. At any minute David would come walking through that door, and here she was with the stuff piled around her like a snowdrift. Frantically, she started picking up the cartons and throwing them back into the closet. She heard Gerda's footsteps descending the stairs and then the uneven stomp of Kripke coming up.

The door opened.

"Wollen Sie etwas, Miss MacMurphy?" as innocent as a cat.

"For God's sake, Kripke, stop asking foolish questions and help me pick up these cigarettes. How many does he want?"

"Fifteen cartons, Miss MacMurphy."

"Fifteen? Fifteen? Why, the god-damned robber, what does he mean fifteen? I only paid thirty for the Tatra itself!"

Kripke's face was serenely sympathetic. "He says fifteen."

She stared at him unbelievingly.

"He says he has to pay 100,000 Reichsmarks for the material alone, which came from a rich man's house near Potsdam, and then he had to smuggle it in through the Russians, and then he had to make them besides. It's high, Miss MacMurphy, det is' wahr. But what can you do? They are already up now."

"That's my advantage, not his. Here, take ten. Tell him I'll pay him ten cartons and that's all. And then tell him to get the hell out of this house as fast as his skinny kraut legs will carry him. Here! Kripke, for Christ's sake get going!"

With an amazing limping alacrity, Kripke grabbed ten cartons and hurried downstairs.

Left alone in the room, Carla went on tossing the cartons and packages back into the closet, slammed the door shut and turned the key. Panting with excitement, she leaned against the closed door. "Thank God!"

Then she heard the heavy hurried stomp of Kripke coming back upstairs. The bedroom door opened again.

"Miss MacMurphy, he says fifteen or he will take them all down again."

"What?"

"He says fifteen or he will take the drapes all down again."

"Why the dirty little bastard!" Her face white with anger she dashed out of the door to the top of the stairs. "Where is he? Gerda!" she yelled. "Send that fool to the bottom of the stairs!"

Leaning over the balustrade, she saw him move into the circle of her vision. A small thin man in a cheap fake-linen coat, he tilted his head way back and looked up at her. "I am sorry, Miss MacMurphy, I must asking fifteen. I am having pay . . ."

"Sprechen Sie Deutsch!" she screamed at him.

He recommenced in German, still looking earnestly up at her. "Miss MacMurphy, I must ask fifteen cartons. I cannot pay even the material, much less the labor, with ten. If you do not want to pay, I will take the drapes down. I do not like to take the drapes down, Miss MacMurphy, but if you do not pay me fifteen . . ."

She stared down at his morose upturned face. "All right, you swindler, I'll pay you your precious five cartons!"

She dashed back into the bedroom, grabbed up the key again and unlocked the little closet. Her fingers were trembling like the prongs of a tuning-fork, but the door finally gave and she snatched up five cartons and rushed back to the balustrade.

He was still standing there, looking up the stairwell.

"So, you cheat, here are your cartons!" With a frenzied energy born of anger she began raining cartons on him. One, two, three, the cartons fell, two hitting his shoulder, the third going wild. Furiously, she threw the fourth.

"Hey, what's going on here?" said a cheerful masculine voice, and David's tall trench-coated figure moved into the circle of hall carpet directly below her.

The little drape man started to explain. "Miss MacMurphy was refusing to pay me . . ."

"David!" said Carla urgently.

He started up the stairs.

With the fifth carton still poised ready to throw, she stared at him and he at her.

At this moment Erika, coming out of the kitchen with a pitcher of martinis and some glasses, started up the stairs below him.

"Carla! What in hell are you doing?" he asked suspiciously. "What is this?"

"Look behind you, David," said Carla in the sweetest tone she could command.

He looked behind him and saw Erika coming up with the martinis.

Handing the last carton to Kripke behind her, Carla advanced to the top step. "Martinis," she explained. "A grand reception for my darling."

He mounted the stairs and kissed her, but the kiss was perfunctory.

"But what is all this? Throwing cigarette cartons down the stairs!"

She put her arm through his. "Just a little fun, David darling. I was giving some cigarettes to Kripke for all the extra work he's done for me. A wave of generosity, that's all." She nodded to Kripke at her side. "All right, Kripke, you can go," and Kripke scurried down the stairs.

They walked together into the bedroom, Erika following.

"Here, Erika," said Carla, taking the tray out of her hands. "I'll take care of it from here."

120

She put the tray down on the cocktail table and began setting out the glasses.

He sat down on one of the loveseats. "Carla, what was going on out there? Who is that guy you were tossing cigarettes at?"

With a great deal of fuss she started pouring out martinis. "Olive or onion?"

"But who was that man?" His handsome face was perplexed.

"I told you, darling. He's a friend of Kripke's and we were just being funny. That's all. Why?"

"Is that all?"

"Of course that's all, silly. Now *you* answer *my* question. Olive or onion?"

"Onion."

She handed him a cocktail.

"How do you like my dress?" she asked coquettishly, making a little turn in front of him.

"Wonderful. We going somewhere?"

"Oh David, you remember. I told you last night. I'm taking Peter to the British Press Club for dinner."

"Peter Rausch?"

"Um-hum. Why?"

"Oh, I don't know. It just seems funny that you'd invite a one-legged young German like Peter to the British Press Club. If you've got a story laid on, why don't you have him here to dinner?"

She looked at him archly. "In front of you?"

"All right. If you wanted to talk to him privately about a story, you could have told me and I'd have arranged to have dinner with the Wilsons or somebody."

She patted his cheek. "David, I do think you're jealous."

He shifted a little on the loveseat. "If he weren't such a thoroughly nice kid, I might be. But Jesus, baby! Can't you see how it looks? Every correspondent in Berlin knows we're living together, and then when you go traipsing in there with some dewy-eyed young German politician . . ."

"David, darling, everyone knows I'm working."

"Sure. But they don't know how, and what with." He glanced around the room. "Where'd the new curtains come from?" He got up and walked over to the windows. "Makes the place look like a Hollywood set."

"Mrs. Horwich. Wasn't that sweet? She sent them over because they didn't go in her place. Colonel Horwich didn't like the color. I think they're perfect in here, don't you?"

"Bob Horwich doesn't know one color from another—even

in women." He was fingering the fabric. "But they're brand new, Carla."

Suddenly he turned around, an impish gleam in his eyes. "Why, you little black-marketing bitch! Where did these drapes come from?"

"I told you, darling. Mrs. Horwich sent them over."

"You're lying."

"I am *not* lying. Eleanor Horwich sent them over because Bob didn't like them."

"All right. I'll just call her up and thank her."

She faltered only slightly. "Go ahead then. Call her!"

He walked over to the bedside table and picked up the phone, looking very pleased with himself.

"David!" She followed him and grabbed his arm. "Stop this foolishness! You know you're just doing this to embarrass me with the Horwiches!"

"Now what on earth makes you think that?" he said satirically. Holding her off with one hand, he began to dial.

She tried to snatch the phone from his hands. "This is my business, not yours, David Hawks! You put that phone down and keep your nose out of this!"

Grinning at her, he pushed her hand away. "All right, I'll make a deal with you. You send your young German gallant away and have dinner here with me, and I won't call the Horwiches."

"No!" If she hadn't already put her mascara on, she'd have cried. "No! You're just trying to blackmail me! That's all you're doing!"

"Okay. Any way you want it," he said resignedly. And recommenced his dialing.

She rushed at him. "David! David, stop it!" Enraged, she lashed out at him with her fists, beating on his back and shoulders. Laughing, he ducked his head under the rain of her blows and went right on dialing.

"David, you put that phone down or I'll——"

He looked up. "Or you'll what?"

There was a knock on the door. "Miss MacMurphy," said Erika from the other side. "Herr Rausch is here."

"Or you'll what?" This time in a whisper, holding the phone just out of her reach.

"Tell him I'll be right down, Erika!" she said through clenched teeth. "You bastard!" catching onto his thick brown hair and pulling with all her might. "You put that phone down!"

With his free hand he loosened her fingers from his hair and captured her arm behind her back. In a quick deliberate twist he dropped the receiver and captured the other arm. "Now, Miss MacMurphy, give up?" He was panting, and a lock of hair hung over his forehead, but the look on his face was as pixyish and unregenerate as that of a small boy in a good-natured tussle. "Give up?"

"Let go my arms."

"Give up?"

"Let go my arms."

"Not until you give up. Give up?"

Her eyes blazing, she looked at him. "You contemptible, smug, dirty——"

"Now, now," he said cheerfully. "Don't let's say something we'll regret. Daddy might pick up the phone again any minute. Give up?"

"All right," resentfully. "All right!"

"And you'll go downstairs and tell him you can't go?"

"Yes. Damn you!"

He released her arms.

Defensively she smoothed down her dress and with a great show of concern examined her wrists and arms for bruises. "You hurt me," she said reproachfully. "And I think you've torn my dress."

"I'm sorry if I hurt you, baby. I didn't mean to." He picked up the receiver and put it back in its cradle. "One thing all this proves—that you think more of a windowful of drapes than you do of Peter. Which is as balm to my heart. But don't worry about the dress. Actually you'll find that I won't mind at all. Always wanted to have dinner with a beautiful woman whose clothes I'd just torn off. Where's it torn?" he asked solicitously. "In the front, I hope."

In spite of herself she began to laugh. "Oh, you *are* a bastard, David! Honestly, you really are!" For a long moment she stood in front of the dressing-table mirror looking at herself and thinking.

"Hadn't you better get down there?" helpfully. "You don't want to keep the poor guy waiting any longer than you have to."

"No." Slowly she walked to the door. "Oh damn you, David Hawks! Damn you, damn you!"

Downstairs she found Peter waiting in the hall, leaning against the wall with his crutches stuck out in front of him. He was wearing a thin, much-pressed blue suit and a neat white shirt, which made him look not quite so young as usual, but when he saw her his face lighted up like a kid's at Christmas.

"Peter," she began.

"Miss MacMurphy?" His eyes were positively starry.

"Peter, I'm terribly sorry, but something has come up——"

Over her head she heard the bedroom door stealthily open, the sound of someone tiptoeing to the banister to listen.

"Peter, I'm terribly sorry. But I just cannot take you to dinner as we had planned. Mr. Hawks is—is quite ill, and I'm afraid I have to stay home and take care of him."

His face fell, whether in sympathy for David or disappointment over the loss of all those calories, she couldn't tell. "Oh, that is too bad! Is there anything I can do for him? Is it serious?" He seemed terribly affected.

"No, Peter, thank you. By tomorrow he will certainly be much better. Erika! Herr Rausch's coat, please."

"It's all right, Miss MacMurphy. I don't have a coat. It is so warm tonight."

It wasn't warm tonight at all, but she let it stand, figuring he had probably sold his coat but didn't want to say so. "Never mind, Erika," she called.

She took him to the door. "Good night, Peter. Thank you for coming. I'll call you in a day or two when I have some more work for you."

"Thank you, Miss MacMurphy." Carefully he swung himself out the door and down the steps. At the beginning of the drive he turned on his crutches and waved at her. "Good night!"

All dressed up in that shiny dark suit and frayed white shirt to go to dinner in an Allied club. Smiling, she waved back. "Good night, Peter!" She felt vaguely ashamed of herself, and of David too, but why she didn't know.

CHAPTER TEN

AND NOW Nuremberg, of all places!

She could kill Norman for making her come down here, murder him, simply murder him, and just when she and David were getting along so well. It was all Norman's fault too, just because he didn't speak German he thought he had to call her down here to sit in this stuffy god-damned courtroom listening to the droning of lawyers and justices and the chattering of interpreters and staring at the dull grey faces of twenty-one war criminals whose plan to conquer the world didn't quite work, while Norman himself sat on his erudite bottom over at the Schloss writing think pieces about the far-reaching significance of the Nuremberg trials, paths we are blazing in international law, precedents and agreements, the terms of the charter, we are writing law, not following it, and nuts, nuts, nuts!

"Just for two or three days," Norman had said on the long-distance phone in his thin squirrelly voice. "Until they pronounce the sentences on Göring and the rest. Then you can go right back." Then, after one of his suggestive pauses: "From your anxiety, Fräulein MacM, I begin to suspect that you have followed my advice and got yourself properly shacked up in Berlin. Who's the lucky man?"

When she'd told David that, he had laughed. "Tell Norman that in Berlin we don't shack up, we villa up," he had said. "But tell him the lucky man is a wild irascible bastard who will beat you if you stay one hour over three days." And when he had tucked her into the back of the Tatra he had kissed her, one of his warm cruel kisses, and said: "As for you, hurry back before I go stark staring rubble-happy without you," and had ordered Kripke to have her back in Berlin no later than six P.M. Wednesday no matter what happened. "That's a Marschbefehl," he had told Kripke sternly, and Kripke's ja-ja had been as happy as her own.

So here she was, sitting in the press-box of the International Military Tribunal at Nuremberg, her head aching from the weight of these damned earphones and listening to the interminable yak-yak of the handing down of four-power justice, looking as sweet and pretty as a young woman with nothing on her mind and missing David so much she could almost cry. She had drunk too much out of that bottle on the way down, that was for sure because she was getting so sleepy and it was all so hard to follow, it was like a masquerade, everybody dressed up like baccalaureate switchboard operators wearing these silly black headphones and talking into the mouthpieces in too many languages as if they were little boys playing telephone. She tried to fix her mind on the slow cultured British voice that was reading the final judgment but all that went through her head was one little two little three little Indians, and she didn't know why except that every time she squirmed uncomfortably in her chair she kept wondering why they didn't just take them out and shoot them like little Indians in a shooting gallery and then she could go home to David.

She tried to focus her attention by staring across at the

famous much-photographed faces, pale and unreal under the blazing blue-white of the kleig lights, the twenty-one arch conspirators sitting stiff and impassive in the prisoners' dock like amateurish and uninspired sketches of themselves, each one withdrawn into the closed and private world of his own earphones, docile and inoffensive. Except Göring, who always sat with his chin in his hand listening avidly to every word and smiling indulgently and switching his earphones from English to French to German and back again, maybe to prove to the court that he really was the Renaissance Man of many tastes and many cultures, maybe so he could hear everything in every language except Russian. Göring, who when the Americans captured him had been a sniveling, dope-sodden, spineless wreck, but who had now been cleaned up and shaven and trimmed of his flabby fat and somehow made respectable and dignified again, who was already living and enjoying his new legend as "unser lieber Hermann, Weltmacht oder Untergang, they'll never get *him!*"

"Therefore, in the judgment of this court, the accused is found guilty under counts one and two, conspiracy to wage aggressive war . . ." Why did she keep looking around at the doors as if thinking that David might walk in past all those snowdrop MP's? David couldn't walk in, that was impossible, David was back in Berlin and it would be two more days before, before . . .

If you shut your earphones off, the courtroom was in complete silence and the trial a trivial and boring comedy without words, and you could watch the gestures, the changing facial expressions, the mouths working—and no sound whatsoever. As in a movie with no sound track and no subtitles, the lawyers would cross the room, the justices would look up from their briefs, heads would turn and mouths would open and shut, people would get up and sit down, everyone imitating himself, and in this labored and unamusing pantomime the only sane man, the only convincing actor, was Hess. Hess the fool, the court jester, a shaggy-eyebrowed comedian whose exaggerated grimaces and crazy antics somehow failed to get the applause they deserved from this staid and self-righteous courtroom of black-robed men in earphones going about the immortal and esoteric business of wordless, soundless and appeal-less justice.

If you turned your earphones back on, it was just the opposite, an ordinary courtroom with delusions of grandeur, indicting a boxful of men not for murder, rape, terrorism or pillage, but all of them at once and in much fancier language. ". . . crimes against the peace . . . crimes against humanity

126

. . . conspiracy to seize power . . ." And Hess was a madman incapable of comprehending the measured multisyllabic accusations of his untouchable judges, and behind the glass cage in the far corner of the room the subdued babbling of the interpreters was like the sound of a simulated waterfall in a forest of black-robed trees.

There was something crawlingly horrible about those twenty-one faces, something chilling and scary, but she didn't know what it was, maybe it was because they were now so familiar, so many millions of words and thousands of feet of photographic film expended in the past ten months to describe every wrinkle, every fleeting expression, that now they seemed like old friends, old friends of the family that one had always disliked. Maybe because they had once been the recognized and accepted leaders of a great state with whom we had done business and conducted diplomatic relations, and then after that they'd been the bogey-men of all the sailors and soldiers and advertising copywriters of the anti-Axis world, and now they were only twenty-one tired bored old gangsters waiting for this legalistic Extreme Unction to be over so they could get on with the business of dying for their crimes. This was what she'd write about, she thought. This was her story. But just when she'd start to organize her thoughts they were gone, like a school of minnows darting away under water, and she couldn't remember what it was that was so horrifying about those dry patient faces staring out straight ahead in the burning courtroom.

At lunch recess she couldn't eat, she had no appetite, so she talked a handsome red-bearded newsman for the *London Daily Mail* into buying her three more drinks, with the result that when she tried to find her way back to the courtroom down those shining white corridors she had to ask for an MP guide. Worse than that, when the correspondents crowded back into the press gallery at two-thirty she had to smile wanly and hang onto the chairs as she picked her way through pretending she was sick and not drunk, but just as she sidled along the aisle toward her place she saw Marguerite Evans of the *Chicago Journal* teetering down to a front seat looking as always like an overgrown Alice in Wonderland and she thought gee, I'd better get sobered up quick, there's too much competition here for my liking.

Somehow she wasn't so sleepy now, those three drinks had jerked her up a little. And everybody round her seemed so tense. So tense and so sure of themselves, sure of what they were going to write. This really was an historic occasion, this was what we had fought for—to prove to the world that what these men had done was wrong and that we, who were right, could and should bring them at last to judgment, and judge them not as men would do, with either vengeance or mercy, but as gods.

The courtroom spaced out into silence. "In accordance with Article 27 of the charter, the court will now pronounce sentence."

Then at last it was over, and everyone was racing into the courthouse pressroom to interview the three who had been acquitted. Sick, and still a little drunk, Carla stood at the back of the pressroom supporting herself against the wall and watched the MP's bring them in, Schacht, von Papen and the propagandist Fritsche, and sit them down to be interviewed by a hundred screaming scrambling pushing journalists. All three were drinking beer and smoking cigarettes which admiring MP's had shoved into their hands, and because she could hear almost nothing over the shouting mob of interviewers she kept looking at their faces—I'm obsessed with their faces, she thought—particularly the smirking yellow face of Schacht. Schacht the thin, the scholarly, the cultivated, who had helped maneuver the Nazis to power and then had broken with them out of pique when they failed to follow his financial advice *("Ah, yes," said Charles, handing her the wine bottle, "but to have been against the Nazis meant almost nothing . . . it's the reasons that count."),* Schacht who sat back now talking about the kindness of the Americans as if he were a departing week-end guest and asking for chocolate for his grandchildren in a voice like the purring of a cat, Schacht whose near-sighted pale blue eyes behind their thick spectacles crawled from face to face of his audience and never rested. Tom Paisley, who had broadcast to Germany on the BBC while Fritsche was broadcasting to England on the Deutschlandsender, who had held a propaganda battle with Fritsche on the air while German and Allied armies battled it out on the ground, shook Fritsche's hand and lit his cigarette, and it was all like the end of a basketball game, everybody shaking everybody's hand and exchanging autographs, no hard feelings, old boy, good try, better luck next time.

Disgusted, she stumbled out of the pressroom and down the corridors and out of the Palace of Justice, and asked a handsome Texan MP which way to the presscamp and set off on foot, on the hazy theory that this would make her feel better. Near some shrubs edging a bomb-demolished corner she thought she was going to be sick, but in a moment it passed and when she'd flagged down a press car and saw ahead of her the Schloss Faber rising in imitation baronial splendor from its sweeping lawns and bright formal gardens, she knew that the crisis was past, she felt better already.

Sedately, because now she was practically sober, she walked up the drive of the castle looking for the Tatra where it was sandwiched in among hundreds of jeeps, dispatch cars and motorcycles that packed the sunny courtyard, and leaning casually against the shining silver hood she saw Kripke, the Berlin city slicker talking with pompous jocularity to a crowd of "Bayrische Hiasl" chauffeurs, and she saw him make his characteristic gesture of pawing the air in disgusted rejection of someone or something, his brown face alive with the pleasure of such an easily impressed audience. Probably giving them his favorite theory of Realpolitik, of how he'd been all for Hitler until 1938, when with all this war production and war training the Nazis had ruined his trucking business by drafting his trucks for Kriegsproduktion and drafting their owner into the Wehrmacht. Enterprising little businessman that he was, Kripke was for anybody who would make the trains run on time and make business good, and he hated war because he had fought in one for six years.

As she mounted the castle steps, the messenger boys lolling around the entrance set up a chorus of wolf-whistles. Smiling a ladylike acknowledgment, she walked in.

And what a joint! A real authentic fake castle, built by the Faber family as a perpetual monument to the glory of Faber pencils, a stone-walled turreted monstrosity now filled to the brim with newspapermen from half-a-hundred nations, rocking with the day-and-night clatter of teletype machines clacking out millions of words to New York, Paris, Chungking, Johannesburg, Moscow, Montreal, Rio de Janeiro, a denazified landmark now transformed into an international billet for the five-hundred-odd men and woman whose job it was to inform the world of the progress of the trials, of Ribbentrop's latest bon mot, Mr. Justice Jackson's newest objection, the superior half-smile on the ugly face of Frick. Its tapestry-hung walls were plastered with press releases and notices, its former drawing-rooms had been made into Public Relations offices. Up and down its wide curving marble staircases correspondents and pageboys raced with copy to go out, copy to go out, who's here for NBC? telegram for Mister Polnitchevski, is there a Chinese News Agency man around? here, boy, copy! Someone with an eye for beauty and a bottle of nail-polish had improved

129

on the castle's ubiquitous Greek statues by dabbing fingernails, toenails and nipples a bright startling red, and at the foot of the stairs a kneeling granite nude held in her outstretched and supplicating hand a copy of *Newsweek*.

In the upstairs dining room as big as a baseball diamond and in its adjoining bar, correspondents jabbered, compared notes, drank, told stories, argued, fought, ate and got drunk in as many languages as there were bottles on the mirrored shelves of the bar. From every floor came the insistent staccato of typewriters, the sound of arguments, the slamming of ancient carved oak doors. And through it all the teletype machines clattered on, the messenger boys raced on their interminable errands, the correspondents argued and wrote and drank.

"Who's the PRO here?" Carla asked a pageboy on her way through one of the draughty cavernous drawing-rooms, just missing being knocked down. "Colonel Kennebunk," was the answer, and when she entered his office he put down the phone, propelled his magnificent belly toward her and embraced her with the glucose affection of an incestuous parent.

"Oh, it's a madhouse, it's a complete madhouse!" he sighed happily. "Nothing like our little place in Munich, eh, Carla? How long you gonna be around? Jesus, only two days? We guys rationed down here? Say, there's a wire around here somewhere for you, from that French guy you met down at our joint last summer. Now where did I put that damned wire? Look, I gotta lay on some transportation for these Canadians here, see you later, buy you a drink at the bar. You seen Norman yet? He's over at the Grand Hotel talking to the prosecution. I'll send him word you're here. You got any transportation?" And then, remembering the Tatra: "You damn well better have transportation, eh, Carla?" slapping his thigh and guffawing with laughter. Over his desk with its five jangling telephones was an ambitious oil painting in the style of the thirteenth century showing two knights in full medieval armor jousting with gigantic pencils—Faber pencils—in place of spears.

She was, she discovered, billeted in the "hen-house," formerly servants' quarters for the castle and now used as a dormitory for the women correspondents. As she crossed the flowered gardens under a blue October sky she was beginning to get angry at being segregated like that, asked to sleep in a narrow army cot with a bunch of press hags undressing and gossiping and cackling around her, and no men allowed, no chance for anything exciting to happen. She could murder Norman for insisting on her coming down here, just kill him, and then she thought what difference does it make? I'm going to be faithful to David anyway, this only makes it easier, but still she was furious at Norman for taking her away from Berlin.

When Norman came over from the Grand Hotel she was sitting disconsolately on her high iron cot, swinging her legs and smoking cigarette after cigarette. The WAC corporal at the hen-house door wouldn't let him come in so she had to clamber down from the cot and come out to meet him. "Well, here I am," she said unenthusiastically, holding out her hand.

He was exactly the same as always, the same Bucks County corduroy jacket, the same bow tie, the same crooked smile and leering yellow teeth. "Now, Fräulein MacM," he said soothingly. "I know you didn't want to come down here, so we don't have to discuss that till later. Come and have a spate of drinks with me in the bar, and we'll talk about what you're to do now. After all, it's only one more day, and according to your own theory a woman doesn't become atrophied until the eleventh day. Come on. I'll wait for you while you go back and put another coat of lipstick on. A half-dozen drinks will make you feel better, and you can see all your old friends clustered around one bar. Practically everybody you know is here."

He was right. Practically everybody *was* here. Correspondents she had known during and since the war all yelled to her from every corner of the bar. She began to feel better. It was like a kind of home-coming, everyone waving and calling to you and saying remember that time in Algiers, Italy, France, England, the Balkans? Quite a delegation from Berlin too, she noticed, seeing Polly and Mike Wilson, Russell Hunt and Bentley Cross at one table, and when Larry Harper came over and absent-mindedly kissed her, she thought oh hell, it isn't really Norman's fault, I'll stick it out through tomorrow and do a good job and when I get back to Berlin David will be just that much happier to see me, and she ordered another double Scotch and tossed it down quick.

Balanced on a bar stool between Norman and Colonel Kennebunk, she drank her drinks and listened to the conversation around her, and the more she drank and listened, the more she caught of the excitement of the place, the bedlam of gossip, contacts, whispers and discussions that hung over these trials, their accused, their employees, their witnesses, their five hundred journalists, like slightly stale marijuana smoke. "Hess

131

was in good form today," said an Englishman behind her. "Bloody fine actor, that chap!" "I've got twenty-five bucks with Tom Riley they'll hang 'em all right here," said someone else, reaching over her shoulder for his drink.

"Carla!" yelled Sally Lodge, rushing up with the bodice of her dress as usual only half-buttoned, her stringy brown hair hanging lank and dirty on her neck. "We're taking a poll of all the women correspondents to decide which of these twenty-one bastards is the most attractive. Then we're going to send a pack of cigarettes and a mash letter to the winner. So here's the question: If you had to go to bed with one of them, which one would you pick?"

"Oh, Hess, I think," said Carla laughing.

"Hess?" screamed Sally, "you mean because he'd be so unpredictable?" The circle around them was widening, the men listening indulgent and amused. "Most of the girls say von Schirach, he's the youngest, you know, and the handsomest. He writes poetry too. But you know who I said? Frank! The butcher of Poland. And you know why?" she went on breathlessly. "Because he's just become Catholic, he spends all his time praying and saying his beads, it'd be so spiritual, like going to bed with a priest!" Laughing, she wandered off, and the circle gradually broke up.

"Hey," shouted someone from the other end of the bar, "anyone seen Bill Somers?" "Jackson has to hang Streicher," remarked a male voice cynically. "Otherwise he'll never be governor of New York."

"Bill Somers?" asked Carla, turning around. "Is he here?"

"Sure, sure," boomed Kennebunk. "Saw him just a couple of minutes ago down on the second floor."

"Try the WP room," a radioman called back. "I think he's down there."

Carla sat quiet for a moment, finishing another drink. Then she slipped down from her stool and made her way carefully, uncertainly, down the inlaid and gilded staircase toward the second floor. I should have eaten something, she thought.

He was just coming out of the WP room with a sheaf of papers in his hand and she thought in his shirtsleeves and suspenders that he looked taller and thinner than before. "Copy!" he called down the stairway. "Get a boy up here, will you?" And then he looked up and saw her on the steps above him.

"Hello, honey," he said, coming up the stairs two at a time and kissing her. "I had an idea you'd turn up here sooner or later. MacMurphy never misses a beat. And how are things in Berlin?"

"Fine." She looked up at him and smiled that full, flashing girlish smile. "And how is Frankfurt?" Slowly, in order to control the words.

"Oh, so-so."

"Yes, sir, Mister Somers?" said the copy boy.

"Here." He handed the boy his copy. "And hurry up, will you for God's sake? That's gotta be off in a couple of seconds." He turned back to Carla. "Gee, you look wonderful, baby. I'd take you up and buy you a drink, only Ed Jones has been waiting for me for half an hour with a jeep. We've got to go out and interview a bunch of Germans in this hell-hole of a city on how they feel about the sentences. Want to come along?"

"Love to. Except I have to write my column. And I have to tell Norman."

"Send him a messenger. Here, boy!" reaching out and stopping a messenger on his way upstairs. "Take a message up to Mr. Brant in the bar. Mr. Brant, got it? Tell him Miss MacMurphy will be back in an hour with her column practically written."

The boy scampered off and Somers went back to get his coat. "Hey!" he called out, motioning to her to follow him. "I got a bottle in here. Let's have one quick one before we go."

There was no one in the room but William L. Brainard sitting quietly in the corner re-reading his own book, *Here Is Germany*. So although no women were supposed to be allowed in the men's rooms she and Bill sat on Bill's bed and giggled at Brainard and finished the bottle, but what they talked about she didn't know.

Outside in the cold dusk all those drinks began whooshing around in her head again and she had to hang onto Bill as they crossed the parking lot toward the jeep. The silhouette of the castle tilted and righted itself, tilted and returned like a ship pitching in a storm, and her feet on the gravel were miles down and moving quite independently. With Bill driving they started out through the customary pattern of smashed houses and rubble-lined streets. The wind that whipped against her face was as cold and delicious as ice-cream, and she tried to sing for them one little two little three little Indians but it made her giggle and she couldn't finish it.

Somewhere out of the dusk came the Palace of Justice, its bluish lights burning into the evening like a thousand white-hot rivets, and Carla felt a twinge of conscience that she still hadn't written anything about the trial and the faces; whatever it was she had intended to write, it had eluded her. Bill stopped the jeep for Jones to get out and get something, the cool wind stopped blowing and everything got hazy again. In the heavy rich indolence of drunkenness she leaned back and watched people hurrying up and down the steps of the courthouse and the big doors swinging ceaselessly in and out in the perpetual action of international justice. In the shadows of the entrance gate several flimsily dressed prostitutes were laughing and joking with some Negro MP's. A German child going past with its mother stooped in the gutter to pick up a cigarette butt: "Guck-mal! A present for Daddy!"

Then there was more wind, blissfully strong and cool, and every time the wind and the jeep stopped, German voices came welling up out of the rubbly darkness—"The trials? Nein, I know nothing of them."—"Mir ganz egal. I have no time for such things."—"Ich? Das is' nicht meine Sorge. I am only a little tradesman." And a ragged old woman, her doleful face twisted with resentment: "Let the Allierten decide. This is not Germans' business." Another, a one-armed PW: "Natürlich, you have the right to hang them. You are the victors."

"Justice?" said a young girl slowly. "What is justice?" She turned and looked around her in the rolling hills of debris in which she was walking. "Was this justice?" Behind her a steeple-less church lay crushed as a decomposed berry-box beside a tiny cemetery under an avalanche of powdered stone and splintered wood. "They tried to be gods and they couldn't. One should not set one's self up as god unless one can continue to the end doing godlike things."

"She's nuts," said Jones.

Monotonously, the girl went on. "What is Germany? A dungheap. A nothing. We are like a people whose god has deserted them." Tears began running down her dirty face. "We have lost faith in everything, in men, in systems, in words. Germany is dead. And it is they who killed her. Let them die too, then, all of them!" She moved up closer to the jeep, her wet face shining in the dim reflection of the jeep's headlights. "And Germans should know what is justice? Who knows? Who cares? You have not a little chocolate, or bread, nein? So. When the stomach is empty one does not think about trials. One looks for food." Still crying, she wandered back into the shattered church.

Grey ruins and grey sky, and Bill's profile floating along in the gloom. More German voices:—"What about the Russians? Who will try them?"—"Politics mean nothing to me."

"Ach, kein Interesse," said a kindly-looking old man. "Let them hang, the Schweinehunde! Through their own stupidity they lost the war and brought Germany to this. Once, a long time ago, in the days when Germany was a great nation, I had a party, a good party, the anti-Semitic party. I helped to found that party in Chemnitz in 1896. Those Nazi blackguards ran off with our platform and then betrayed us by not living up to it. Hitler promised to wipe out the Jews. But did he do it? There are still Jews in Germany! Maybe not so many any more, but enough to start the same trouble again. And what about die Schwarzen, the Catholics? They are as bad as the verrückten Juden, and where are they? Everywhere." In the deathly quiet of the Marktplatz, in the grey rubble, his gentle soft voice went on. "Ruining the nation, dividing it, setting German against German."

The unmuffled roar of the jeep motor cut savagely into that sweet reasonable old voice spinning out its soft web of theory. Carla was jerked suddenly to one side and nearly fell out onto the pavement. And then the cold wind came back and the night was bigger and full of stars swimming around upside down.

The marble staircase of the Schloss revolved around her like a corkscrew, but she hung onto Bill's arm until there she was in the bar again sitting at a little table next to Norman, and Bill had raced off to file a story or something.

"Well, Fräulein MacMurphy," said Norman, smiling his faint suggestive smile and ordering two double Scotches. "I see you have fallen back into the waiting arms of a former love. Tell me, is warmed-over coffee any good?"

"Oh, Norman!" she said.

The bar was crowded with people, the noise of voices so loud that it had become an entity, hundreds of voices blended in drunkenness or argument falling around her like a heavy curtain, walling her in alone with Norman at the little table.

"Did you get a column out of it?" asked Norman.

She drank her Scotch. "Out of what?"

"This jeep trip with the devoted suitor."

"I think so."

"Good," he said. "Then you can file tonight?"

"Tonight," she said. The word tasted funny, as if it filled her mouth to capacity, and she swallowed quickly. "I think I'm a little drunk," she said.

"Nonsense," he said, ordering another round of drinks. "That's just what a growing girl needs." Smiling his yellow

135

smile, he settled back in his chair. "Now, Miss MacM, now that we are alone together, geben—as we German teeps say. What's happened to your French Marxist and have you given up the idea of taking the socialist veil?"

She put her elbows on the table. "No-o-o."

"Rumor has it, you know, that your affections have recently established a bridgehead in Berlin."

Unconsciously she tossed her Scotch down. "What if I have?" in that little-girl voice. "What if my heart is breaking? Who gives a damn? As long as I keep on working and slobbering out—slobbering out articles for the great American public, who cares? Her eyes were shining with unshed tears. "Let's have another drink."

"Fine," said Norman. "Same thing, Otto." He reached over and patted her hand with his own thin freckled one. "Now, tell Uncle Norman all about it. Having never made a pass at you in my life, I think we can consider me qualified as a first-class confidant." His sharp brown eyes were traveling around her face, recording the unshed tears, the tragic-comic pout to her mouth. "Come now, Fräulein MacM, tell Uncle Norman all about it."

Her eyes on the table and its half-empty glasses, she failed to notice the eagerness in his face. "What does it matter?" she said desperately. "What does it matter that I'm so unhappy I could die! You don't know what it's like. You can't know. To be torn as I am between the love of two wonderful men. You don't know. Nobody but a woman could understand. Not these bitches around here but a woman who has known sorrow, and sacrifice, and—and the terrible responsibility of being loved. Too much adored all her life long, and now——" She picked up her Scotch. "Venus, Helen of Troy, someone like that—Lola Montez—women for whom men lived—and died."

"Otto," said Norman softly, and with his hand indicated a repeat on his last order.

"I brought it all on myself! Go ahead, tell me! I'm responsible! I'm responsible for both of them. For their lives, their work, their happiness. Happiness. Charles, sitting there waiting for me from day to day. How can I desert him? His very life is dedicated to me. Without me—— Oh you don't know, you can't know! And yet every time I even think of leaving David ——"

"David?" echoed Norman, leaning over to hear her better. "Dave Hawks, you mean?"

"Yes," she said softly. "David. Oh, I had no intention. If I'd had any idea. Started so innocently, two hungry young

136

people yearning for just a few moments in each other's arms. How could we have known that—how far it would go? That I'd be torn like this, torn between them. You don't understand, how broken he'd be. Think of a mind like that, that brilliant mind of his, tossed on the refuse-heap of history because I have another destiny, destiny in the arms of another man." She put her head down on her arms and began to cry softly as a child. "I can't do it, I can't, I can't."

Bill Somers came up and pulled out a chair. "Okay, Norman," he said. "How about that drink you promised me? Hey, what's the matter with Carla?"

"Ssh!" said Norman, and then soundlessly with his round fishmouth forming the words, "Crying jag."

She lifted her tear-stained face. "Until now I never knew what love was. Other men don't make love, they commit it. But not David—or Charles." Her hair, which had gotten mussed up in the jeep ride, tumbled about her face. What had originally been a pompadour curling high over her forehead was now a sausage-roll over her right ear. "I am split in two, and the two halves of me bleed for each other. O God, O God!" And she put her head back into the cradle of her arms.

"Maybe we ought to get her over to the hen-house and to bed," suggested Somers.

She lifted her head again. "What I could say to ugly women right now! Women who always envy women like me, think they'd give anything to be in my place. They don't know! They don't know how lucky they are! Oh, what I wouldn't give to be just an ordinary unattractive woman who could love one man in peace, not be always torn like this. Trying, like somebody's wife—don't remember whose, doesn't matter—be all things to all men. Two men. Two wonderful, wonderful . . ."

"Miss MacMurphy!" called a messenger, plowing through the crowds around the bar. "Telephone for Miss MacMurphy!"

"Think that's me," said Carla, stumbling to her feet.

"Come on, Carla, I'll give you a hand," said Somers. "Where, boy?"

"Miss MacMurphy?" asked the boy in a crisp nasal voice. "Booth number three."

"Okay, here we go," said Bill, taking a firm hold of her arm.

She started off with him, then suddenly turned back to Norman. "Caesar's wife, that's who," she said. "All things all men."

They walked unevenly through the bar. At the door, Carla looked up and recognized him. "Bill," she said thickly. "Wonderful Bill. Think I'm drunk, don't you? You don't know I

137

still gotta write a story. Something about faces those twenty-one bastards. Had it all thought out, then forgot about it. Imagine! Column. Eighteen hundred words."

Carefully he guided her toward the telephone booth. "Your column?" he asked, holding her shoulders. *"Look Here, America?"*

"That's right. Promised Connell I'd write damn thing tonight but forgot what was gonna say. Something about faces. Bill." She stopped short just at the door of the booth and smiled at him weakly. "Write a column for me, this once. Write anything. Just sit down, put words on paper, eighteen hundred of 'em, sign MacMurphy. That's all. Simple." She reached up to kiss him but her kiss smacked wetly in mid-air. "Bill, you're 'n angel. Always wanted to write a column, didn't you? Well, here's chance."

He held her tightly upright. "Yes," he said thoughtfully. "I always did. Especially about the Nuremberg trials. I got a lot of things I'd like to say about this trial, but never had space to say them in." For a long minute he stood silent, supporting her with one arm, as if thinking over what he would write. "It'd be a scorcher."

"Don't care," she said. "Don't care. Write anything. Anything. Just sit down, sign MacMurphy."

"Okay, honey," he said, opening the door and switching on the light. "I may only commit love, but I can do all right with a column. Okay, don't worry about it. I'll get over to the courthouse right away and get it started. What about you, though? Sure you're all right? Let's see you get in there and take that call."

"Sure I'm all right," she said. "Watch. Perfec'ly all right."

She took down the phone. "H'llo! H'llo!" The evenly matched white teeth flashed but the smile was humorless and feline. With her right hand she waved him a limp farewell and closed the door.

"H'llo! H'llo!" she said.

"Miss MacMurphy?" said a sharp soprano voice. "Hold on, please. Berlin calling." The line buzzed, a series of electric signals beep-beeped along the wire. The booth was hot and close and her head began to spin, but she held on tightly to the receiver and with her other hand supported herself by clinging to the phone itself. On the brown wall of the booth were lettered names, telephone numbers, line drawings of nude women and men in different stages of desire. A fly crawled determinedly up the wall in front of her. "Fly," she said aloud.

The drawings were swaying from side to side, and one time

138

a crude sketch of a rump-sprung Negress almost bumped into her nose. Then the line cleared and she could hear David's voice. "Hello. Nuremberg?"

"David!" she said. "David!"

"Hello, Carla? Hello, baby, how are things going? When are you coming home?"

She was about to tell him when his voice came in again. "I suppose you're beating the pants off everybody there. Did you get a good story off?"

"Tonight, got one off tonight."

"Wonderful. What about?"

"About——" She stopped to think. "About little Indians, twenty-one little Indians, four little five little——"

"Carla! Are you drunk? Carla baby, what's the matter? Are you sick?" His voice was low with anxiety.

Then suddenly the line clicked and the buzzing started up again. "David!"

There was no answer. "David! H'llo! H'llo!"

The booth was quiet. The fly started just as determinedly down again.

"Hello, Nuremberg," said the operator. "I'm sorry, the connection's been broken with Berlin. If you'll hold on a minute or two I'll connect you."

"I'm a fly," said Carla to herself in the muffled silence of the closed booth, and she thought she ought to walk up the wall and out of the booth and go and find Bill who was toiling away somewhere in that courthouse like a men's privy writing her column for her, because now she'd almost remembered what it was about the faces and she ought to tell him, but all she could do was just keep holding the receiver and saying over and over Charles, David, Charles, David, one little two little three little——

"Jesus Christ!" said Norman, opening the door of the booth. "What a mess! Is she all right?"

"Yeah, she's all right," said Somers. "She's just sick. Look, Norman, I'll clean her up and get her across to the hen-house. Why don't you go on back to your table and leave it to me? We don't want to attract any more attention than is absolutely necessary. Okay?"

"Well if you don't mind, Bill, I think perhaps I'd better. The stench of something like that always makes me so ill. My stomach, you know." He backed away. "You're positive you can handle her all right?"

"Positive. You run along, Norman, I'll take care of this."

"Right you are. Goodnight then."

"Goodnight, Norman."

Somers got down on his knees, took a handkerchief out of his pocket and began wiping off her chin and throat and wet sputtering lips. He unbuttoned the bodice of her dress and carefully, efficiently wiped off her breasts. Then he rebuttoned her dress and putting his arms under her armpits got her up off the floor. "Out cold," he said to himself. "Poor crazy kid!" Grunting a little, he hoisted her up in his arms and started down the stairway toward the hen-house.

CHAPTER ELEVEN

THAT DAY—Christmas Eve—was the day they decided to dig up the Russian soldier.

Carla was standing at the big French windows of the living-room, holding back one satin drape and looking pensively down toward the frozen lake. "I hate winter," she said fretfully. "Winter bores me. All you can do is drink or go skating. Kripke!" she called, hearing his loud cheerful voice in the kitchen. "Kripke!"

"Ham Se mich gerufen, Miss MacMurphy?"

He always looked so ready for anything, stomping in like a wiry little Boy Scout to push his hair back out of his face and grin at her. "Kripke, how long would it take to dig up that Russian soldier?"

"Ach, Miss MacMurphy, only about half an hour."

She turned back to the window and gazed down across the snow-covered lawn. "With the ground all frozen like that?"

"Ha!" he said scoffingly. "That is not difficult! He is stiffer now and easier to dig up. Also he will stink less."

David looked up from some military government reports he was reading. "What did you say, baby?"

"Nothing, darling. Kripke and I were just discussing the tomb of the unknown looter."

"Our Russian DP down there by the lake?"

"Um-hum. All right, Kripke, that's all I wanted to know. Is Luisa fixing us some tea?"

"I think so, Miss MacMurphy. She is baking cakes right now, Torte and Brötchen and things like that. I know because now I am assistant cook," he added proudly. "I do the greasing of the pans."

She looked up. "Why doesn't Erika take care of things like that?"

"Erika is sick, Miss MacMurphy. She is in her room upstairs."

"Oh." She thought it over for a minute. "All right, Kripke, that's all. Tell Luisa to make tea as soon as she can."

After Kripke had left the room, David got up and came over to the window beside her. "What's the matter, baby? Bored?"

She sighed. "I guess I am. I'm also upset about all these robberies, everybody stealing food and coal all the time. Do you realize that last night was our fourth robbery in one month?"

"Oh, hell!" he said easily. "As long as they confine themselves to food and coal, I have nothing against it. If I were a German with a couple of starving and freezing kids, I think I'd do some stealing myself. After all, for all the stuff that guy got away with last night, all we have to do is go back to the commissary and order some more."

"But why us all the time? Why does it have to be *our* food they're always stealing?"

"Actually," he said, "it isn't us all the time. It's all over Berlin, thousands of housebreakings and robberies every week. Personally I think we've come off pretty lightly."

"Another thing," she said, troubled. "I'm also worried about Erika. David, I don't like the idea of her being sick all the time. I think she's lying down on the job. She used to be such an excellent maid, and now she's so absentminded she never even hears what you tell her. And she's getting so fat she looks terrible serving at the table. She can scarcely fit into her uniforms any more. Honestly, I'd can her tomorrow. Except then I'd have to use Lubowa for everything, and Lubowa's so damned awkward, always spilling things and tripping over her own feet."

He looked at her sharply. "Don't you know what's the matter with Erika?"

"No. Except I think that ever since her precious American captain got sent home, she feels so damned sorry for herself that she can't do any work any more."

"She's pregnant."

"What?" She turned and stared at him.

"Jesus, baby, I thought you knew. I can't see how you could have missed it. For weeks Kripke's been teasing her unmercifully about being belegt with an American bastard, and the poor kid's been so embarrassed she's tried to keep out of sight as much as she could."

Carla turned away from the window. "Well, the dumb little cluck! Why didn't she come to me and tell me about it? I could have arranged for an operation as easy as that! If there's anything in this country easier to get than V.D. it's an abortion. How many months?"

"About five."

She shrugged her shoulders. "Well, it's too late now. All she can do now is go ahead and have the damned thing and get it over with. But if she thinks she can go on working for me when she's waddling all over the place like a duck, she's got another think coming!"

"Look, Carla," he said patiently. "I'm sorry I forgot to tell you, but when you were in Nuremberg she came to me and told me about it and asked me what to do. And I said the only thing for her to do was go ahead and have her baby and we'd see she was well taken care of. And then I told her she could go on working for us here until she was ready to have it. Actually, the poor kid——"

"The poor kid, nuts! Why'd she get herself in such a predicament in the first place?"

"Carla, let's be fair! Jesus Christ, she isn't even eighteen years old yet! She probably didn't even know what sex was until she met this guy. An innocent kid like that——"

"Innocent? Don't make me laugh! I know these Fräuleins, I've watched them operate."

He walked away across the room. "All right, Carla, we won't talk about it any more." He sat down in his chair and picked up his reports. "Go ahead and fire her, then, and I'll take care of her from here on out."

She stood for a moment looking at the back of his head, the soft thick brown hair and his straight broad back. "What do you mean, take care of her?"

His voice was quiet. "I mean find her a place to live, pay her bills, get her a good doctor and a hospital reservation and see that she gets enough to eat to live through it."

"For Christ's sake!" she said. "Why don't you marry the girl and be done with it?"

He didn't even turn his head.

"Honestly, you make me sick," she said. "Making excuses for a common little kraut who just through her own carelessness has got herself knocked up by some American soldier who never intended to marry her in the first place! If she needs help so bad, what's the matter with her mother, Frau Lochmann? Why doesn't her mother do something for her?"

"Carla," he said coldly. "You know that's impossible. You know how that family lives. Why, Frau Lochmann has to work nine hours a day cleaning up rubble and then two hours more doing our laundry. Her family *can't* take care of her. No German family could. They haven't got the medicines or the food or anything else. Under the circumstances, since the baby is half American, I don't see why we shouldn't do what we can."

"How do you know it's half American? How do you know what else she's been running around with?"

He didn't answer.

"And even if it were!" she said. "Even if it were, I don't see why we have to take the burdens of the world on our shoulders. And just because he was an American captain we have to pay for and take care of his illegitimate brat!"

The room was quiet. Except for the soft scraping of his pages as he turned them, there was no sound.

"Miss MacMurphy," said Gerda unobtrusively, coming in from the office. "Your copy is ready to go out now, if you'd like to proofread it."

"Thank you, Gerda," she said coldly and distinctly, still looking at the back of his head.

She took the typewritten sheets and skipped quickly over the first two paragraphs. "Fine, Gerda," she said. "Just send it off like that."

She wandered back to the window.

The garden was immersed in ice, only the tops of Kripke's patiently tended raspberry bushes stuck up black and impudent through a crusted dead sea of grey snow. Beyond the barbed wire in the woods to the right that belonged to somebody else she saw three women whacking murderously with knives and fingernails at the stumps that dotted the ground while a fourth woman walked around the bare black trees stripping off small branches and tying them into bundles. They have no right there, she thought. Military government law says they can only gather wood in public parks, and then only with a license.

"David," she said slowly. "I'm sorry I got so upset about Erika. I think I was just annoyed that after all I've done for her she didn't come and tell me about it in time to do something."

There was no answer.

"But what the hell! It's done now, and it's too late to get her fixed up. So honestly, darling, what do you suggest we do?"

Only half-mollified, he got up and came over to the window. "Just what I said, I guess. Give the girl what little help we can. She's got a tough row to hoe all right, living in this god-forsaken country of hers with an illegitimate kid to support _____"

Suddenly Carla caught his arm. Her face shone. "David! I've just had the most wonderful idea! I'll adopt her! In the column! In *Look Here, America!* My God, why didn't I think of that before? The most marvelous human-interest copy you could get—the story of a GI-Fräulein romance. Describe her and her family, their whole case history, how and where she met the captain, his departure, her getting pregnant, and then follow her week-to-week through the whole thing—what kind of doctor, what hospital, what medicines, her troubles getting food and clothing for the baby—David, isn't that a wonderful idea?" she concluded breathlessly.

"Jesus, I think you've got something there," he said. "Why don't you write them a letter in Washington and propose it?"

"I think I will." She made a quick little whirl of delight. "Has Gerda gone?"

"I think so. I told her she could leave early because it's Christmas Eve. Why?"

"Oh, nothing. I'll dictate the letter to her in the morning."

"That's the girl," he said. He put his arm around her. "Still mad at me?"

"Oh, no! David, of course not!"

"Well, come on. It isn't four o'clock yet. Let's cancel the tea, get our coats on and go down to Berlin-Mitte. Get some air and some Christmas 'color.' How about it?"

She looked up at him, her eyes dancing. "Wonderful! I'll go get my new coat."

Humming a tune, she raced up into the blue-velvet-and-white-tulle bedroom, pulled down from the hanger the mink coat that mother had sent her for Christmas, dug around for her new mink hat, took a quick delighted look at herself in the mirror and raced back downstairs.

He was still at the window looking out over the icy garden. "Look what one word from your pretty lips does to our man Friday."

A small wiry figure in an American army fatigue jacket was working with pickaxe and shovel over the corner of the garden nearest the lake, breaking up the ground and then shoveling it away. As they watched, he put the shovel down, reached down and pulled something up out of the ground. Amused, they watched him tugging, pulling in this direction and that, and

144

then saw him almost fall over with the sudden giving-way of whatever it was he was tugging on. Impatiently, he threw everything on the snow-covered ground, walked limpingly over behind the boarded-up boathouse and came back with a wheelbarrow.

"What the hell!" said David suddenly. "The thing's disintegrated."

Working fast and with concentration, Kripke started piling onto the wheelbarrow first a leg, then another leg, then a torso with an indistinguishable muddy head, then an arm, then the pickaxe and shovel. The barrow loaded, he bent over, took up the handles and started ploddingly up the walk toward the house.

"Where's he going with the damned thing?" said David.

He rounded the corner of the house and was lost from sight.

"Come on," said David, and they started for the front door.

He opened the door just as Kripke was coming around the front of the house. "Hey, Kripke!" he yelled. "What happens here? What are you doing with that corpse?" A freezing wind blew into their faces.

Kripke turned his head and grinned. "Putting our Kamerad in the trash barrel, Mister Hawks."

"Wait a minute. You can't do that. We have to phone the Russians and give them a chance to come get it."

Kripke put the wheelbarrow down. "Ach, Mister Hawks, die Russen don't care about another Russian corpse. On the east front we used to wade through them, and nobody even took the trouble to shovel them under. What difference makes one more Russian soldier? In the morning the garbage service will take it away and Schluss! Nobody will be any the wiser." His grin was knowing and he winked owlishly across the wet snow.

"Never mind about the east front," said David. "You just let that wheelbarrow stand there for the time being while I call up Karlshorst."

A messenger came up the steps. "Miss MacMurphy?"

"Yes?"

"A wire for you."

Shivering, she accepted the wire and watched Kripke disgustedly set the wheelbarrow to one side and start back toward the house. He limped up and stood on the walk below her. "Does Mr. Hawks really think the Russians give a damn about one Russian corpse?"

"Perhaps not," she said soothingly. "But he thinks we have to make sure, Kripke."

145

His lower lip stuck out, he looked longingly back at the wheelbarrow. "Wait till the Russians come back, then you'll see what I mean. One more body—German, Russian, American—it makes no difference to the Russians."

She looked at him. "What do you mean 'when the Russians come back?' They're still here."

"Ja, ja, det wees ick. I mean when the Americans leave and the Red Army comes."

The young messenger nodded his blond head in agreement, and Carla looked from one to another. "That's enough of such defeatist talk," she said sternly. "The Americans have no intention of leaving Berlin—ever. At least, not until everybody decides to leave at once and give Berlin back to the Germans."

"Ha!" said Kripke scoffingly. "That will never happen. The Russians will never agree to give Berlin—or Germany—back to the Germans. They are fools, die Russen, but not so big fools as that!" Swinging his arms, he walked back toward his corpse-loaded wheelbarrow.

Carla tore open the stapled edge of the telegram, expecting no more than a service message from the Globe or the usual Christmas greetings from the publisher. ARRIVING SIX PM TONIGHT BERLIN WANNSEE STATION TO TAKE YOU BACK PARIS WITH ME STOP JE TEMBRASSE CHARLES.

O my God!

For one moment she stood there with the wire in her hand. Then she walked back inside the house and stood in the warm darkness of the hall leaning against the door.

Her heart was beating like a short-wave signal. O my God! Of all things to have happen at this particular moment! And I was just planning to go to Paris as soon as the holidays were over! She looked at her watch: almost four o'clock. In less than two hours and a half Charles would be arriving. And what would she say? What would she do? David—Charles—they'd kill each other if they ever met.

"Ready, honey?" said David, appearing behind her in his big GI overcoat.

"All ready," she said with forced brightness, and shoved the telegram in her coat pocket.

"Kripke," said David, walking out into the yard. "Leave the wheelbarrow right there for the time being. I just talked to some Russians and they're going to send a car down in a few minutes to collect the thing."

"Maybe they'll put him back together again and make him the political Kommissar of Wedding," suggested Kripke wickedly. "Okay, Mister Hawks. I leave our comrade here and go get the Tatra right away."

They waited while Kripke backed the Tatra out of the garage, watched it emerge tail-first like a gleaming silver shark swimming slowly in reverse, then watched it turn around in the drive and point its long tapered nose toward the gate. In spite of her excitement over Charles, Carla felt a ripple of pride, as if the Tatra were some enormous aquatic animal that she had personally caught and tamed and taught to obey her, a human Nereid astride her own faithful sea-Pegasus.

Noticing the expression on her face, David smiled. "You love that car, don't you?"

"Me?" a little annoyed. "No, not particularly. I just think it's a beautiful car and a lot pleasanter riding than a damned jeep."

"Now don't get mad, baby. I was only teasing you. I think it's a pretty beautiful contraption myself." He helped her in. "Just like its owner."

Snuggled together under their thick velvety auto robe, they rode down to the center of the city, past frozen streets empty of either traffic or pedestrians. "Everything seems so deserted," said Carla. "Where is everybody?"

"Probably at home in bed," said David. "Trying to keep warm."

Not until they got out of the car near the grandiose tumbled ruins of Hitler's Reichskanzlei and started walking down the Wilhelmstrasse did she broach the subject. Then:

"David," she said softly, holding tight to his arm. "Do you remember that French writer I used to tell you about? The one named Charles Poignon?"

"That ex-fiancé of yours? What about him?"

"He's arriving at Wannsee station at six o'clock. I just got a wire from him."

"He is?" His breath was like white smoke on the winter air. "Well, there's plenty of time to go and meet him if you want to."

All the way up to Unter den Linden they walked in silence. Carla was amazed, and in some funny sense disappointed, that he had taken it so easily. What did he think she was, a streetcar that he didn't have to run after any more because he'd already caught it?

She removed her arm from his and walked a little way away from him. "I'm going to ask him if he doesn't want to stay with us." And glanced at him sharply.

He didn't seem even to have heard her.

147

In the pale wreckage of the Pariser Platz where the Brandenburger Tor stretched its gaunt triple-vaulted shadow, a few snowflakes drifted slowly down through the cold air. Under the Tor a crowd of black-marketeers lugging sacks of goods moved together, broke away, swirled like dirty water around the arches of the battered gate. Otherwise the center of Berlin was as empty and uninhabited as an arctic wasteland.

"But what's he coming here for?" asked David.

"Darling, I told you before. He's writing a book about Germany."

"Carla, you know what he's coming for. He's coming to see you. To try to get you away from me and get you to come to Paris to marry him. Isn't that so?"

"Could be." With her foot she kicked at the frozen gutter and dislodged a small piece of ice that skidded across the street toward the snow-topped heap that had once been the American Embassy. She smiled mysteriously. "Could be."

Below the new mink coat her legs through their nylon stockings ached with cold, a dull muscular cramp, and the tips of her fingers tingled. But her body inside the coat and her head where the little mink bonnet covered it felt luxuriously warm, and happier now because David was angry. With one hand she stroked the soft cold fur of the other sleeve. "Charles is a wonderful person, and he has every right to come here if he pleases."

"And stay in our house? A former lover of yours to stay in the house with us?"

Luckily, there was no one around to hear his shouting.

"David, I'm cold. Let's start back toward the car."

He took her arm and wordlessly they passed under the purple shadow of the big gate, past the whirlpool of dingy curbstone trafficants and out on the other side.

"Now where are we?" asked Carla. "Are we still in the Russian sector?"

"We were just then. Now we're in the British sector. As a matter of fact, we're now in the center of the city. Boy, it's a dead center too."

She looked around her, trying to distinguish one quadrant from another as he pointed them out—the Russian sector beginning there behind the Tor, the British sector out here, the French sector running that way, the American out there, like slivers of a quartered pie—but all she could see were frosted ruins under a grey sky, a still grey purgatory of desolation as far as the eye could reach in any direction.

He took her arm again, the cold breathing against their

148

faces, and they started off down the deserted east-west axis toward the gilded Siegessäule sticking up out of the devastation like one yellowed tooth in the gums of a grinning old hag. "Look, Carla," he said, tucking her hand into his pocket. "Try to give me the benefit of a little sense. I don't care how wonderful this guy is, you just cannot bring him out to stay at our house. It isn't fair to him any more than it is to you and me."

"Actually," said Carla irrelevantly, "you'll like each other. You'll probably disagree on a lot of things, but you'll like each other just the same."

"How can we, for Christ's sake?" he shouted. "He's a goddamned Commie, isn't he? And he's out after my girl!"

"He is not! He may be a Marxist, but he certainly isn't a Communist!"

"What do I care what he is? In a triangle like this I don't care whether he's a Marxist or a Seventh Day Adventist! All I know is that he's coming here for the sole purpose of getting you to quit your job and leave Berlin."

Again she smiled, a soft mysterious smile. "Could be."

"Well, what are you going to do, then? Damn it, Carla, be reasonable! You're a grownup girl now and this isn't dancing class. You've got to make some kind of decision! You can't keep two men dangling at the ends of your strings forever!"

"I *have* made a decision."

"To ask him to stay somewhere else?"

"No." Looking down at her trim little fur-lined boots.

"Well, what, then?"

"I've decided to keep myself apart from both of you until I can decide quietly and without pressure which one of you I love most."

"What!" He stopped short in his tracks and stared at her. "You mean to say you don't know? You mean to say you're still considering going off to Paris with that guy? And leaving me? After all the things you've told me in the last five months?" He began to laugh, a hard, dry laugh. "Jesus Christ! What asses men are!"

"David!"

"What a bunch of horses' asses! And all this time, I suppose, you've been telling him the same thing! All about how until he came along your love had no face. Love was just an impersonal thing of physiological need. Until *he* came along. To give love meaning. 'This face, Charles, your face.'" He was mimicking her. "Boy, I'd like to bash his goddamned face in and see how you felt about it then!"

"David!"

149

She glanced up at him, at his grey eyes murderous with anger, the clean tangential line of his chin, a little frightened of him but warmed and delighted by the fire of his temper. Somehow, in the intensity of his jealousy, he had the same driving boldness that he had when he was sexually excited, and she welcomed it and reached out to it just as she did those other times, feeling now as then that if she didn't she would be missing something. She felt her thighs tighten, and she glanced up at him again.

"Boy, your love's got a face all right!" he was saying. "And anytime you want to see it, Miss MacMurphy, all you have to do is go look in a mirror!"

She put her hand on his arm. "David———"

"Well, what is it?"

"David, darling, please listen. You misunderstood me. I have no intention of leaving you, or going to Paris with Charles. I just———" The appealing little catch in her voice was there, so much there that she choked a little over it. "I just don't want to hurt him any more than I have to. He's so wonderful and so—so sensitive, David. I'll just have to try very hard to pick the right time to tell him."

He watched closely the passing expressions on her transparently white heart-shaped face, the wide green eyes brimming with emotion. In the distance behind that adorable face he could see shawled and bundled figures grubbing for potatoes in the wasted stretches of the Tiergarten. "To tell him what?" he asked sourly.

"That I can't go away with him because I'm going to stay here with you." She turned her face quickly up to his. "Oh, David, you really will like him. I know you will."

"Like him?" said David. "I hate his guts."

"No, you don't."

"No," he said grudgingly. "I guess I don't. After all, it's Christmas Eve and I suppose I should be charitable. But I still don't see why he has to put in an appearance right now, like a wad of half-chewed gum sticking to our shoes." He took her arm again. "Ordinarily I wouldn't mind meeting him at all, if he's the guy that wrote that book about the Congress of Vienna. Oh, hell, maybe it won't be so bad. Come on. If we don't get going, you'll be late to meet him."

When she let him out at the ranch-house door, he kissed her hand and held it against his cold cheek. "You've just got time to make it," he said, looking at his watch. "I'll have some drinks waiting for you when you get here. And don't worry!"

kissing her again. "I'll be so civilized and gentlemanly you won't recognize me. After all, he and I have a lot in common —a profound and no doubt exaggerated admiration for you, for example."

As he was striding toward the door, he turned and gestured toward her, his hat shoved back onto the back of his head and his handsome face beaming.

She rolled down the window of the car and leaned out into the cold.

"I guess Kripke was right!" he shouted across the icy yard, motioning toward the wheelbarrow which still sat there with its macabre load half-dragging in the snow. "It doesn't look like the Russians are in any hurry to reclaim the poor bastard!"

"Ach!" said Kripke suddenly, pulling on the handbrake and dashing out of the car. "I manage this, Mister Hawks."

Like a housewife setting the table for dinner, Kripke bustled happily around the wheelbarrow, readjusted the torso, piled an arm in a more balanced position. "So geht's," he said proudly, surveying his work. "If I know the Russians, he'll sit there for a long time. He may as well be comfortable."

"Kripke!" said Carla severely.

Officiously he limped back to the car and got behind the wheel. "That's the Russians for you!" he said. "They're probably having a political conference about it right now." He started the motor. "Where to, Miss MacMurphy?"

"Wannsee station. And we're late, Kripke."

"Keine Angst, Miss MacMurphy. I'll get us there in time." And with his usual confidence he rolled the Tatra smoothly out of the drive.

They were halfway to the station before either of them said a word. Then: "I'll be glad to see Mister Poy-nong again," said Kripke conversationally. "For a Franzosen, he is not a bad fellow."

She sat bolt upright. "How do you know that, Kripke? Where in hell do you pick up these things?"

"Ha, that's easy, Miss MacMurphy. The messenger boy said someone was arriving from Paris. And then when I saw Mister Hawks getting so angry, I figured——"

"Well, you just stop figuring and tend to your driving."

"Jawohl, Miss MacMurphy."

CHAPTER TWELVE

ALL THE way out from the station Charles held her hand, seemingly so moved at being with her again that he could find nothing to say, his eyes luminous and tender and so articulate with adoration that she herself could do nothing but smile shyly and cling to his hand.

Past scores of Germans pulling little carts of scavenged wood, the Tatra moved through the bleak winter twilight like a comet in an inexorable orbit, its passengers silent, its interior a secret closed world of high-voltage emotion.

Meltingly she looked at him. And something in her heart went soaring away, lifted beyond the bare treetops of everyday good and evil into the fleecy heady realm of pure silent glandular understanding. She felt almost the way she had felt as a little girl loving the Christ Child at Christmastime, or the way she and Dad had been before the divorce, wrapped in a cocoon of inexpressibly sweet sweet warmth.

Her eyes shining, she squeezed his hand.

"I had forgotten how beautiful you are," he said at last, his voice husky and low. And then he held her mink-clad shoulders and kissed her softly, delicately, up and down her throat and all over her face, and the sweet sweet warmth became almost excruciating, and she didn't feel like a little girl any more.

And he was so wonderfully humble, something David with his fierce and merciless honesty had never been. Not one word of reproach that she had stayed five months instead of three weeks, or that she had written to him so seldom. No anxious questioning on whether there was another man. Not even a hint of resentment because she had broken her promise to come to Paris and he had had to seek her out like a recalcitrant child. Which is what I've been, she thought; I've treated him miserably.

They rounded the curve in the drive and the ranch-house came in view, so she sat up and straightened herself a little and smiling gallantly, as if this were just another day in her life, let him help her out of the car. And then there was Lubowa running out to help Kripke unload the bags, and the first thing the little dope did was drop Charles' shaving-case and half the things tumbled out on the snowy walk. "Tollpatsch!" yelled Kripke in his rasping Gefreiter voice. But again Charles was amazingly patient, assuring the stammering Lubowa that it didn't matter, nothing was broken.

"Seh'nse mal, Mister Poy-nong!" yelled Kripke cheerfully in back of her. "Wait till you see what I've got here!"

In the shadows of the houselights it was hard to see what he did have but Carla knew with a furious certainty that it was some portion of that dug-up Russian soldier. Damn him! she thought. Then, shouting, "Kripke, put that back!"

Stopped in mid-action, holding just what she had thought— a frozen mud-caked leg—he looked at her with the crestfallen disappointment of a small boy who has been caught stealing apples.

"What on earth has he got?" asked Charles, peering into the shadows.

"Nothing, Charles, nothing," she said, quickly taking his arm. "He's just trying to show off. All it is, is a Russian soldier that——"

Charles gave an unbelieving laugh. "You mean you've already started shooting them? Or dismembering them, rather?"

"Of course not!" she said, a little annoyed. "It's nothing but a Russian soldier that was buried down by the lake, and Kripke—— Oh, I'll tell you later. Kripke, do what I tell you! Take that horrible thing and put it back in the wheelbarrow!"

Limping and muttering, Kripke trudged back over the yard carrying the leg over his shoulder like a musket, and she and Charles entered the house.

The first thing that Charles saw was the fire, a bright crackling wood fire that threw ripples of light along the walls and reflected in all the pieces of pewter and copper that she had brought back from the Russian Zone to adorn the bookcases. "Oh," he said, pleased, "a fire!" And walked toward it rubbing his hands.

Out of an easy chair near the fireplace, David stood up. Outlined against the light he looked towering in height, and on his face was a dignified unfriendliness that made her blood freeze.

She took a long breath. "Charles," she said prettily, "I'd like you to meet David Hawks of the *New York Press*. David, this is Charles Poignon, a very old friend of mine who has just arrived from Paris."

"How do you do?" said Charles, extending his hand.

"Carla has told me a great deal about you," said David with cool courtesy. "But sit down while I get us a drink. Scotch, Carla?"

"Please," she said, settling down in a big wing chair.

A door to the right banged open to the sound of loud panting and groaning.

"What weather!" said Kripke, bustling in behind a towering armful of logs. "My old Anna is probably frozen in her bed, such a cold old goat she is anyway." With a dull thud he dumped the logs on the hearth and got down on his knees to sort them out.

"What would you like, Mr. Poignon?" asked David. "I have some cognac and some pretty good French vermouth."

"Scotch also, if you don't mind," said Charles, walking around in back of the divan and looking down toward the lake.

Precociously, talking to himself and glancing from time to time at Hawks, Kripke worked over the fire. "I put this big one on for a Julklotz, to make you a fine big fire on Christmas Eve. For Weihnachten a man needs only a fire—and a bottle of Schnaps." He looked up again at David. "Of course it is better to have both, but if a man has no fire, then a nice warm bottle——"

David pretended not to have heard. "Kripke," he said, going over to the bar. "As a small Christmas present from Miss Mac-Murphy and myself, would you be willing to accept——"

"Don't give him whisky, David," said Carla sharply. "Give him some of that sweet stuff that we don't like, that bottle of apricot brandy, for example, that one right there in the front."

From over by the windows Charles was watching the scene with puzzled interest.

"Oh danke, danke, Mister Hawks," said Kripke, bowing and grinning with open delight. "Danke, Miss MacMurphy. Ach! Wunderbar! Schnaps!" Holding the bottle as if it were a baby, he limped jubilantly out of the room.

David went back to mixing Charles' drink. "A Frenchman who likes Scotch, that's rare, isn't it? Where did you learn to like Scotch?"

For a moment there was no answer. "Oh, I'm sorry," said Charles in a strangely husky voice, turning back to the room. "This young lady," nodding toward Carla where she sat motionless and beautiful as an ivory figurine in front of the fire, "was my institutrice. You can see how convincing a teacher she was."

David handed them each a drink and then sat down. "How was your trip down from Paris?"

"Interesting certainly," said Charles, settling back on the divan, "although not very happy. Before the war they would have talked to you on a train like that. Now they huddle together in their dirty rags and stare out at you like frightened dumb animals, because you are an Ausländer, a Frenchman, and whatever your sympathy you cannot share in this which is a strictly German misery. They are very jealous even of their own misery."

"You rode in the German coaches?" asked David, surprised.

"I wanted to talk to them. Besides," he added humorously, "I am so much against military government I even dislike its trains."

"Carla tells me you are writing a book about Germany."

"Yes." His black eyebrows were raised, his face serious. "It is a critique of the occupation. It is almost finished."

"You don't think the occupation of Germany is much of a success, then?" His voice was sharp.

"Frankly, no," said Charles. "I think all occupations are bad; that is implicit in their nature. But this one I think is not only bad but unsuccessful."

"How both bad and unsuccessful?"

Carla sighed and crossed one nylon-clad leg over another.

"I can see you are a very good journalist, Mr. Hawks," said Charles. "Well, then, unsuccessful because it has made no real progress toward its pretended goal of making Germany a democracy. And bad because it has produced so much fear in the world."

"I agree with you one hundred percent on the first," said David. "But fear? Fear of what, for God's sake?"

"Of Russia, of America. And of war. Europeans, for example, are now so afraid of being conquered by the Russians and then liberated again by the Americans, or vice versa, that it has become almost an obsession. Russia is afraid of America, and the Americans of Russia. Everywhere now there is fear of men, of systems, of machines. And certainly the tensions built up over Germany are responsible for much of it."

Sitting very erect with shoulders back and breasts lifted, Carla looked idly around the room. Those green drapes really looked wonderful in here.

"But I'm not sure that fear of war is a bad thing," said David. "As a matter of fact, I think it's a hell of a lot better than a desire for war."

"It would be if they weren't so nearly the same thing." He reached into his pocket for his pipe and tobacco pouch and looked inquiringly at Carla. "It will trouble you if I smoke this in here, Carla?"

"Not at all, Charles," she answered graciously. "You know

155

how I've always loved the smell of your pipe." And glanced defiantly at David.

But he was engrossed in the discussion.

"Cigarette please," she said with sweet impatience, holding out her hand, and when Charles offered her one and lit it for her she held his hand lightly with her fingers, as if steadying the light, and lifted her black lashes and looked straight into his eyes. Almost as if hurt, he turned away.

"Ah!" he said suddenly, picking up a small booklet from the table. "What is this? *Nuremberg: Formula or Fiasco?* by Carla MacMurphy." Interested, he opened it to look at the first page.

"Oh that!" said Carla with unconcealed pleasure. "It's a column I wrote from Nuremberg, about the trials, you know, and it became so famous they reprinted it as a booklet." That brilliant smile of shy girlish delight animated her face. "It's already sold over a million copies."

He was beginning to read it.

From the depths of his armchair, David spoke up. "Do you know, Mr. Poignon, I don't think you and I agree."

"Perhaps not," putting the booklet away. "But on what subject?"

"About the roles of America and Russia in the postwar world. You seem to think that Communism is just another economic system that you can fight with votes. You don't seem to see that the only reason those bastards understand is the sweet reason of a machinegun."

Carla leaned her head back so that the flames of the fire outlined her lovely childish profile and looked from one face to the other, from her handsome and temperamental young David to her mature, tolerant Charles. Such a stupid discussion, and the way they were carrying it on one would think it was the most important subject in the world to them, instead of—as her unerring female instinct told her—only an argumentative camouflage of their real rivalry. She smiled to herself. Men were so transparent.

Charles leaned forward in his chair. "Attendez. I am a Socialist, Mr. Hawks, since I am twenty-one years old. We Socialists in Europe have been fighting the Communists beak and claws from the moment that we saw that they had abandoned all democratic principle—and for that reason. Now you have taken our ideological quarrel and made it into a nationalist one, and you are surprised that we do not get so hysterical as you. But in reality you are beginning very late to fight, and for the wrong reasons, and in the wrong way.

156

We have been at this a much longer time. And we know, d'expérience brutale, that one cannot fight Communism with hysteria."

Carla rested her chin on her fist, leaned over and lit herself another cigarette and amused herself by trying to blow the smoke into the fireplace.

"In fact," continued Charles, "we think our complaint against them is much stronger than yours. You are against them as a nation against another nation, because they are almost as powerful as you and because they are interfering with the free play of that democratic-capitalist system of yours. We are against them as a method and an idea, because they betrayed the working classes of Europe."

David was getting angry. "That isn't true!" he said, his forehead flushing with the heat of his argument. "We are against them because they represent and support the most brutal and cynical dictatorship the world has ever seen!"

Sighing, Carla crossed her legs again.

Charles sat back a moment or two puffing on his pipe. "No," he said finally, and his face in the firelight was shadowed with contemplation. "You must excuse me if I do not agree with you. That dictatorship is no more brutal and cynical now than it was from 1941 to 1945, and during those five years you indirectly supported it yourselves by allying yourselves with it. Additionally, that dictatorship is no more brutal or cynical than Hitler's, and you did business with Hitler for eight years. No," he said again, shaking his head. "I believe that as a nation you know what you are doing. But I do not believe that as a people you know why you are doing it."

Carla shifted in her chair. On and on! An intellectual sparring that meant nothing and got nowhere.

"But to get back to Germany," said David. "So granted that we've made a hell of a lot of mistakes, what else could we have done?"

Charles was relighting his pipe, the flame of the lighter flickering briefly over his rugged features.

"Knuckle under to the Russians?" pressed David. "Return to the isolationism of the twenties? Sit back and let Germany and Russia establish that combination of industrial and agricultural might that Bismarck dreamed about, and let them conquer the world?"

Disgusted, Carla watched him, the stubborn belligerency of his well-boned intelligent face, the swinging gestures. He's ruining everything with this silly argument, she thought resentfully; once he gets started like this he never stops until he falls down drunk. And now look. All the high elation of Charles' arrival, the exhilaration of being fought over by two men, of being desired and adored and petitioned, everything had been drained off, the evening flattened out like an old toothpaste tube and all the joy and excitement squeezed out of it.

"Or," he paused rhetorically, "send in a couple of divisions of crack troops to hold the line of the Elbe? Draw a line and say. 'Okay, you bastards, one step over that line and you've had it!' "

From the office came the sound of the phone ringing.

"Oh, excuse me," said Carla, getting up. "Excuse me a second," and disappeared into the office.

"No," said Charles quietly. "I think both of those possible solutions are too extreme. And extremes are like rabbits, they always produce more extremes. Why not do something more rational?"

They stood up as Carla came back into the room. Without a word she picked up her drink and dropped back into her chair, one leg tucked gracefully under her, and leaned forward in front of the fire in that lovely radiator-cap attitude of hers. Paying no attention to the conversation, she sat quietly sipping her drink and playing with Charles' cigarette lighter.

"After all," continued Charles, watching David pour out the whisky, "the only thing that can defeat Communism is democracy—real democracy, not just the symptoms of it. I was a Communist once myself. I know them. There is no ruse they will not use to get their system established. But if once you begin to adopt the same ruses——"

"Then you've had it, eh?"

"Absolument foutu," said Charles. He tapped his pipe out against the ashtray. "That's what I mean when I say hysteria won't work."

Carla looked at her watch and stood up. "Could you excuse me again for a few minutes?" And without waiting for an answer she left the room.

David was dropping ice into the glasses with his fingers. "I know this isn't hygienic, Mr. Poignon, but I can't seem to find the ice-spoon."

Charles' voice was deep with amusement. "Actually, some of the best things in life are unhygienic."

"Aren't they though?" said David, grinning. He leaned back in his chair. "But to get back to Germany——"

As quietly as she could, Carla made her way down the

158

entrance hall, grabbed up her mink coat and let herself out into the icy dark. Looking carefully to right and left she proceeded up the walk toward the street, stepping delicately so as not to get snow in her little high-heeled slippers, and just as she rounded the turn she saw him waiting beside the gate, his crutches under his left arm, his Tyrolean hat pulled down a little over his face.

"Peter," she said in a low emotional voice.

He took her hand. "I am sorry to disturb you, Miss Mac-Murphy," he said contritely in his sibilant German accent. "I would not call on Christmas Eve like this except I have something important for you to know."

"Oh," she said disappointedly. "And I thought you'd come just to see me," and looked up at him with a teasing smile.

"That too. Of course."

He seemed embarrassed at her teasing. His clear boyish face was pulled down in consternation.

"I'm glad you came, Peter," softly. "I really wanted so much to see you tonight." Her voice choked with an inexpressible sadness. "I've been so terribly lonely."

"Lonely?" he echoed, surprised. "An American is lonely in Berlin? With everything the Americans have, such wonderful Christmases, I thought only Germans were lonely."

"One can be lonely, Peter, even in the midst of plenty," she said chidingly.

"Yes." He thought about it for a minute and then laughed an envious half-laugh. "I would like one time to be lonely in the midst of plenty." Unconsciously he stroked the sleeve of her coat. "But isn't Mr. Hawks there?"

"Yes, he's there. I guess—I guess he's just too busy to care. He's in the house talking to some French socialist he's got there, all about Communism and Germany and European Socialism."

Peter looked down the drive toward the lights of the house. "A French Socialist?" he repeated. "I would like to meet a French Socialist and talk to him. Does he speak German?"

"Fluently," she said.

He continued to stare down the driveway. "What does he think of Germany and of German Socialism?"

"Oh, I don't know, Peter," she said impatiently. "I didn't listen very carefully. Come along, let's walk a little down toward the lake and you can tell me about your important news."

Haltingly, they started off. "Lots of French are very much against the Germans," he said thoughtfully. "And I suppose

159

they have every right to be. But I heard that the Socialists are different and want to make contacts with German Socialists so that later on——"

"Peter," she interrupted. "Tell me about your news."

"Oh," he said. "Oh yes." He was straining a little over his crutches. "It is quite a story, and I have all the proof to it. Well, you know in the Russian zone they have just reorganized the police department, and no one knows why. Until just today, when——"

Scarcely listening, she walked beside him in the bitter cold, her head bent, watching the movement of his crutches over the ice, the tips so exactly set down, the forward swing of his leg like a long black pendulum within a moving frame.

He finished his story. Then: "You are quiet tonight, Miss MacMurphy. Is something wrong?"

"No-o-o." She sighed. "It's just—it's Christmas Eve, Peter."

"Yes," he said. "And I have no present for my little mother." For a few labored steps he was silent. "Well, it is not a happy Christmas for anyone, and she knows that. At least she is not as cold as some are, since I found her a little coal last week."

They had reached the end of the street and were proceeding slowly down a sloping path toward the frozen lake. In the dim winter light the lake shone like a disc of polished steel and the rim of wooded land around it was black and hostile. A sweep of cold wind blew across the lake into their faces.

"Take care, Peter. Your footing," whispered Carla.

"Ah, Miss MacMurphy," his young voice crystal clear over the still air. "I am better on my three legs than before on two. I am more than eighteen months now with these Krücken."

She put her arm through his and looked up at him. "Not Miss MacMurphy," she said in a sweet low voice. "Carla." With one gloved hand she reached up and caressed his face.

"Carla?" he repeated, starting a little. "But I cannot call you that when Mr. Hawks is——"

"Please," she coaxed. Her adorable face, tilted provocatively close to his, shone in the frosty half-light. "Please, Peter. Always, when we are alone, call me Carla."

For a full minute he looked at her. Then he set his crutches forward for the next step. "Also dann, when we are alone I call you Carla."

Near the edge of the lake she saw a bench, and ran over to make sure but turned back disappointed when she saw that the wooden planks of the seat had all been removed. "Schadet nichts," Peter said philosophically. "I only hope it is hot-burning wood. That means it is keeping somebody warm." In the darkness his voice sounded whimsical but tired. "We should start back anyway, don't you think? When we stop walking it is too cold." And she could hear his crutches turning in the gravel.

She came and stood in front of him. "Peter——"

"Yes?"

"It's Christmas Eve, Peter. Aren't you going to kiss me a merry Christmas?"

"Kiss you?" he said uncomprehendingly.

"Please. In a minute it will be Christmas."

Hesitant, he stood still.

"Peter—" The name whispered like an audible caress.

Resting on his crutches, he looked at her. Then he bent and touched his lips to her cheek.

In a rush of emotion she slipped her arms around him and put her head against his thin worn coat, and felt his body shivering next to hers. "Peter—dearest—Liebling——" Her hands moved up from his shoulders to the back of his neck, and she held his head in her hands, her eyes shining in the darkness.

Braced by the crutches, he pulled back.

"Peter——"

Over her head he was staring at the cold grey flatness of the lake, the ring of silent shore, the lights of American-requisitioned houses twinkling in the refractive cold.

"But I am a German," he said slowly.

"It makes no difference, it makes no difference, Peter—Liebster——"

As if drawn by a magnet against his will, he inclined his head and looked down at her imploring white face, the softly opened lips almost black in the purgatorial dimness of the lake.

"I——" he began.

Like a black orchid, the lips came closer and closer, the soft fleshy petals of a beautiful carnivorous flower. Across the lake the glimmering lights of the American houses receded in a thunderous mist, the air burned like dry ice. Velvety and near, the petals of the flower parted in sweet imploring hunger.

"Peter—Liebling——"

As if mesmerized, he put his mouth against hers.

"The tragedy of Germany," David was saying, "is that it's a bone of contention. And bones of contention invariably get chewed to pieces."

161

Carla stood for a moment just outside the livingroom door, listening.

Now Charles was talking, his deep masculine voice relaxed and slow. "Exactly. The tragedy of Germany is the tragedy of western Europe. Being western she cannot accept Sovietization. Being European she cannot accept Americanization. I have never been to the United States, I can only talk as a European, which I am. But I can tell you how it looks to us——"

Ready to step into the room, she sighed and stood where she was. Conceited fools, they hadn't even missed her.

"We don't want our souls saved," Charles' voice went on, warmed with the pleasure of his thought. "We've seen too many reformers come and go, all the way from Savonarola to Hitler, and out of their Messianism all we inherit is the mess. We are the world's voyous—— I don't know how you say that in English."

"Dead-end kids," said David.

"Dead-end kids," he repeated, as if mentally setting the words up in type. "We are the world's dead-end kids; we are suspicious of all saviors and social workers. Of the Russian faith-healer at one end of the street and the American salesman at the other. We would like to believe the Russians but we cannot. We know they are false priests. We would like to live like the Americans, with soundless toilets and refrigerators full of canned beer, but we know that we cannot. So, voilà! There is the Fifth Freedom that Europe won in the second great world war—the freedom of dilemma."

Taking a big warm breath, Carla walked into the room and over toward the fireplace, pulling her coat off as she came. "Hello, everybody!" she said brightly. "I've been for a walk in the cold cold winter weather!"

Both of them stood politely and watched her toss her coat onto the divan and sit down in her accustomed big chair. "And I'm absolutely starving too!" she said, smoothing down her hair. "What would you think if I ordered us up some sandwiches and coffee?"

Charles sat down.

David remained standing. "Where did you say you were?" he asked, his voice curdling with anger.

"For a walk. Why?"

"With whom?"

"Why, with no one, David," she said innocently. "I just went for a walk alone. You were both so engrossed in your conversation——"

162

"Never mind our conversation! If you had one iota of womanly understanding in that stupid head of yours, you'd know damned well what we were talking about and why!" He was beginning to shout. "Now you walk in here like a common little tramp——"

Startled, she turned to Charles, but Charles was sitting with his head down looking at the floor.

"—with lipstick smeared all over your face——"

Unconsciously, she put her hand up to her mouth.

"Yes!" he shouted. "With two men sitting in here waiting for you, you can go traipsing off with God knows who! Like a bitch in heat, you never get enough, do you?"

Furious, she stood up. "You shut up!"

"You never do, do you?" he repeated.

She threw her glass at him but it missed and hit the wall and a splattering of glass, water and Scotch trickled down over the bookcases. "How dare you talk to me like that!" she screamed. "You big foul-mouthed bastard!"

Quietly Charles got up and left the room.

"You sonofabitch!" she shouted. "Talking like that in front of my guest, *my* guest you understand——"

He pushed her back into the chair. "Now sit down and keep quiet while I tell you a thing or two about *your* guest and what your behavior has already done to him. If you had one bit of consideration for that guy—and a wonderful guy he is, too!—if you had given one small thought to his feelings——"

"You leave me alone! Get away from me!"

She started to get up but he pushed her back into the chair.

"Do you know what he's doing? Do you know what he's doing this very minute?"

Eyes distended, she stared at him.

"He's packing his bags to get the hell out of here! That's what he's doing!"

"You're lying!"

"Okay. You think I'm lying." He strode over to the door leading to the cellar and yanked it open. "Kripke!" he bellowed.

"Ja-ja," came a voice from below. "Komm' gleich, Mister Hawks."

Cold as a statue she sat still in her chair.

"Ham Se was——" began Kripke, emerging from the cellar.

"Kripke," said David sternly. "Go upstairs and ask Mr. Poignon if you can help him. And then come right back down and tell me what he's doing."

"Wird gemacht, Mis'er 'awks," said Kripke mutteringly,

and stomped through the room toward the stairway reeling like a sailor.

"He's drunk," said Carla dully. "He's drunk as a goat."

"Of course he's drunk! What the hell else do you expect in this house when you're off gallivanting with some——"

"You shut up!"

"At least you could wipe the lipstick off your face! Here!" He pulled a handkerchief out of his pocket and shoved it at her.

Her face white with hatred, she accepted it and began wiping off her mouth.

Kripke limped back in. "Mis'er Hawks," he said, bowing so low he almost lost his balance. "Mis'er Poy-nong is packing his bags. Asked me to find out when the next plane leaves. Next plane one hour I told him. Plenty time to get Tempelhof." Expectant, cheerful, he hung onto the edge of a chair and waited for orders.

"Then get the Tatra out and bring Mr. Poignon's bags down." David's face was a cold rock of discipline.

He turned back to Carla. "Now sit there and figure out what you're going to tell *your* guest!"

Sullen and unmoving, she sat in her chair and watched Kripke trudge drunkenly out and listened for sounds upstairs which would mean Charles was coming down.

All right, maybe it hadn't been wise. But how was she to know that Peter was going to get out of hand over just a simple little kiss? That was something David could never understand, but Charles could. Charles, with his wise commiseration for all things human—she ought to go upstairs and explain it to him, that's what she ought to be doing and she knew it. She could never explain to him in front of David. David would only hoot with scorn and bring up all the times she had flirted so "outrageously" with Peter. Yet she couldn't move, she couldn't. And her clothes were sticking to her, all her lipstick was off. Christ, what a mess!

And then she heard the sound of his footsteps coming down the stairs.

He entered the room, and David turned.

He was wearing his camel's hair traveling coat and holding his beret in his hand. As. he walked across the floor toward them she saw in his face the same deeply tragic expression that had first struck her in the garden of the press camp at Munich, a dispassionate indulgence of all folly, all faiblesse, as an inescapable condition of human existence. Like the time he had talked of the concentration camps with sadness but no hatred and had even in his strange humanist way made excuses for the Nazis. Fragments of things he had said spun like meteors in her head: "I am a man without ambitions, except the ambition to make love to you. It is only for the others that I have ambition." And: "You do not know how human I have become with you. Always before I was too busy fighting for what I thought was right, I had no time to be made human by loving someone."

My heart is breaking, she thought, sitting up erect. My heart is breaking.

"Carla," he said, and his voice was deep and steady. "Carla," he said, "I am sorry to ask favors, but could you possibly ask Kripke to drive me to the airport? I have discovered that I must go back to Paris immediately. You have been so generous, and I do not want you to think that I am impolite, but it is necessary that I go."

She could scarcely move the words up out of her throat. "Of course, Charles, Kripke can always drive you anywhere. But must you really go?"

"I am afraid that I must."

From the front of the house came the sound of Kripke huffing and swearing and banging the bags around, and then the slam of the front door. A cold breeze crossed the room and blew up the chimney.

"Charles——" she began.

"How about one for the road, Charles?" said David suddenly in a brusque comradely voice. "It's a cold night." He was standing exactly as he had been when she and Charles had first come in, but on his face now was a friendly and sympathetic respect.

Charles' blue eyes shone in the lamplight with a moist sadness. "If you don't mind, David,"—— When did they start calling each other by their first names?—— "I would like that very much. I have the habitude to be always hung over in airplanes, and because I am an old man now I do not want to change."

Emotion evidently threw him back into the French idiom; his English was not as smooth as it had been in his conversation with David. Suddenly he looked and talked not like her gentle Charles but like a man who had spent his life fighting and working, and the restrained violence that she had sensed before in Bavaria was only shallowly below the surface of his urbane politesse. In one fleet moment she saw the battle-history that lay behind him, the prisons, the concentration camps, the exile, the apartment that was "so wonderful for

165

revolutionaries" because it had so many doors, the tested and disciplined strength-within-himself that allowed him to condone the weaknesses of others. "I have been so many times betrayed," he had said once, "that it does not surprise me any more." She looked at him. He was a magnificent stranger.

David was pouring three more drinks.

Cap in hand, Kripke stood in the doorway. "Alles fahrbereit, Mis'er 'awks," he said with exaggerated deference.

"Thank you, Kripke," said David absently. "Put the car keys on the table and then you may go."

Kripke advanced weavingly across the room, looking inquiringly at Carla, at David and at Charles. Having attained the divan, he stood supporting himself by holding on with one hand; with the other he brushed the hair back out of his eyes. Dumfoundedly, he looked at David again. "But who is to drive?" he asked thickly.

"I will drive Mr. Poignon to the airport, Kripke," said David, without even looking up. "Leave the keys here and go along to bed."

His square unshaven face perplexed, Kripke stood where he was.

Carla accepted the drink that David put in her hand. She leaned forward. "Charles," she began, in that childishly pleading voice, "I think I must explain to you what happened here tonight and why I——"

"Ah, non," he remonstrated, his eyes shining. "You need explain nothing to me, Carla. I have known everything since the first step I made in here tonight. We are adult people."

"Charles, please listen—I want to tell you——" With David standing right there, her voice became more and more plaintive.

"Non, chérie."

He says chérie again.

"Non, chérie." He came over and took her hand, and looked down into her upturned face. "Life is often bad, and sometimes it is good. If for one moment it was beautiful, one should thank le bon Dieu, and not curse him." He patted her hand. "Now soon we will say adieu, you and David and I, as the good friends I think we are."

The blue eyes were ringed with red, the winged eyebrows more angular than ever, but on his face was that same look of wise and gentle comprehension, and he smiled at her the way he used to do.

"Mis'er 'awks!" said a loud stentorian voice. "Ick bin Ihr Chauffeur!"

166

Startled, they all looked at Kripke. He was holding the keys as if about to drop them on the table, but his tragic brown mask of a face was as grim as that of a witness for the defense. "Mis'er 'awks. If I give you the keys to the Tatra and let you drive Mis'er Poy-nong to Tempelhof, denn bin ick morjen janz versackt. So. I have drunk maybe the bottle you gave me for Weihnachtsgeschenk. But I am still your chauffeur!" Tears came to his bleary eyes as he faced David. "If I am a bad driver, Mis'er 'awks, then fire me and I go away."

There was a silence.

"I am driving Mister Poignon," said David sternly, "and you are going to bed. Those are orders, Kripke."

Tearfully, Kripke put down the keys and turned to leave the room. Then he saw Charles looking at him. He hobbled around the table. "Mis'er Poy-nong!" he wailed. "Ick bin Deutscher, Mis'er Poy-nong," passionately tapping his own barrel chest. "Mis'er 'awks is' meen Chef. Miss M'Murphy is meene Chefin. I am their kleiner chauffeur and it is my business to do as they say and never think and never argue. Ick bin keen Dummkopf. Mis'er Poy-nong, I am in the Wehrmacht six years, I know what obedience is. I have five slugs in my belly and I do not know how many more in my legs. But I can still drink like a dog. And I can still drive like a— like an angel."

Charles looked at David. "He seems to be in a very unhappy state," he said.

"What difference does that make?" said David. "He can't drive you, he's drunk as a fool. How do I know he'd even get you there alive?"

Charles put his hand on David's shoulder. "Let Kripke drive me, David. This is a fine thing. An ex-Wehrmacht soldier who knows the meaning of obedience but who still— when he is drunk enough—makes an appeal."

David stood still, considering. "Well, Jesus, Charles, if you really prefer——"

"I do," said Charles. "It is a horrible cold night and I do not want to make you come out into it. In addition, I am a very observant man, and I see that if you do not indulge me you are likely to lose an excellent chauffeur who is taking this matter much more seriously than you and I."

David looked at Kripke's desperate face, the touseled hair and sad puppy eyes. "All right, Kripke," he said in German. "Mr. Poignon, who is a friend of yours, says you may drive him."

In sudden elation, Kripke grabbed up the keys and started for the door.

"Well," began Charles embarrassedly, pulling on his gloves.

Kripke turned and exultantly addressed all three. "Wir sind alte Kumpel, Mis'er Poy-nong and me. I am German. Mis'er Poy-nong is a French. The French do not like the Germans. But Mis-er Poy-nong likes the Germans, he is a friend of Germany, det weess ick. So he is also a friend of Kripke." Happy as a kid, he broke into a pidgin German-accented French. "Bong jour! Voolay-voo cooshay 'vec moi, Madam-azell?"

"You can see he was a soldier in France," David explained in German.

"Have I been in France?" echoed Kripke, his voice loud with pride. "Have I been in France! My outfit led the break-through at Sedan, we were the first to enter Paris, before even the Gestapo came. We were the armored guard when Hitler marched up the Champs-Elysées." He straightened up to what he thought was military bearing and almost lost his balance. "Except me personally," he recollected sadly. "I was in the guardhouse for finding some bottles of French cham-pagne. But my company was there." For a moment he lapsed into a thoughtful silence. "In those days *we* were the Besatz-ungstruppe, the occupiers."

Charles took Carla's hand again. "And so good-bye. Please do not come to the door. I like better to say good-bye here, like this, where I can remember later that I have left you in a safe warm place."

"Charles——" she said chokingly.

He bent over to hear.

"Charles, I know you heard a terrible quarrel between David and me tonight——"

He straightened up and smiled that tired understanding smile. "Ah, it is nothing. You are like husband and wife. It is a form of love-making."

Kripke watched the scene with distant blood-shot eyes. "I liked the French," he said nostalgically. "We all liked the French. What we could never understand was why the French didn't like us." He sighed. "Now when I am back in Germany and the war is over, I understand much better."

"David," said Charles, stretching out his hand. "Thank you for a wonderful evening and a wonderful conversation. Per-haps we meet again someday."

"Goodbye, Charles," said David. "I certainly hope so."

His eyes moist, Charles looked from one to the other. Then

without another word he walked quickly to the door and out of the room.

"Goodbye, Charles," said Carla in a dead low voice, and buried her face in her hands.

David stood unmovingly by the fire.

From the vestibule they could hear Kripke prattling on as he opened the door. "Do you know, Mis'er Poy-nong, sometimes when we came in a café they wouldn't even talk to us? Just sit there and stare at us and say nothing, until a man couldn't even swallow his beer! Denk'n Se nur mal! So a man would even put down a good drink!"

Another freezing wind blew in across the warm lighted insularity of the room. Then they could hear the front door close and from the outside, faintly, the sound of Kripke whistling cheerfully "Über Metz, bei Paris, in Chalons," and the tight wheezing finality of the slamming of the Tatra's door.

CHAPTER THIRTEEN

"DAVID," whispered Carla, stirring in the warm cradle of his body. "David!"

"Um." Without waking, he stretched his long legs down under the blankets, groaned, rolled on his back and threw one arm out toward the wall.

"David!" she whispered again in the darkness.

Sighing, he turned back, hunched his legs up around the curve of her buttocks and pulled her closer to him. "Um?"

She nudged him with her elbow. "David, wake up! I think I hear something."

"Nonsense." His hand felt around in front of her and instinctively cupped itself around her breast. Contentedly he sighed again, his breathing becoming deeper and more relaxed.

With hushed urgency she tried again. "David, please! Wake up! I know I heard somebody moving around downstairs."

"Kripke, probably." His voice was hoarse.

"Ssh! He'll hear you."

They lay quiet, listening.

"There! What was that?" Cautiously she propped herself up in the bed. "David, there *is* somebody down there. You better get up and get your gun." Sniffing and coughing, she reached out for the Kleenex box and found it empty.

"All right, all right." Grumbling, he got up, felt for his robe and tied it around him. Walking softly, he went over to the bureau and opened it and came back carrying his .45. In the dim light of the window he inserted the clip, flicked off the safety and cocked the hammer. "God-damned ridiculous having a gun like this," he was muttering, "too heavy and too dangerous. Blow a guy's head off as easy as not. Wish to hell I had my carbine."

Silent, shivering, Carla stood beside him.

He bent down to whisper in her ear. "Hadn't you better get something on, you with that cold of yours? If we're going to play cops and robbers all night, it might be a good idea to get out of the nude." He gave her a little prompting pat on the bottom.

"David!" With hushed indignation she pushed him away. "David, please! If you don't go down now, he'll be gone before —what was that?" She stuck her head out the open window and looked down. "My God, there he is!"

In the bushes just below them stood a dark figure carrying something square and black under its arm.

"Halt!" shouted David, shoving Carla to one side. "Du! Was machst Du da?"

There was no answer.

"Speak, or I'll shoot!"

For one long second the figure stood motionless. Then suddenly it started racing across the grey expanse of yard, twisting and turning like a frightened jackrabbit.

"The safe!" screamed Carla over David's shoulder.

David waited just long enough to see that the figure didn't limp. Then in the darkness of the bedroom the .45 spat fire. There was a deafening shot, then another and another. The figure tottered, dropped and lay sprawled out on the livid carpet of the yard.

"You got him!" breathed Carla. "Thank God!"

David's arm with the .45 fell to his side. "Yeah." As if numbed by his own action, he stood staring out of the window. "He isn't moving."

"Neither is the safe," she said gloatingly. "Let's go down."

Still staring out the open window: "Wait a minute."

From below came the sound of someone running along the hall, lights flicked on that reflected out into the yard and cast shadows over the still dark figure that lay there. "Mister Hawks!" yelled a stentorian voice up the staircase. "Are you all right?"

"We're all right, Kripke!" said David. "I'll be right down."

170

He turned to Carla. "I guess I better get down there and see if the poor bastard's dead or not." He started for the door.

"I'm coming too," said Carla, struggling into a housecoat.

He turned on her. "Please, baby, stay right here where you are and let Kripke and me handle this. You can't tell what accomplices a thief has or what kind of trouble might start now."

"But I want to see!"

"Carla," anxiously. "Please do as I tell you and stay up here until I call you. I'll let you know the minute I think it's safe. Will you do that for me, please?"

"All right," she said glumly, turning back to the window.

Behind her she heard him leave the room, then an upstairs door opened and Erika's voice called across: "Was it a burglar, Mister Hawks? Is there something I can do?"

And David answering tiredly: "No, Erika, nothing. Just stay in your room. Kripke and I will tell you about it later." And the tread of his footsteps going downstairs.

Standing in the cold of the open window, sniffling and shivering, she held the collar of the housecoat tight about her throat. She heard the back door open and saw a long bar of light fall across the yard, then the quick dark flash of Timmy bounding into the shrubs, then the silhouettes of the two men walking into their own shadows, the tall one in a bathrobe that reached not much below his knees, the little one limping painfully at his side clad only in a pair of pants, his tubby chest bare to the damp early-spring air. She saw Kripke kneel down at the side of the robber and turn him over on his back and put his ear to his chest. "Tot!" she heard him say awedly. "Der singt nich mehr."

Dead, she said to herself. And a good thing too!

Gun in hand, David was standing over the corpse looking down at it. "A kid," he said in English. "Nothing but a kid. Nur ein Kind, Kripke."

Kripke looked at the boy's face. He started back. He looked again, and began to howl like an animal in pain. "Oh Gott! Oh Gott! Oh Gott!"

What is it? she wondered. What's Kripke getting so upset about?

Kripke's voice rose in a tragic wail. "Ach mein Gott! Mein kleines Güntherchen! Was hast Du getan!" Still on his knees, he looked up at David, and she thought she saw tears shining on his face. "Was für eine Pleite! Was für eine Pleite!"

"What is it?" she called out the window. "What's the matter?"

The two men were talking in low tones, she couldn't hear what they were saying. Irritated at being kept in suspense, she leaned out and called again, her voice mucky from her stopped-up nose. "What is it, David?"

He looked up. "I'll be right up, Carla. Please close the window and get out of the cold." There was a crispness to his voice that she didn't like, the uncompromising I-will-be-obeyed of a company commander in an emergency.

"But what is it?"

Authority sharpened his voice. "Carla, will you please do as I tell you! Shut the window and get inside!"

Infuriated, she slammed the window shut. "To hell with you!" she said aloud. "I'll do as I please!" Excited and angry, she pulled some slacks out of the closet and struggled into them, kicking her housecoat off into a corner. Men were all alike! If there was anything they loved it was a nice fat male secret, the chance to "protect" a woman from a perfectly ordinary thing like a corpse! As if nobody'd been around during the war except themselves!

In the downstairs hallway she passed Kripke carrying the safe. "Mister Hawks says for me to go get the police," he explained curtly, his face haggard and expressionless, and hobbled past her toward the office.

She continued on through the wide-open back door and across the yard.

"Carla, didn't I tell you——" began David, seeing her coming, and with that same harsh authority in his voice.

"Yes," she said sweetly, coming up to join him. "Yes. I just decided I'd come down anyway." She looked curiously at the body. "He's dead, isn't he?" The boy's face and hair were covered with blood and dirt on one side, clean on the other. "Where did you get him?"

"In the middle of the back," said David dully. "Look, Carla, will you please——" He took her arm.

"No," she said, removing his hand from her arm. She continued to look down at the body. "I'd say he's about fourteen years old, wouldn't you?"

"Carla," exasperatedly. "Will you please——?"

"Please what?" She looked up at him defiantly. "What on earth is the matter with you? You and Kripke walking around here like a couple of professional keeners at a wake! Of course, it's too bad the boy is dead. But he asked for it, didn't he?"

In the grey chill of pre-dawn he took her shoulders in his two hands and pulled her attention around to him. "Carla," he said gravely, "there's a complication to this that's more

172

serious than you think. I may as well tell you, this boy's name is Günther Lochmann. He's Erika's little brother."

"What? You're kidding!"

"I wish I were."

She turned her head and looked down again at the body. "Erika's brother Günther! Are you sure?"

"Kripke knows him well, and it was Kripke who recognized him." His voice was tired and flat. "It's my own fault for keeping a gun like that in the house. Anyway, you can see what we've got on our hands. I've sent Kripke to go call the police, so we can get the body out of here before I have to go up and tell Erika." He let go her shoulders. "Funny thing is I was just shooting at his legs, just to stop him. That god-damned .45 must have jumped on me. If I'd had my carbine ———" His shoulders sagged, and he looked down regretfully at the corpse and the spreading pool of blood that had darkened and clotted the grass. "If I'd just had my carbine———"

"If I'd just had my carbine!" she mocked. "Jesus, to hear you talk, you'd think it was you who had robbed the house, instead of him!"

"Carla!"

"Well, I don't care! Of course, it's too bad he's dead. And it's too bad he's Erika's brother. But what else could we have done? Let him get away with it? When someone breaks the law, it doesn't matter how old he is or whose brother he is, he has to be apprehended just the same. Doesn't he?"

"Carla———"

"Well, doesn't he?"

He didn't answer her. "Come on. We'd better go in and get dressed before the police get here."

They walked back toward the house.

"Did you ever stop to think," she went on, "that every criminal is somebody's brother or son or whatever? Suppose we ran the world according to your system, what do you think we'd have? Criminals and thieves and rape-artists all running around free just because they're somebody's brother? Is that the way you'd like to see it?"

"Carla," he said sternly. "I just don't want to talk about it. If you don't mind."

"All right, have it your way! You always do!"

He opened the door of the office for her.

"I'll wait in here while you get dressed," she said, sinking into a chair. "Leave me some cigarettes." Without a word he put cigarettes and matches on the desk next to her and mounted the stairs toward the bedroom, his footsteps heavy and slow.

"Timmy," she said, and the dog bounded into the armchair next to her and curled up sighing with the innocent fatigue of a job well done.

The grey-green light of dawn was pushing against the windows. Abstractedly she looked around the office, at the confusion of papers and typewriters and reference books spread out in the glimmering light of the coming morning. Faintly from overhead she heard the dull padding of David getting himself dressed.

So David's mad at me! All right, so he's mad at me! Certainly I feel sorry for the boy, for being so stupid as to think he could get away with a trick like that. And certainly I feel sorry for Erika. But the fact is, I'm right. And David's wrong. You can't let your sympathies run away with you. Right is right, and wrong is wrong. And when people break the law, they have to be prepared to accept the consequences.

From the radiator in the dim corner of the office came the comforting little clackings of the furnace going on. In imperceptible wavelets the pale light of morning suffused the room. Leaning back in the chair she lit a cigarette, inhaled the first dry caustic drag, and the journalistic disorder that she and David had left last night was as remote as refuse on the bottom of the sea.

CHAPTER FOURTEEN

LETTING the cold water run, she squeezed a tiny ribbon of paste onto her brush and started to brush her teeth. She was very proud of her teeth and it took her all of three or four minutes to brush them, the way the dentists said.

From below came the sound of the phone ringing, and she had a funny premonitive sense of something unpleasant about to happen, some oracular eye in the back of her brain blinking its long disastrous lashes. I'm getting like the Germans, she scoffed at herself in the mirror; like Kripke, with his braggart claims that the shrapnel floating in his knee tells him what kind of day it will be.

"Miss MacMurphy," called Gerda up the stairwell. "It's a long distance call for you."

"From where?" Her mouth full of lather.

"From Munich, Miss MacMurphy."

Carla opened the bathroom door wide and called across to the bedroom. "David, could you take that call for me? It's probably some PRO with a story about something. All you have to say is that I'm not here and can you take the message."

"Okay, I'll get it." He was lying in bed reading the morning newspapers and waiting for her to finish in the bathroom. "All right, Gerda! I'll take it for Miss MacMurphy up here."

From the bedroom she could hear his voice as he picked up the phone, that purposeful shouting with which people begin a long-distance telephone call. "Hello, hello! Yes. Well, I'm sorry Miss MacMurphy isn't here right now, Corporal. Could I possibly——"

Watching herself in the mirror, she went back to brushing her teeth. When she had finished, she rinsed out her mouth with a mouthwash, drank her morning glass of water and went back to the bedroom. David was just finishing the conversation. "Okay, I'll tell her. Okay, Corporal, thanks very much. Goodbye."

"What was it?" she said, putting her perfume bottle down on the dressing table.

"I don't know," said David. "Some complicated business about an automobile ring. Another of those Bavarian scandals. The M.G. down there wants to check the papers on your Tatra."

Her face dropped. "What?"

"Well, I don't think it's very much, baby. All they seem to be doing is catching up with a bunch of car thieves, and they just called you because your Tatra was originally registered in Munich and they want to check the papers. I told him you'd call him back as soon as you came in."

"And who is 'him?'"

"I don't know. A corporal named Simpson or something like that. I got the phone number here."

"Samsen," she said.

"You know him then?"

"Yes, I know him." With great deliberation she took a cigarette out of the silver cigarette-box on the table and with equal deliberation lit it, and unthinkingly held the match so long that it almost burned her fingers. She sat down and tapped with her fingers on the table. Then she got up and went to the top of the stairs and called down to Gerda. "Gerda! Will you call up the airport right away and find out when's the next plane to Munich?"

David sat down on the bed. His hair was still touseled from the night and his voice was husky. "Honestly, baby, don't you think that's kind of silly? What do you have to go to Munich for? Just call them up and tell them you'll send the papers in this afternoon's mail. That's all you've got to do."

She turned on him. "I know what I've got to do a hell of a lot better than you do, Mr. David Hawks. And I've got to go to Munich. That's all there is to it." Her green eyes narrowed, she paced up and down in front of the window contemplating the problem.

"But what the hell for? When it's your own car legally acquired? When you paid perfectly good legal francs for it? Damn it, Carla, if I hadn't seen the papers myself I'd think you had something to hide. I tell you, all you have to do is just send the papers down so the Provost Marshal can take a look at them. That's all. Simple as ABC."

Paying no attention to him, she went back to the head of the stairs. "Gerda!"

"Coming right away, Miss MacMurphy."

She recommenced her pacing.

In her usual shy but efficient manner Gerda rapped at the half-open door but stood respectfully outside. "I have your information now, Miss MacMurphy."

"Yes?"

"There's a plane at nine o'clock that arrives in Munich at ten-twenty, Miss MacMurphy. After that, there isn't another until the day after tomorrow. They only fly every other day."

Halted in the middle of the bedroom, Carla listened, her head down as if staring at the carpet. "And what time is it now, Gerda?"

Gerda looked at her wristwatch that she was so inordinately proud of, that David had given her last winter as a Christmas present. "Almost eight o'clock. In other words, the plane leaves in about an hour."

David sat quiet on the bed, smoking.

"I don't see how I can make it!" Then, decisively: "Yes I can!" She began to talk fast. "All right, Gerda, now listen carefully. Call the airport right away and reserve me a seat on that nine o'clock plane. Then call up Corporal Samsen at the Munich press camp and tell him I'll be arriving at ten-twenty or whatever it is, and to have somebody out at the airport to meet me. Got it? All right, now get to it."

The minute Gerda had left the room, Carla flew into a zigzag of frenzied activity. Forgetting David's presence entirely, she threw off her housecoat, grabbed up a garterbelt and some stockings and started buckling them on, yanked open a drawer and found a brassiere and slip. "Damn!" She

176

ripped off a torn stocking and started pawing around in the drawer for another.

"Honestly, Carla," said David, watching her from the bed.

Opening the closet door she pulled out a suitcase and began tossing into it a suit and some dresses, stuffing them in pell-mell in rolls and bunches. In the quiet room her breathing was rasping and forced.

"Honestly, Carla, don't you see how silly this performance is? All this melodrama about nothing——"

"Will you leave me alone?" she exploded. "I know what I'm doing. And I can do it a lot better if you'll stop arguing and start giving me a little help." She went on energetically packing clothing. "Now let's see, stockings, lingerie——"

Unconvinced, he sat watching her. "On top of that, you're signed up to go on that tour of the Russian Zone tomorrow. You backed out of the last one too, if you remember. How you can go on being an expert on the Russians and the Russian Zone without ever going down there, I don't know. And now you take this particular time to barge off to Munich——"

Dashing back in from the bathroom with her arms full of jars and bottles, Carla regarded him with impatient exasperation. "David, do you suppose you could possibly do something besides stand there and think up arguments? I know what I'm doing and I'm going to Munich, and I don't give a damn what the Russians or anybody else thinks about it. *I am going to Munich!* Now will you please shut up and go down and tell Kripke to get the Tatra out? I'm not even sure I'm going to make that plane."

Without another word he dressed and left the room, and when she raced down with her bag packed and ready to go he was at the wheel of the Tatra himself. Erika set the bag in, David threw the car in gear and with a hail of gravel they were off for the airport. "Where's Kripke?" she asked, lighting herself a cigarette but in her excitement forgetting to offer David one. "Off on some errand," said David. "Now don't worry, I'll get you there."

The rest of the way he said nothing. Pulling nervously at her cigarette she glanced at him from time to time, but his face showed nothing more serious than the challenge of getting her to the airport on time: his jaw was set with stubborn good humor. Not until they were chasing across the hot dusty landing-strip toward the waiting plane did he make his last patient protest: "To look at you, chasing off this way, a guy might think your life was at stake! Wasting all this time and trouble, scratching the last chance you've got to go through the Russian Zone, walking off without even an explanation. Naturally, Carla, it's your business. But don't you see how completely nuts——"

"You're right, David, it *is* my business," she said, stepping with breathless but firm relief on the gangplank of the waiting plane. "And I'm handling it the way I see fit."

He sighed. "Okay, baby." He handed her her suitcase. "Have you got the Tatra papers with you?"

She patted her purse. "Right here."

"We're ready to take off now," said the flight sergeant politely.

She started up the ramp.

"Don't I even get a goodbye kiss?" asked David looking up at her.

She turned around and came back down and absent-mindedly kissed him on the cheek. "I'll phone you from Munich and let you know how I get along," she said. "Take good care of the Tatra while I'm gone. And don't worry, darling."

"All ready for the take-off, Miss," said the flight sergeant.

She started back up the ramp, remembering just as she went through the door to wave back at him and smile.

There were only eight other passengers in the plane, six middle-aged men in civilian clothes sitting together up front and two GI's sprawled half-asleep in the tail. After some flattering concern by the flight sergeant over her comfort, Carla chose the second row in back of the civilians and leaned exhaustedly back in her seat. As the plane taxied slowly, bumpingly across the field she caught a glimpse of David still standing by the terminal door looking like nothing in the world but a newspaperman—sleeves rolled up, shirt collar unbuttoned—and for the first time she felt a stabbing worry over the disapproving coolness with which he had let her go. A year ago when I went to Nuremberg he was like a man forlorn. I wonder if he'll miss me, sleeping alone like that, I wonder what he thinks—hell, it's too late now. I hope he just thinks I'm nuts. Stretching forward to look back through the annoyingly tiny window of the plane, she peered toward the terminal. Maybe I should have been less brusque. But the plane had already turned onto the runway, the terminal building was out of sight. Oh hell! She settled back in her chair. I'll be back in a week anyway.

In the stuffy airless interior of the plane she began to perspire, partly from the let-down of having caught the plane and partly from the heat. It's all right, she thought: this was the only thing to do, even if I couldn't tell David about it. A big fuzzy pendulum was swinging nauseatingly back and forth in her stomach, and she held the muscles of her abdomen tight in order to slow it down. Well, at least I caught the plane. Now the only thing is to get around those damned investigators in Munich, and do it cleverly enough so no one will know; it's not so much a question of the Tatra itself as it is of my entire reputation. I could get kicked out of the whole theater for this, and my accreditation revoked and lose my job besides. If only General Blakely hadn't left last spring, maybe I could have worked an angle there. General Hughes is so goddamned moral!

The flight sergeant came by. "Ready for the take-off. Fasten your seat-belts, please."

The fur-coated pendulum stopped, hesitated, and then sickeningly started up again. With cynical disinterest she watched the six old men in front of her buckling on their seat-belts and murmuring among themselves as to which end went with which. As if it mattered! For some reason or other, the shorter life got and the more insignificant, the more tenaciously people clung to it. "Who are they and what are they here for?" she whispered to the sergeant. "I dunno." His fresh young face was close to hers. "Just a bunch of senators and congressmen investigating something-or-other. Same thing," he added in explanation.

"Do me a favor," she pleaded. "Ask one of them what they're investigating." Her smile was dazzlingly appealing.

"Okay," he said cheerfully and with a conspiratorial nod moved to the front of the plane.

They were now in the air. Breathing more easily, she regarded the bald heads in front of her, six polished Easter eggs in six beds of hoary desiccated moss, and the longer tendrils of the moss combed and spittled into elaborate whorls and filaments, like giant fingerprints on slick paper. From the back, their heads seemed wax-like and artificial; their freshly shaved skin had the embalmer's-fluid pinkness of the already dead or the still unborn. If these old fuddy-duddies were the ones investigating that auto ring in Munich, then she had it made. Luck, she said to herself, the MacMurphy luck.

The flight sergeant sauntered back. "Dismantling," he said, leaning over to whisper in her ear. "They're investigating dismantling."

"Dismantling? Really? All right, sergeant, thanks." She gave him a quick impersonal smile and turned away quickly to cut the conversation. Oh well—still looking at those webby bald-heads—I suppose it was too much to expect. Maybe I'll get along all right just the same. But then sweat broke out all along her back and trickled along her scalp, her entire glandular system seemed to curdle, the contents of her bowels churned against her anus in a series of warm sickening waves.

By an extreme force of will she kept her eyes fixed on the six congressmen. Why couldn't it have been they who were investigating this so-called auto ring? Why couldn't I get a break once in a while? She felt irritated at them, and as her irritation mounted her nausea began to go down. Bunch of superannuated old biddies wearing trousers only because their mothers put them in trousers in the first place and since then they've never had either the curiosity or the courage to investigate why. So they investigate dismantling.

The plane droned on. So they investigate dismantling.

The sign "Munich Press Camp" was covered over by vines, but otherwise the place was exactly as she remembered it.

The same heavy iron gate, half open, led down to the same wide expanse of gardens and lawn, the same neatly clipped evergreens like pawns motionless on a pale green chessboard. Driving with the expert ease of familiarity, Corporal Samsen pulled the jeep through the gate and down the white-stone drive and came to a squealing stop in front of the steps. The gravel dust settled down again. A languid summer silence closed in.

Carla swung her legs over the side and stepped out. Her muscles felt milky and untrustworthy, her mouth dry as powdered aspirin. I wish it were over, she thought; oh Christ, I wish it were over.

The morning was moist and cool, with wisps of sunpailletted mist trailing over trees and shrubs. In the early morning sunlight the garden droned with lazy insect-activity; beads of dew glistened on every blade and leaf. Charles. She almost said it aloud: this is where I met Charles. Behind its timbered balconies the house seemed closed and hostile, uninhabited except for the swallows that still murmured sleepily under its eaves. In the distance the operatic backdrop of the Bavarian Alps communed silently with the clouds. And right down the center of her fear the realization swept—maybe it's just as well about Charles. I never could have lived up to him anyway.

She turned impatiently away. "I suppose we may as well go in," she said, and in the quiet preoccupation of the garden her own voice sounded as sharp and inappropriate as laughter in a cemetery. "Colonel Kennebunk is upstairs?"

180

"I imagine he is," said Corporal Samsen laconically. "I doubt if he's even up yet."

She noticed that he made no move to carry her bag in for her, so she left it where it was in the back of the jeep and soberly they walked up the steps, through the vestibule and up the big staircase.

"But isn't Colonel Kennebunk expecting me?" she ventured.

Samsen's freckled unsmiling face turned. "Sure he's expecting you," he said shortly, and they continued up the stairs.

At the top of the stairs they turned left, toward the big corner bedroom that she had stayed in when she was here before—the bedroom where she and Charles had been so happy—and the Corporal knocked once on the door and they went in.

Colonel Kennebunk was sitting up in bed in purple silk pajamas. "Pete?" he grunted. Then: "Oh hi, Carla. Come on in. Apologize for receiving you like this. Little informal, to say the least, but can't be helped. Been feeling punk lately, haven't I, Pete? Have to keep to bed in the morning." The room was dark, its shutters closed against the sunlight outside; it reeked of whisky and male perspiration and stale cigarette smoke. "Pete," said Colonel Kennebunk, "run down and see if Otis has got that coffee ready yet. You take cream, Carla?"

"If you've got cream," she said.

"Sure. Sure, we've got cream. Place is running with cream. Tell Otis to bring up a pitcher of cream too, Pete. But sit down, Carla, sit down."

All available chairs and tables were littered with men's clothing, trousers and shirts and underwear tossed helter-skelter over every inch of horizontal space. In the corner, catching one thin streak of light from the balcony, stood the Louis Quinze dressing-table where she used to make up her face; now it was piled with liquor bottles and glasses, and two of the beveled mirror-panels were broken.

"Just knock that stuff off a chair and sit down," boomed Kennebunk. "You and I got a lot to talk about. But first we'll have some coffee. Get us out of the dumps a little, eh, Carla?" His joviality was forced. In the subdued light of the room his face looked like spoiled ham, mottled red and grey. "What a mess, what a mess! And you don't know the half of it yet. Did you see this?" He reached out to the night-table, exposing a fat hairy white arm, and came up with a folded newspaper. "Take a look at that, if you don't think we got troubles."

She carried it over to the balcony to read in the streaked light of the shutters. It was a newspaper story by some AP correspondent she didn't know, and as she read it she felt the heat pushing against the underside of her skin. "—a scandal involving more than half a million dollars in automobile frauds. Monday morning three Germans will go on trial here before a Military Government court charged with selling stolen vehicles to Americans . . . trial is expected to crack open the entire ring, including two top-ranking Military Government officers who issued false papers to enable Americans who bought the stolen cars to register them as legal——" Her eyes blurred, she read on. "How many Americans are involved is not yet known, but it is rumored that among them is the foreign correspondent of an important U.S. newspaper——"

She turned hysterically on Kennebunk. "Is that me? Does he mean me?"

"Afraid he does. Now stop that screaming and come over here and sit down. I think old Daddy Kennebunk has got a plan. Can't promise anything, but—oh, here it is. Come on in, Otis. You remember Miss MacMurphy, don't you?"

She threw the newspaper on the floor. "But where the hell did he get that? Who told him that?"

"Right here, Otis," said Kennebunk, hunching himself up in the bed. "Here, give it to me. I can put it right here on my lap." He looked up at Carla. "I suppose he got it from Schaeffer, little garage-keeper in Dachau who sold you the Tatra in the first place. He's one of the three being tried. Now for God's sake sit down and stop screaming. Have a little coffee here."

The tray tilting precariously in his hands, Otis staggered across the room and deposited it in the Colonel's hands. Over his GI uniform he had on a long once-white apron covered with grease spots and blood, and he was very drunk. Having set down the tray, he straightened up. "Hello, Miss MacMurphy," he said with slow concentration on his syllables. "Nice to see you. I remember you very well. I fixed some sandwiches for you one day, and you were standing in the kitchen window, all golden fire. Like a Tintoretto angel, or the Rubens Andromeda, all gold——"

"All right, Otis," said the Colonel sharply. "That'll be enough. Miss MacMurphy and I have things to talk about."

"Thank you, sir," said Otis. He started wobblingly for the door, but on the way stopped in the middle of the room and looked longingly toward the Louis Quinze dressing table where the bottles were stacked together. "Colonel, sir?"

Kennebunk looked up from pouring the coffee. "Well, what is it?"

Otis rubbed his hands over his dirty apron. "I was just

thinking about our agreement, that if I didn't say anything about——"

"Don't you have anything down there to drink?" boomed Kennebunk.

"No. That is, no sir, I don't."

Kennebunk frowned. "All right, Otis, you can have that bottle of rye on the right."

In one beautifully coordinated movement, Otis scooped up a bottle of rye and started for the door.

"But what the hell are we going to do?" said Carla, the minute the door closed. "Jesus God, you don't understand! My job, my reputation, everything in the hands of these squealing krauts! How do I know what that Schaeffer has already spilled? Or how to stop him from doing any more of it?"

"Now, look here," said Kennebunk. He was pouring coffee, his tiny hands fluttering over the cups like two white moths. "You just sit down somewhere, have a cup of coffee and I'll explain the whole thing. Don't get so excited. Here," as she stood in the center of the room trembling like a rabbit, "come over here and sit down on the bed."

Still she hesitated. Then, as if hypnotized, she came over and sat down gingerly on the far corner of the bed.

"Cream?" he said.

"Please." Her stomach was rolling with hunger and she eyed the tray hopefully for a sign of toast or something, but all there was was coffee. "Lots of cream," she said in a small tense voice.

He handed her a cup and poured his own. "Now," he said, settling back against the pillows and pulling his purple pajama-top tighter over his enormous stomach. "I'll explain the whole business. It's a mess all right, but maybe we can figure out some way to beat it. Pete and me, we're in the clear. Last night I had a long talk with the P.M., Colonel Peters, old friend of mine. You know him? Anyway, I got Peters' promise he'll protect Pete and me all along the line. Let the krauts take the rap." For a fraction of a minute his old jovial smile returned. "They got nothing to lose. Couple of years in jail'll do them good. Peters knows the prosecution, he's a brown-nose captain who could get busted if he doesn't do what Peters tells him. So Peters can call the turns on all the charges and say who's going to be called, and so on." He leaned over. "Just between you and me, Mil Gov isn't happy about the thing at all. They're trying to shut it up themselves. Too dangerous right now, with Congress sitting over there right at this minute debating appropriations for the whole occupation and everything. Anyway, Peters has got it all set to prove that we licensed these cars without ever knowing where they came from. Inefficiency, they're going to call it. Which isn't going to do me much good when I go back Stateside, don't forget that." He slurped noisily at his coffee. "Still, it's better than getting caught."

"But what about me?" asked Carla shrilly. "What about me?"

"About you." Colonel Kennebunk put his cup down on the night-table. "About you, maybe—just maybe—we can work an angle. Where's the Tatra now?"

"In Berlin."

"Um-m-m." When he frowned his spoiled grey face clamped shut. "Anyway we can prove to the trial J.A. that you don't own it any more? That you only bought it as a kind of prank? Whose name is it in?"

"Mine," she said. "Although," she faltered only slightly, "although at the moment another correspondent has it."

"You see, the whole goddamned trouble is they gotta nail one American. If they don't, it looks like it's been fixed. Which it has, of course. But still you can't indict a bunch of Germans for selling cars to Americans without producing at least one American. Otherwise you'd have the whole CID down here and a bunch of investigating congressmen and everything. So the only thing we got to prove to the J.A. is that you're not the one to pin it on. They got to have one horrible example, that's all right. All we got to do is convince them that it oughtn't to be you." He poured himself another cup. "So if we can just talk Colonel Peters and his captain into believing that you're just a cute little trick that didn't know any better—who's got the car now, did you say?"

She stared down at her empty coffee-cup. The room was quiet. "A correspondent in Berlin named Hawks."

"And what did you charge him for it? On paper, I mean."

"Nothing." _

He wriggled back against the pillows. "Wonderful. Perfect. My guess is that'll just do it. We go down to see Peters this afternoon and give him the story. You didn't think the Tatra was much of anything. You already gave it away to this guy in Berlin. That may be all we need." He reached over and chucked her under the chin. "Now just trust old Daddy Kennebunk. Peters'll do practically anything I say. It's t.s. for the next guy, but it'll spring you or I miss my guess. You just trust old Daddy Kennebunk to fix it up. If you're nice to him, that is." He put his arm around her and drew her toward his end of the bed. "You're a sweet little thing, you know that?"

His jowls hung on either side of his jaw like unformed eggs; looking at him and smelling the sweaty moisture of his body she thought he was like an enormous overfed baby pleading for something it wanted. Holding her breath, she allowed him to pull her over into his soft billowy lap. "Really, Colonel Kennebunk——"

Blunt pink tongue protruding from his mouth, he tried to kiss her.

"Please, Colonel——"   .

His mouth almost found hers, his tongue wetting the side of her chin.

Again she pulled back. "Colonel Kennebunk——"

From close up, his mottled face was pock-marked and bristly. His one-day beard scraped against her neck. "I always did have a yen for you," he said, his right hand exploring under her skirt. "You're a cute trick, you know that? A little snobbish, but a beautiful dame just the same." In the greyness of the room his smile was as webby and moist as seaweed. "Say, whatever happened to that Frog you were running around with when you were down here before? You were pretty sweet on him, weren't you? Guy named Poy-gi-nun."

She thought for a moment. "He's back in Paris, I think."

"You were pretty sweet on him, all right. That's why I never had a chance in those days. You take a nice American girl like you, I suppose she's got to try everything. See what these continental Romeos got that everybody raves about. Sooner or later, though, you come back to good clean American men. That's what I told myself then. Sooner or later, I said, she'll drop this Frog and get herself back on the American standard. Then I'll have a chance." Against her right hip she could feel his thick warm stomach rising and falling and wriggling lasciviously toward her. "So here we are, eh Carla? Just the way I said. You scratch my back and I scratch yours." His diminutive right hand was proceeding over her thigh. "You really are a sweet little trick, you know it?"

"Colonel Kennebunk——" she protested, trying to pry his hand away.

"Put your arms around me," he breathed against her neck. "Put your arms around me!"

"Colonel Kennebunk——" With all her strength she managed to detain his hand at a point just above her knee.

His round pink tongue reappeared reaching for the corner of her mouth. Like an obscene hungry infant he strained toward her panting and drooling.

185

For a moment she sat deathly still. The bed, the Colonel and the Colonel's breath all smelled the same, the sour curdled smell of an unwashed child. The fetid obscurity of the room swam around her.

CHAPTER FIFTEEN

AND THAT was the way you did it.

In the daytime you ran around military government corridors with Colonel Kennebunk straining and panting at your side. In bare offices with tiny U.S. flags growing in vases on the desks and pictures of Eisenhower on the walls, you dimpled and smiled at every transportation and legal officer within reach while Colonel Kennebunk explained to Colonel Peters and Colonel Somebody-or-Other what a shame it would be for "a sweet young kid like this" to get "foisted" with the blame for a bunch of professional crooks. And besides, "the poor kid" thought so little of "that old jalopy of a Tatra" that she had long ago given it away for nothing to another Berlin correspondent named—— "What did you say that guy's name was, Carla?"

That was the way you did it in the daytime, and although your nerves ached with the ague of a perpetual hangover it wasn't so bad. Not like the nights, the nights when you came home to sit down to Otis' sodden dinners and swill your quota of whisky in front of Corporal Samsen's rigid unfriendly stare—sitting in the same place that Charles had sat that first night, "Tiens! Vous parlez français?" Only now no candles curtseyed and danced in the soft evening wind; life was as merciless as the 200-watt lightbulb that beat down on the dirty tablecloth, the gravy-splattered plates and Colonel Kennebunk's balding head, and as unrelenting as the heat. You drank and drank until finally the bottles were empty and then you proceeded haltingly upstairs, the Colonel's heavy arm hanging along the edge of your hips. That was the way you did it in the nights.

Until, two days before the trial was to take place, something happened to her, fever or shock or something, and she had to take to her bed. The same bed in the big corner room, and the Colonel surrendered it to her with some little-boy disappointment and a lot of fussing about blankets and hot-water bottles. "Now don't you worry the least tiny bit, my pet. Daddy knows a lot about these bad dirty cramps that sometimes happen to little girls," he would say, carefully wrapping a gurgling red-rubber bag in a dirty towel and placing it just so, "Just so, right here on our little tummy. My, my, what a luscious figure we have," reluctantly pulling the blanket back up over her. Then he would lean down to give her one of his wet secretionary kisses. "Now Carla's going to be a good girl and stay right here while Daddy goes back to take care of these damn trials," and tiptoe noisily out of the room.

For awhile she thought she knew what it was, that she was pregnant by David, but after awhile that passed too and all that remained was the fever, a half-delirium in which Otis, reeling with drunkenness and a tray of unappetizing food, and Colonel Kennebunk, smoothing the blankets and feeling her knees in an effort to "cheer her up," reappeared and disappeared and reappeared again like extremely familiar ghosts, the bed held her like a shallow warm stream in which she wished she could drown but knew she couldn't, waking each time washed up on a floating white bank of damp sheets and sticky granular pillows.

The afternoon of the trials she lay awake sweating and shivering waiting for the Colonel and Pete to come back, waiting for the screech of the Colonel's car in the driveway, the slam of the front door. I'll know as soon as I hear their voices, she thought. When she was too nervous to lie still any longer she got up, got into a housecoat and made her way out to the balcony, so weak that she had to hang onto chairs and the jamb of the door as she half-walked, half-propelled herself through the darkened room and out into the glistening sunlight.

Below her the garden lay tepidly stewing in the slow spermatic heat of summer, the air was moted with swarms of bright insects going about their business in a methodical humming heaven of flowers and grasses gone to seed. The sun beat down, flattened against her like a rough heavy blanket, heating her skin to the burning point, while inside she shook with chill and a wet liquescent fear.

Far beyond the dark pines of the garden the pinnacles of the Alps stood aloof and superior, wrapped in a silver sun-threaded mist. So near you could almost touch them, lean over and with one long extended arm knock them over like the fake props they were, scatter them all over Austria—and Berchtesgaden with them, that lofty eagle's-nest where Hitler used to stand and contemplate his godhead. That bastard! He's the one responsible for it all—Germany, the war, the Tatra

187

that stinking military government court down there, that god-damned Schaeffer who may be squealing on me this very minute just to save his own kraut neck, all, all, everything. That sonofabitching Hitler and his sonofabitching Germans! In the bright sun she shook with fury and with cold.

At just that minute she heard them on the stairs, Colonel Kennebunk's booming voice: "Twenty years will do 'em good, teach 'em a goddamned good lesson!" She heard them enter the bedroom. "Tight squeeze, God knows, and mind you I'm damned glad to be out of it. But at least it'll teach those bastards not to get ideas about blackmailing people who're stronger than they are! Hey, where is she? Carla!"

"Here," she said, surprised at the strength of her own voice. "Out here on the balcony."

"Now look, my pet," waddling good-naturedly out onto the balcony. "Didn't Daddy tell you to stay right there in your little beddie-bye while he went to bring home the bacon? And boy! Didn't he bring home the bacon this time! Eh, Pete?" His wink was broad, his guffaw as jovial as ever.

Sending Pete off for some martinis, he sat down and per-spiringly told her all about it. The three Germans had gotten twenty years each and an American lieutenant of the Trans-portation Division had been given six months. "He was a bastard anyway, always putting the bite on Pete and me for a bigger cut every deal we made. And he won't hurt for much. He'll get sent home and reprieved right away. He's lucky he didn't get something serious." Laughing with energetic ap-preciation of an ordeal that now lay safely behind, he prattled on of their "tight squeeze" as if somehow it demonstrated the sterling qualities of their characters, his mottled pink face laughing and talking at the same time. Still chilled and a little sick to her stomach, she heard only those portions of his con-versation that concerned her.

"Takes a couple of snakes like us to wriggle out of a trap like that, eh, Carla? Gotta get up damned early in the morning to catch two rogues like us!" Then, patting her knee: "As for you, my pet, with all those cigarettes you were lavishing on poor old Schaeffer, it's a wonder they didn't indict you for spreading nicotine poisoning!" His round stomach shook with laughter, his delicate little hands meanwhile exploring her thigh. "Lost some weight down here, didn't you? Shouldn't get too skinny, you know. You were good the way you were."

When Pete came up with the martinis, he started making plans for a special dinner "to celebrate our triumph over the forces of law and order. Now that our little Carla is well enough to sit up and take a little nourishment," pouring her another martini, "we got to lay on something special."

Quiet, considering what she would do, she looked from face to face. The mantle of worry had fallen off Colonel Kennebunk like a tinsel cape off a strip-tease dancer; bustling over the martini tray, he was unchanged from the jovial, tail-wagging goldbrick she had met on this very balcony a year and a half ago. Even the sullen Pete had recovered some of his old freckle-faced pleasantness. Time to get out, she thought, this is where I came in, and announced regretfully that she had to catch the next train back to Berlin. "There's one that leaves just two hours from now."

Colonel Kennebunk's face fell. In his role as "Daddy Kennebunk" he advised her seriously to stay over at least another day or two. "Too strenuous a trip for somebody in your condition. How about it, Carla? Two days and you'll be fit as a fiddle."

She shook her head. "No," she said with sweet firmness. "You know I'd love to. But no, I really can't. I really have to get back to——" She had almost said David. "I have to get back to work."

In the end of course he gave in, and he and Pete helped her pack and drove her down to the Munich Hauptbahnhof and walked her toward the train. "We going too fast for you, Carla?" the Colonel would ask.

"I'm all right, I'm all right," she answered perfunctorily, straining to peer ahead to the tracks. "Are you sure it hasn't already gone?"

"Nonsense," said Kennebunk, supporting her with one arm. "Two minutes to go. Lots of time."

Like submissive cattle, shabbily dressed Germans drifted back and forth in front of them, their voices and footsteps whispering in the lofty broken-glass vacuum of the station's dome. "One side!" said Kennebunk, impatiently shoving through the crowds. "For Christ's sake, will you bastards get out of the way? Can't you see we're in a hurry?"

Other Americans were rushing past them, military government officers and civilians and girls in WAC trench coats, all heading for the track where the American military train waited. The crowd of Germans tangled up, then, like sheep before a trained shepherd-dog, divided to let the Americans through. "Hurry up, you dumb bunnies!" yelled one girl shrilly, racing up the platform. Laughing and panting the rest of the group raced after her, twisting and turning through the apathetic Germans.

189

Then at last, with relief, Carla saw the train, the two American flags hanging limply from the back of the observation car, the locomotive in front coughing up steam into the already steamy twilight of the station. But the exertion of walking was telling on her. The little lights of the dining-car winked sickeningly at her as she dragged along on Colonel Kennebunk's arm, and when they arrived at her car she had to support herself weakly against the handrail while the Colonel scrambled pantingly inside to arrange for the making-up of her berth. The loud exhalations of the station pressed against her ears. She thought she might faint. But then Colonel Kennebunk reappeared to help her aboard and sit her down on her berth, the first shudder of the locomotive shook the train, and with a wet kiss and a "So long, Carla!" he was away and gone.

Alone in her compartment, amid that peculiarly lonely smell of aged upholstery, she looked out to watch the waiting German coaches drift slowly backward on the next track. The German train was packed to the ventilators with people, four to eight heads sticking out of each window, and as her own train moved out, its thousand-headed body crawled slowly behind her like an enormous human caterpillar back-tracking itself out of danger.

Overcome by nausea, she lay back on the bed. I should get up and unpack my bag, she thought; in a minute, in a minute . . .

Sleeping and waking, moving fitfully back and forth across the line of consciousness, she was dimly aware of a great deal of time passing. Once, when she opened her eyes, it was still daylight and the train was gliding smoothly past the ruins of some city. Once she got up and stood in a kind of dream talking to herself in the mirror over the washstand. It was almost dark outside now, and she could scarcely see. Her stomach still felt queasy and her knees shook underneath her. "You do look thin," she told herself, listening to the strange quaver in her own voice. "And pale too. Maybe the paler and thinner you are, the more David will fuss over you." Holding onto the washstand, she stared at her swaying reflection. "And look at all you've accomplished," she said to the girl in the mirror. "And no tears, no hysterics. The Tatra, your whole reputation ——" A saw-tooth knife of pain ripped through her head. "The Tatra——"

Her knees buckled and she reached out blindly for the bed. Still I don't feel very well. I don't feel well at all. I wonder if the Colonel was right, if there was some reason I shouldn't

190

have tried to make this trip so soon. Her forehead burned. Her skin felt tight to bursting. She thought she might vomit, and twice she retched but nothing came up. A chill washed over her like running water. Completely indifferent, the tiny compartment in which she was shut up chugged doggedly along through the dusk, a capsule prison endlessly rocking, endlessly pushing through space.

When she woke up again the train was slowing down in the outskirts of a town, ticking quietly past ghost-like fragments of buildings and mountainous piles of rubble.

Weakly she forced herself to a sitting-up position and with her head in her hands sat watching skeletonized buildings drift past in the blue darkness. Her fever, she thought, was lifting. She felt nothing but an immense pervading tiredness. To give up, to stop everything—thinking, breathing, intending —seemed the easiest thing in the world to do. Just to lie back and pass quietly out of existence. Not to die; that would require effort and energy. Just to cease.

Her own compulsion in life escaped her. What makes me keep going? What keeps me racing after trains, looting Tatras and then defending them, dashing after stories, rushing from Berlin to Munich to Berlin? Is it David? No. Something beyond David and beyond all the others. Some consistent thread on which individual men are as incidental as a row of strung pearls. A calculated trajectory that leads unerringly—— In the gloom of the compartment she saw the hundreds of front-page stories falling one on another like they do in the movies, illuminated headlines, headline after headline, by carla mac-murphy . . . By Carla MacMurphy . . . BY CARLA MAC-MURPHY, regular, unceasing, inexorable. Four years now since she had first made the front page, with that first thrill of triumph! And now almost every day, and always the same triumphant satisfaction, never mitigated, never lessened. Her mother's composed, consciously sweet face swam up in the darkness as real as a vision, the immaculate breakfast table with its bowls of spring flowers, the maid hovering in the background with fresh coffee, the morning *Globe* folded at the side—and morning after morning the frown of irritation, the struggle to control her jealousy as the perfectly manicured hands opened the *Globe* to read: DP'S BATTLE GERMANS, BY CARLA MACMURPHY . . . KRUPP GETS TEN YEARS, BY CARLA MACMURPHY . . . LOOK HERE, AMERICA! BY CARLA MACMUR-PHY . . . BY CARLA MACMURPHY . . . BY CARLA MACMUR-PHY. And not only mother, she thought, but all the rest of those gossiping fishwife Washingtonians who said Charlotte

Murphy could never be as beautiful, talented and successful as her beautiful, talented and successful mother. Mustn't frown, mother, she said aloud with murderous solicitude; it makes wrinkles.

Clanging and hissing, the train groaned to a stop. Feeling a little better, she let the window down and the cool night air flooded the compartment. From the din next door it was evident that six or eight Americans were having a party. The wall vibrated with their shouts and laughter, snatches of war songs they were singing. Sitting there in the darkness, smoking a cigarette, she looked across to the station. MAGDEBURG, said a freshly painted sign on a smashed gable, as if announcing to a disinterested world that this skeletal railway station still represented a living city. We're in the Russian Zone, she thought. Under dim overhead lights the station platform looked as starkly unreal as a deserted theater-set. Far in the west, over the bomb-gnawed station-roof, hung a curved fingernail moon.

The window in the next compartment went down with a bang. "Not so fast," warned a good-natured male voice. "Not so fast. You wouldn't wanta get raped right here in front of all these Russians, would you?" The sound of laughter and a struggle echoed out against the ruined station.

"Roll me over, roll me over," sang one of the girls, and the others joined in: "Oh, this is number three——" "Hey, where's the liquor?" somebody demanded.

Across the empty station platform came a Red Army soldier, his heavy boots clacking on the boards. Stiffly erect, shouldering his rifle, he marched resolutely by under the feeble lights and went down the steps on the other side.

"Hey, vuss iz loose?" screamed one of the girls out of the next window. "Vuss iz loose?" "That's all the German she knows," said a male voice and the whole party broke into uncontrollable giggles. "Well, what're we waiting here for?" the girl wanted to know. "Lookit here! Train's stopped! Somepin's sure as hell loose!"

The lights of the train streamed across the tracks. Still feverish, Carla leaned out the window to taste the moist air and then suddenly, startled, ducked her head back in again. A man was standing directly under her window, standing motionless in the shadows leaning against a stick. Cautiously, she looked out again, caught the square outline of his jaw against the buttresses of bright lights from the other windows. She wondered what he was doing there, and before she realized it she said aloud: "Gut'n Abend."

192

He turned his head and looked up. "Gut'n Abend," he said. His face was thin, his eye-sockets round and owl-like. As a streak of light fell across his face she realized that he was blind. He cleared his throat. "This is the American train, no?"

"Hey, vuss iz loose?" screamed the girl next door. "Aw, shut up, Peggy!" said one of the men. "Nuthing's loose but the nuts in your head." More guffaws of laughter. "Her name's Ruthie," corrected another girl.

"Ja," said Carla. "It is. Why do you ask?"

The German spoke hesitantly. "Excuse please that I come here. I do not wish to make trouble. But if you would have perhaps a very small Stückchen of bread——"

"Vuss iz loose?" screamed the girl again, giggling. Then as if in sudden panic. "Hey, there's some Russkies here! Right under the window! I heard 'em talkin'! Hey, you guys! We better get the MP's right away! Before they try to hijack the train or somethin'!"

Paying no attention to the girl, Carla turned back to the compartment, got two candy bars out of her bag and returned to the window. "Hier," she said, leaning out. "Etwas Schokolade."

He reached up his hand, and after one or two false passes took the chocolate and shoved it quickly in his pocket, a surreptitious gesture that meant that in the Russian Zone it was verboten to beg from American military government trains. "Danke," he said hoarsely. For one minute more he stood there, then he reached out with his stick and tapping ahead of himself crossed the tracks and disappeared.

"See there?' yelled the girl next door. "See there? A Russky! Just like I was saying, and you guys wouldn't believe——"

With a jolt the train started up again; the noisy voices of the next compartment receded behind the creaking of the couplings and the steadily rising clicking of the wheels. Still sitting at the window, Carla watched devastated warehouses and wrecked factories drift by under that sharp little moon. On a siding they passed a DP train, twenty to thirty freight cars with their doors open and human bodies piled up inside sleeping. On each freight car a leafy branch was nailed, put up by the DP's themselves to signify that there were people in this car, not cattle.

She closed the window and sat down again on the bed. With explorative fingers she touched her forehead. Much cooler. Her fever was gone, her head was clear.

And now the compartment was no longer a claustrophobic terror, it was a safe warm American place against the dark unknown of Eastern Germany, a closed and winged chariot carrying her swiftly and surely back to Berlin and David. She snapped on the little bed-light and looked at her watch. By tomorrow morning I'll be back in the ranch-house. By that time I'd be all well and David and I can begin all over, like we did after Nuremberg—except that that time I was only gone four days, and this time I've been gone almost four weeks. This time it'll be even better, almost like a brand new love affair.

Smiling and hugging herself, she settled back against the pillows. That poor little blindman! she thought. That was a good act, to give him that chocolate. An act of contrition. A corporal act of mercy: to feed the hungry. Somehow, by that one act, she had washed away the Tatra business, Colonel Kennebunk, all the bad things she had had to do in the past month. The miracle of penance, she whispered to herself. It even broke my fever.

Lulled by the steady rockabye of the train, she fell into a beatific sleep.

CHAPTER SIXTEEN

STRANGE. Nobody met her at the train.

The moment she stepped down she scanned the row of waiting cars. No Tatra. For almost fifteen minutes she stood on the platform in the brisk morning sunlight, peering down the road. The air was cold and clear, streaming with that early bronze pallor that marked Berlin in spring and fall as an eastern city rather than a western one. One after another, private cars and army sedans pulled up to load in their passengers. Still no Tatra. The waiting crowd began to thin out, the parking lot emptied. Finally, still looking over her shoulder, she asked a ride from a State Department official whose wife had come in on the same train. "Not at all," he said cordially, leaning over to open the car door. "You're Carla MacMurphy, aren't you? Sure, right on our way." In the back seat his wife moved over and said nothing.

All the way out she kept a watchful eye on all oncoming traffic, hoping to see David and Kripke whipping past late on their way to the station. Traffic was light, even for so early in the morning. Wheezing German charcoal-burners and big lumbering British and American army trucks rolled noisily through the deserted streets. Here and there a broken-down Russian vehicle, one of those crab-like three-wheeled trucks which the Berliners called "Dreibeene," stood by the curb with its Russian driver stamping impatiently up and down beside it. Once in awhile a shiny new American "Herrenvolks-wagen" flashed by. But still no Tatra.

Then didn't David get my wire? But he must have. It was sent from Munich yesterday. He's probably overslept. Forgot to set the alarm——

"How do you like Berlin, Miss MacMurphy?" the State Department man. was asking politely.

Her eyes fixed on the road: "Oh, fine." But Kripke would never oversleep; Kripke would certainly have awakened David. Even if they were late, they'd have passed us by now. Then what could have happened? What could have gone wrong?

Her own street seemed strangely secretive, the American press houses closed behind their shutters, the interjacent ruins sunken deeper into the ground under their blankets of brown vines and shrubs. At the ranch-house gate they let her off and with a "not at all, perfectly all right," slammed the car door shut and roared on down the street. In the quiet of their wake she stood in the drive, as if hesitant to go in. Then she clicked open the gate, picked up her bag and started through.

The garden glowed with color, the unhealthy and beautiful bloom of incipient decay. Already the slow disease of autumn had touched the late asters, the yellow chrysanthemums, had reddened the ivy and shored up the fences with a froth of tawny oak-leaves. Kripke should have raked up those leaves and started burning them, she thought, proceeding down the drive. Makes the place look almost abandoned.

Under the rustic little carriage-way she set down her bag and unlocked the door, and pushed it open and went in.

The hall was dark, the drapes still drawn over the windows. "Hello!" she called. "Hello!"

There was no answer.

"Hello!" Her voice bounced against the wall and came back to her.

Still no answer.

She listened. Faintly, from behind the closed door of the living-room, came the sucking whine of the vacuum cleaner. She crossed the long hall and opened the door. "Erika!" she said.

The drone of the vacuum cleaner filled the room.

"Erika!" louder.

The girl turned around. "Miss MacMurphy!" she said, her

face brightened with surprise. She snapped off the machine. "Sie sind zurückgekommen!"

"Of course I've come back," said Carla curtly. She looked around the room. "My God, what's happened here?"

The room was a pictorial description of a hang-over. The area around the fireplace was littered with broken glass. Half of the books had been taken out of the bookcases and piled up on the floor. Over everything hung the pungent smell of whisky. Frowning, she started opening windows. "Where's Mr. Hawks?"

"I—I don't know, Miss MacMurphy," said the girl embarrassedly. "I—— He was here until about nine o'clock last night."

She turned on her. "You mean he didn't sleep here last night?"

"No, Miss MacMurphy."

"You're sure he didn't come back in late last night? Have you looked upstairs?"

"Yes, Miss MacMurphy. I've already cleaned the whole upstairs, and he isn't there."

"Well, where is he then?" Irritation sharpened her voice. "Where is he then?"

The girl blushed. "Honestly, Miss MacMurphy, I don't know." Her small rough hands twisted and untwisted around the handle of the vacuum cleaner. Her face was a mirror of oncoming tragedy. "All I know is he left here about nine o'clock last night. Then the baby was sick again, and I had to——"

These people! thought Carla. They always act as if they're on the very brink of hysteria. As if the S.S. were on its way to beat the door in and drag them off! "All right, Erika," she said, taking one more look around the disordered room. "Clean this up as best you can. Kripke will give you some gasoline from the Tatra to use on the carpet."

Still flushed with nervousness, the girl just stared at her. "The baby's been so sick, Miss MacMurphy——"

"Thank you, Erika," coldly. "That will do." Closing the door behind her, she was on her way toward the stairs when she heard the doorbell ring.

But it was only Gerda coming to work.

"Good morning, Miss MacMurphy," said Gerda in her pleasant unruffled voice, taking off her coat and hat and hanging them in the vestibule. "Did you have a good trip?"

"Fine, thank you," without enthusiasm. "Gerda, have you any idea——" The words were already in her throat when

196

she decided not to say them. "All right, Gerda, you can go on in the office and get started on the newspapers. I'll be in shortly. I just——" From somewhere upstairs she heard Timmy whining and scratching to get out. "I just want to let the dog out." She put her foot on the first step, watched Gerda go into the office, and then, feeling like an intruder in her own house, started up the stairs.

The bedroom door was closed, and for a minute, standing in the hallway, she could feel his presence inside, she was sure he was in there sleeping. Quietly she turned the knob, as if not to awaken him too abruptly, and out bounded Timmy, crying and leaping up against her. "Stop it, Timmy!" she whispered. "You'll tear my suit! Stop it, I tell you!" Wriggling with joy the dog circled around her legs, almost upsetting her as she walked in.

But the room was empty. It was just as it should have been —clean and in perfect order, the bed made, the blue velvet spread untouched—except that David wasn't there. Like a ghost revisiting an old haunt, she walked slowly across the room, her eyes confirming every piece of furniture, the love-seats, the white rugs, her dressingtable just as she had left it, nothing changed, nothing unusual. At the windows she stood staring down at the brown waters of the Teich stagnant and still under their floating leaves. *Of course I may be getting all upset about nothing. He could have been called out on a story and just hasn't come back yet. He could have stopped in at Bob Willstrom's or somebody's for a drink and decided to stay the night. After all, he might not have gotten the wire.* Opaque and glassy, the lake stared back. *Lots of wires get misdelivered, sometimes.*

Except what about that brawl that took place downstairs last night? Even when a man's lonely, he doesn't sit and throw glasses at the fireplace. To reassure herself, she went over to his wardrobe and opened the doors. And then she jerked back like a frog on a string. It was almost empty. Like a row of regimented scarecrows, a few khaki uniforms hung loose and swinging on their hangers. Her heart riveted to her ribs. Frantic, she raced over to his bureau and yanked out the top drawer. Empty! She pulled out the second. A few old keys, a Second Armored Division patch, some crumpled papers, that was all.

The quiet of the room swam over her.

Then it's true! He's walked out! Walked out bag and baggage and left me an empty house to come home to! After everything else that's happened this month, everything I've been through!

197

But how could he? He's found some other woman, moved in with her? No, it's unbelievable. David? Why, never in all the time I've known him has he ever even looked at another woman, much less—— And those goddamned little krauts downstairs, telling me they didn't know anything about it! Erika—and Gerda!

Her entire anatomy churned with rage and hurt. She dashed downstairs and threw open the office door. "Gerda!"

The girl looked up from her newspapers, her scissors poised for a clipping. "Yes, Miss MacMurphy?"

"Gerda, why did you lie to me?"

Puzzlement and disbelief fused on Gerda's sallow serious face. "Lie to you, Miss MacMurphy?" she repeated.

"Never mind the acting. Answer me! Why've you all been lying to me? Did it ever occur to you that sooner or later I'd catch up with you? Didn't that ever occur to you?"

"Miss MacMurphy, I don't think I understand. Lying to you about what?"

"About what!" She mimicked Gerda's slow dignified syllables. "About what! So you've told so many you don't know which one I'm talking about!" Her green eyes flashing, she advanced toward the desk. "About Mr. Hawks, you fool!"

Her eyes on Carla's face, the girl rose from her chair and backed slowly toward the wall. "Miss MacMurphy, I think you must be mad. I don't know what you're——"

"No, of course you didn't! You didn't know he'd moved out of here! You never saw him packing his bags and moving out everything he owns, his clothing and everything else! You, with your simpering Nazi faces, you didn't know a thing about it, did you? Perfectly innocent! You didn't know where he was, did you? You didn't know anything!"

The girl's eyes were like marbles, round and black. "Miss MacMurphy, we didn't know. We knew he'd spent several nights away, but it wasn't our business to ask. We never knew he'd moved his things."

"And Erika didn't know anything about it either, did she? No, of course not! Well, let me tell you, Miss Gerda Breitstein, when somebody works for me and accepts what I pay her and what I feed her, then she works for me! And then it's her *business* to know! So now suppose you just gather up your belongings and get ready to get out of here. Because you're fired! And when you get over that, you can march out to the kitchen and inform Luisa and Erika that they're fired too! And if they want to know why——"

Behind her she heard the front door open and heavy footsteps proceed along the hall. The door in back of her opened and she spun around. "David!"

But then abruptly the door closed again and the heavy foot-steps went on down the hall. She looked at Gerda standing stiff and motionless behind her desk. "And if they want to know why, you can tell them that I just don't happen to like being lied to, that's all!" Breathing deeply, she turned and raced down the hall after him.

He was already in the half-cleaned-up living room, setting down his suitcase next to the bookcases.

"David!"

He looked up. "Hello, Carla," he said dully, and got down on his knees and started sorting out the books that were piled up on the floor. From his behavior she thought he was a little tight. His balance as he stooped over the books was unsteady. He supported himself on the floor with one hand, like a sprinter waiting for the gun, and his face was completely, inscrutably, blank. With the other hand he was piling books mechanically into the suitcase.

"David," she said softly, her voice dropping into a husky emotional appeal.

He made no answer.

"David," she said again. "David, what are you doing?"

An interminable wait. "I'm getting my books," he said at last in the same dull half-drunken voice. And went on piling books into the suitcase.

Watching him in the sunlit room stooping like that in the shadow of the divan, she thought of his lovemaking, of the towering bulk of him crouched over her at night, and the very thought of it honed her voice to a split-edged sharpness. "I should think you could at least tell me where you're taking them."

He made no reply.

"David!" Her voice dropped. "David, please——"

He went on stacking the books into the bag.

"David! Can't you at least have the politeness to answer me?"

"It's all right, Carla," he said tiredly.. "There's nothing to say."

"You've moved out?"

He nodded without lifting his glance.

"Where?"

"At the moment I'm staying with the Wilsons."

Pulling a pack of cigarettes out of the pocket of her suit, she paced back and forth in front of him. "Couldn't you——"

Her voice caught on an imploring note, "Couldn't you at least tell me why?"

Sitting back on his haunches, he regarded her. "I think you know why, Carla."

She stopped pacing. "But I don't know why!" she said, tears coming to her eyes. "David, I don't know why."

"Look," he said patiently. His voice was thick. "Look, Carla, you're a lot of things. But one of the things you aren't is dumb. You know damned well why."

Her eyes were now brimming with tears. "But I don't, David! I don't know why."

"My God!" he said quietly, and went back to packing books.

"But why?" she wailed. "You've got to tell me! David, you've got to tell me! The Tatra?"

He didn't answer.

"The Tatra? Is that it?"

As if preoccupied, he opened a book and flipped over the pages. "Carla," he said wearily. "Does it ever occur to you a guy can just get his belly full? Yes, it's the Tatra. It's everything. The Tatra and everything else." He shut the book and turned it around to look at its title. *"Das Konzert Europas,* von Charles Poignon. Good book." And carefully stacked it away in the suitcase with the others.

The whole silly business spilled over in her heart. "You!" she said. "You don't know what I've had to go through! Saving the Tatra from those cut-throats——"

He looked up. "Saving the Tatra?" he repeated. "Saving the Tatra? Where'n hell do you think the Tatra is?"

She stopped crying long enough to look at him. "In the garage, I suppose."

Infuriatingly he went back to packing books.

"Well, where *is* the Tatra then?"

He sat back and looked at her and in doing so almost lost his balance. He righted himself. "Lady, I hate to bring you bad news. But if the Tatra is in the garage, it sure as hell isn't in the garage you think it's in."

"Where is it, then?"

He looked at her coldly. "I have no idea. The last I saw of it, it was being driven off by the C.I.D. Maybe it's in one of their impounding lots."

"The C.I.D.?" disbelievingly.

"The C.I.D."

"But they have no right——"

"They have every right. Particularly since I called them up and asked them to take it."

200

"You—you what?"

"I called them up and asked them to take it."

"You don't mean—— David, you didn't!"

He nodded. "I did."

An avalanche of fury and frustration tumbled over her. "You big—Jesus Christ! After everything I did to save that car, and you could do a thing like that. When it wasn't yours to begin with! Who the hell do you think you are anyway, to get so free with other people's automobiles?"

An ironic squinting humor lay on his face. "According to the C.I.D., the Tatra belonged to me. And they had documents from Munich to prove it." He staggered to his feet. "Is there nothing in this house to drink?"

She could have murdered him.

"So," he added, moving unevenly toward the bar. "So I gave it to them." He turned and grimaced at her. "Bad rubbish, good end." In the streaming sunlight of the room his face was a grey Mephistophelean mask. "Good end, bad rubbish." By some amazing system of tacking, he attained the bar, reached inside and found a bottle. "All of which fine. Except it's made one guy so profoundly unhappy—Kripke. It becomes apparent that our Kripke had a social stake in that looted piece of junk. Gave him dignity among his fellow chauffeurs to drive a de luxe crate like that, two steps above an American Cadillac." With a precise attention he held the bottle poised over two glasses. "Drink, Miss MacMurphy?"

She could not answer.

"Poor Kripke!" he sighed. "Non-vested interest. It never pays off. Like all the rest of the Germans, who got nothing but non-vested interest in Germany any more. Americans and British got all the Westen now." Wobbling only slightly, he filled both glasses. "Still, he could have done worse. He could have got caught driving the thing, for example. After all, it isn't everybody, Miss MacMurphy, who has your amazing facility for getting other people to take the rap for you." With a courtly bow he presented her with her glass. "Your drink, madame."

As if hypnotized she took the drink from his hands and started to bring it up to her mouth, looking all the time at his handsome drunken face as if through five feet of smoke.

"A drink," he said, carefully composing his words, "a drink to those dirty dishonest Germans down in Munich who got twenty years, and thereby saved the flower of American womanhood from shame and public scorn. Twenty nice long years in which to contemplate democracy and democratic justice.

That'll teach 'em what this whole wonderful occupation's been teaching all the Germans—the one great postwar lesson—not to go around losing wars."

Suddenly she reeled back and threw it at him, glass, liquor, water and all. It hit his shoulder and splattered all over his neck, face and chest. "You smart-alecky bastard!" she breathed. "You and your goddamned fake morality, I hope you choke! Get out of here! Take your goddamned books and get out! I never want to see you again!"

She thought he would hit her. His face, dripping with water, was screwed up in a conflicting combination of hilarity and rage. But all he did was pull a handkerchief out of his pocket and mop off his face and then get down on the floor again and recommence sorting out the books. "Carla, baby," he said, stacking another book in the suitcase. "You always were impressive when you were mad. It's the only real emotion you've got."

And that's the way it ended.

For a few weeks she thought he might come back, and twice at the Press Club she saw him at the other end of the bar drunk as a goat with Polly and Mike Wilson. She began running around with Peter, but although that had its compensations—Peter was so full of inside information on Berlin politics that week after week she was beating the *New York Press* almost without trying—she tired of that quickly. Peter was too young to be any good in bed, and after awhile all that devotion became cloying. And he was never jealous of anybody, even of David. There was no fun to it.

Then too, as the months wore on toward spring, everything seemed to get progressively worse. The new secretary who had taken Gerda's place was missing story after story in the Berlin press. The new cook got sloppier and sloppier until her meals were almost inedible. The new maids, she was sure, were stealing everything they could lay their hands on, yet although she laid trap after trap she never succeeded in catching them. Only Kripke—the only one of the entire household crew who had not deserted her—remained indispensable and always comforting.

Of course he still goofed off from time to time. Every Sunday morning as regularly as a churchbell he would get himself blindly and cheerfully drunk on Pfefferminzlikör and reel into the office to call her "meene Chefin" and kiss her hands until they were all sticky with that damned sweet liqueur. "I tell you why the Nazis were so mächtig in Germany," he said grandly

202

during one of these Sabbath demonstrations of his staggering but unswerving loyalty. "Because, as any Dummkopf knows, it is the best thing in life to have one boss and then to stop thinking and just do everything he tells you to do. Of course," he added, ruminatively, "Det is man klar—even better is to have a Chefin, a pretty young woman as your boss, and be her slave and her Beschützer." His grin was infectious but his smeary kisses on her hand were like glue.

Still, with all of Kripke's amusing prattling and Peter's very profitable adoration, she was bored, bored, bored. The ruins of Berlin began to depress her, sodden grey hulks that they were. It was no longer fun to browse around in the enormous junkyard of Stadtmitte looking for "color" for her stories or bargains in diamonds or etchings or anything else; she had already accumulated so much stuff she was beginning to worry about whether she'd ever be able to get out with it. And now it was getting to be spring again, the winter receding and the inhabitants of Berlin emerging from their ruins like bears out of caves, their faces pale and thin, their overalls and jackets wearing neat winter-lamplight patches. Now there would be sunlight falling slantwise over the Teich and tiny green tongues licking out of the shrubs and fruit-trees. And now, one pale spring evening when she was standing at the office window, it became too much for her.

For hours she wandered back and forth, drinking Scotch. Then she went into the office and picked up the phone. "Give me Nuremberg, please," she told the military operator. "Nuremberg urgent. Yes, it's official."

She lit a cigarette. I wonder what he'll say. She heard his voice: "Hello. Hello."

"Hello, Norman," she said.

"Fräulein MacM!" pleased. "Well, I must say this is a rare treat! What's on your mind this time of night? Besides the usual thing, of course." His voice had that same agreeable thin humor.

"Norman," plaintively. "Norman, what can we do about getting me transferred out of Berlin?"

"Out of Berlin? As I remember it you loved Berlin. Couldn't wait to get back there to your little snuggery by the Waldsee and zero yourself in between the sheets with the big competition."

"Norman! Seriously, Norman, can't we get me a reassignment? After all, I've been here almost three years now. I think I've written myself out. Why can't the *Globe* send me to the Middle East or someplace like that?"

His voice faded off the line and when it came back it was saying just what she wanted to hear. "——which I will certainly do if you're sure you want me to. I'll wire old Connell tonight and call you back as soon as I get a reply. Perhaps tomorrow or the next day. Right you are! Still, Miss MacM, you realize this means I can no longer keep my fatherly eye on your nymph-like antics."

Feeling somehow quieted, she hung up. Well, for all of Norman's lip-smacking, at least you know he'll do the best he can. Anyway, it doesn't depend on Norman, it depends on Connell. And I've always been Connell's favorite, ever since that time his wife went to Indiana to visit her folks—or was it Ohio? That time in the Willard Hotel, and it was so hot we actually stuck together. No, it was Indiana she went. Muncie, Indiana.

As if in a trance she crushed out her cigarette in an embossed ashtray. "Grüss Gott," it read through the blackened ashes, and for a moment she had the impression that she couldn't read it, it was in Arabic.

On the shining white apron of Tempelhof twenty big C-54's were lined up for the take-off. Under the early summer sun the field swarmed with German workers in overalls, GI overseers, army trucks and jeeps scooting over its surface like nervous little beetles. Everywhere the air vibrated with the hot rasping breath of planes warming up.

Bored and hung-over, Carla wandered down the near edge of the apron, her topcoat carried over one arm, her beret in her hand. "Stop it, Timmy!" she said, pulling back on the leash as the dog strained to investigate an orange peeling. "Stop that tugging!" Shading her eyes against the sun, she looked across the field to the far runway where, like mechanical toys playing follow-the-leader, planes were swooping down out of the clouds, gliding in and landing, taxiing into place to be set upon immediately by trucks and workers and unloaded at breakneck speed. A warm breeze scurried leaves and crumpled candybar wrappings over the squeaking cement. Behind the barbed-wire fence to her right, in the piles of rubble that edged the field, barefooted German kids were playing as contentedly as children in a sandpile, stopping every time a plane came in to nudge each other and point. As Carla came nearer they sat back like startled gophers to stare at her.

With a grim smile she jerked up Timmy and started back. German kids were such unattractive little runts, pale and colorless and totally lacking in that wholesome energetic deviltry that made American kids so lovable. Half of them tubercular and the other half scabrous with skin diseases, you couldn't feel any sympathy for them if you tried. Well, let them stare! They don't know it but the pretty pretty lady they're staring at is getting the hell out of this godforsaken country as fast as her legs and the American airlift will carry her.

In the raw sunlight her head throbbed. Every sound shrieked at her, every movement was a deliberate stab. "Okay, Mac, let 'er go!" yelled a GI in back of her, and she spun around like a trapped animal. She had a funny feeling that she wasn't here at all, that this enormous teeming airfield was something she had dreamed up for use in some future nightmare, and an equally funny feeling that she'd been through all this before. Everything was at the same time screamingly unreal and drearily familiar. And when five German workers crossed in front of her to enter the terminal warehouse, their wooden-soled shoes clacking on the pavement, she knew that she had been expecting those five workmen all along. If they hadn't appeared at just that moment, she would have been startled at their absence.

A sergeant came running up to her. "We're ready for the take-off, Miss MacMurphy."

"Oh." Instinctively she looked over to the sunset sky into which they would fly. "Oh fine, Sergeant. Thanks. All right, Timmy, come on." And followed the sergeant back to the loading area where her plane waited.

At the bottom of the gangplank the flight lieutenant took her ticket. "You're going all the way through to Cairo?"

"That's right."

"Okay," he said. "You change at Frankfurt. I'll see your baggage gets transferred."

"Thank you, Lieutenant," she said sweetly, and mounted the plank into the waiting plane and chose a seat well forward along the side.

The interior of the plane was stuffy and hot, and she folded her topcoat and put it to one side before settling gingerly back into the uncomfortable steel hollow that the army called a bucket-seat. "All right, Timmy. Right here."

Against the throbbing of her head the plane's motors started revving up. Automatically she reached for her seat-belt and buckled it about her, and then, her heart beating against her ribs, suffered through the one moment she hated most, that dizzying transference from earthbound to skybound.

As the plane banked for its turn into the air corridor she peered back out of the window for one last look at the barren volcanic mooncountry that people called Germany, this Central European boneyard with its six million arrogant dead and its sixty-eight million arrogant living. She knew she would be expected to write a summing-up piece, the final conclusions of a seasoned reporter on what it all meant. But her mind was completely blank. Oh hell! she thought comfortably. I can always dig out that first piece I wrote the day I got here. A few new facts, a quick rewrite, and they'll never even recognize it.

Through the roseate haze of the sunset the city of Berlin turned and spread out below her its three hundred and fifty square miles of rubble. From the ground, as she knew, it looked like the end of the civilized world by a necrophiliac painter, and one was surprised not to see mastodon jaws and dinosaur bones sticking up out of its moss-grown ruins. From the air all it looked like was an enormous messed-up grey jigsaw puzzle.

The plane continued to bank and climb. Through thin pink clouds the jumbled ruins of the city fell back to the east. An anachronism and an augury, remnant of the last war and already the Brückenkopf of the next, Berlin dived backwards and disappeared.

Relaxed, she unclamped her seat-belt and leaned back. The next war! And tingled a little at the thought. What theater would I cover this time? Maybe the Far East, maybe even Russia itself. Anyway, one thing is certain. Not this one. This is one kitten who knows when she's had enough.

The co-pilot opened the control-room door and strolled through the plane. "You can unfasten your seat-belts now." On the way past he stopped in front of her. "If you're interested in the air corridor, Miss MacMurphy, you can come up front whenever you'd like and see how we chart." He had the typically lanky Air Force build, and when he bent down to pat Timmy his blue eyes looked up at her with unconcealed admiration. "Say, did anybody ever tell you how snappy you and this dog look together? I was watching you walking over on the ramp just now. The exact same color of hair, did you know that?"

Her smile was disarmingly modest. Putting her book and newspaper to one side, she prepared to follow him into the control-room. Gee, an awfully attractive guy, she decided. An awfully attractive guy. Wonder if he's going to Cairo.